BURY THE PAST

ALSO AVAILABLE BY JAMES L'ETOILE:

At What Cost

for L.J.
the past
isn't done
with us yet!

BURY THE PAST

A Detective Penley Mystery

James L'Etoile

CROOKED
LANE

NEW YORK

Published in the United States by Crooked Lane Books, an imprint of The Quick Brown Fox & Company LLC.

Crooked Lane Books and its logo are trademarks of The Quick Brown Fox & Company LLC.

Library of Congress Catalog-in-Publication data available upon request.

ISBN (hardcover): 978-1-68331-442-4
ISBN (ePub): 978-1-68331-443-1
ISBN (ePDF): 978-1-68331-444-8

Cover design by Andy Ruggirello
Book design by Jennifer Canzone

Printed in the United States.

www.crookedlanebooks.com

Crooked Lane Books
34 West 27th St., 10th Floor
New York, NY 10001

First Edition: December 2017

10 9 8 7 6 5 4 3 2 1

We may be through with the past, but the past is not through with us.

Bergen Evans, *The Natural History of Nonsense*, 1946

ONE

Larry Burger was a night shift worker by choice. Evenings at the truck stop didn't require people skills beyond handing a shower key to a tired long-haul driver. Tonight was no exception. Larry ended work minutes before the morning commute that would require making small talk with the truckers coming in for coffee and amphetamines.

It wasn't that Larry felt superior to the pill poppers. In truth, he was one of them. The two dozen white OxyContin pills in his pocket promised to deaden his senses, a welcome relief from the cesspool life had become. That was the plan the minute he got home: pop a couple Oxys and disappear for a few hours. He felt the outline of the pills in his pocket, and they gave a warm reassurance that something better waited for him. He told himself he wasn't an addict. Larry could quit anytime he wanted to—and he would, just not right now.

The door lock on his Corolla had been drilled out months ago, the remnants of a bad repossession job. The upside was that Larry didn't need to worry about locking his car anymore. The engine coughed to life when he turned the key. A bill from the power company with red letters proclaiming this was a final notice sat on the seat next to him. It was either the electric bill or the Oxy, and the pills had won out—again.

Fifteen minutes from home, he took the Garden Highway exit and chewed on one of the pills, thinking it would start to mellow him out by the time he got home. An unexpected hassle from a cop during his

shift justified a second Oxy to tamp down the anxiety and old paranoia. The riverside road was dark and deserted in the predawn, leaving
him alone with his demons. He wasn't always like this, popping pills
to forget the pain. Next to the warning from the power company was
a card reminding him to meet with his probation officer. He was supposed to give a urine sample. The bitter Oxy taste in his mouth said
that wasn't going to happen today.

A sudden roar erupted from under his car. The entire front of
the small import shuddered. The rearview mirror didn't show an
animal carcass in his wake, and the steering wheel's violent jerk
didn't let up. He limped the car to the shoulder.

"Damn it all. I don't need this."

The door screeched against rusty hinges when Larry kicked
it open. He went down on a knee and inspected the underside
of the front wheel well. Something was caught up in the wheels
and had made a mess of his tire, brake lines, and God knows
what else. Fluid leaked from severed hydraulic lines, and the
smell of hot oil and radiator coolant wafted from under the car.

A blur shot past Larry, accompanied by footsteps in the loose
gravel. His reactions were dulled by the opiate, and when he
turned, a boot caught him on the forehead. The jolt sent Larry
sprawling to the gravel shoulder. He raised his arms to ward off
another blow as he crawled backward, until his back hit the car's
fender.

"Someone tells me you've been a bad boy."

Larry struggled to focus on the man standing above him. Dazed
from the blow to the head, he couldn't make out his attacker's face.
A slick sheen reflected moonlight off of the man's steel-capped
boots. It took Larry a moment to realize it was his blood. The boot
tip shot out again and caught Larry on the temple. The impact
bounced his head off the fender, and pain blossomed behind his
eyes despite the Oxy kicking in.

"What do you want? I don't have anything." Larry held a hand
up to protect himself and dug in his pocket for the baggies of pills.
He tossed them to the ground in front him. "Here, take these."

A gloved hand retrieved the pills and stuffed them into a
pocket. "That's not what I'm here for. You've been talking. You

were supposed to keep your mouth shut." The other hand gripped a yellow-handled hammer.

"I haven't said anything."

The attacker shuffled forward, and Larry curled up in a ball against the car.

"You were supposed to do the right thing. We trusted you, and now you're a damned junkie, shooting your mouth off." The cold metal claw hammer pressed against Larry's cheek.

"No. It wasn't like that."

"Who did you talk to?"

When Larry didn't instantly respond, the tool snapped at his head, the metal claw tip tearing a ragged gash is his cheek.

"Who?"

"It's not supposed to go down like this. I did what I had to do. I lived up to my end."

"Who did you talk to?" The hammer pulled back.

"Wait, wait! Newberry! It was Detective Newberry."

The hammer dropped to the attacker's side. "Now see, wasn't that easier?"

"I promise I won't say anything more. I'll go away; they'll never find me again."

"I know, I know." The man bent over Larry and cupped the injured man's chin with one hand. The other snaked from his pocket with the bag of Oxy and dumped them into Larry's mouth. Larry tried spitting them out, but the hand held his mouth closed. When he tried to take a breath, the attacker shoved the plastic bag with its pill residue down Larry's throat.

Larry resisted, attempting to push his attacker away, but a quick knee to his chest made Larry inhale sharply, lodging the torn bag of Oxy in his windpipe. His eyes widened, and he slapped at the man who held him down. Panic turned to resignation, and the last thing Larry felt before his world turned black was regret. Regret for so many things. Past sins welled up, and the promise of redemption crumbled to dust under their weight. Regret for trusting her.

When Larry went limp, the attacker took another baggie from his jacket and opened it. He smeared a dark substance on the lifeless junkie. The empty bag went back into the killer's pocket while he stood and considered moving the body into Larry's beater of a Toyota. The body might go unnoticed for days, written off as a homeless guy sleeping in his car. That wasn't the point. The sooner someone called in a dead guy on Garden Highway, the better.

TWO

Detective John Penley picked up his partner, Paula Newberry, at her midtown Sacramento home. The sharply renovated Victorian triggered an amused smile on Penley's face every time he saw the place. Its perfectly manicured gardens and carefully restored gingerbread woodwork were a regular feature on the local home tour circuit. His amusement came from the fact that Paula was anything but neat, tidy, and all put together. Not that she wasn't a good cop—she was. It was that Paula's work persona was the polar opposite of the person who lived in this well-maintained home. On the job, Paula was spontaneous, almost to a fault. It was one of the things that made her an effective investigator, one unafraid to follow the evidence, wherever it led—and whoever it pissed off. Her disaster zone of a workspace reflected a brash, outspoken woman who didn't waste time with decorative picture frames—or clearing empty coffee cups from her desk. Her perfectly ordered home was Paula's refuge away from the daily toll of crimes, victims, and bloodshed.

Paula saw John pull the city-issued Crown Vic to the curb and locked up after setting the alarm. Under five-and-a-half feet tall with her boots on, Paula more than made up for her small size with the grace of a bear fresh out of hibernation. She got in the passenger seat and slammed the door.

"Well aren't you a little ray of sunshine this morning," John said.

"Just drive."

John pulled the car from the curb and navigated around lines of trash cans that had been left out for collection. In another hour, the garbage trucks would be finished with their demolition derby through the neighborhood, leaving cans scattered halfway in the street.

"What time did the watch commander call you?" Paula asked.

"About an hour ago."

"I got my call twenty minutes ago."

"So?" John said.

"Why do they always do this last-minute shit to me?"

John turned north on Sixteenth heading toward the warehouses and adult bookstores that marked the city's edge. "Marsden is a good guy, but not always the most organized. I wouldn't read anything into it."

"It's been over a year since I left internal affairs, and they still find subtle ways to fuck with me all the time. Last-minute calls, or forgetting to copy me on case files."

"You did your job, and that's all it was—a job. Some people have a hard time seeing that."

"That doesn't make it right." She crossed her arms and looked at the morning homeless migration from the river to the shelter on North C Street.

"No, it doesn't. But it builds character."

"Well then, I'm motherfucking Joan of Arc."

John grinned, then decided it was time to switch subjects and go over the scene as it was described to him on the phone. "Our crime scene was called in by a woman on her way into work. On Garden Highway, a guy sitting outside his car. It didn't look right to her, so she called nine-one-one. She stayed in her car and waited for the first officer to respond—about ten minutes. She's still on scene, waiting for us to interview her. You wanna take her statement?"

"Sure. Medical examiner called out, I take it?"

"Yep, her people should be there by now. The watch commander said they were finishing up a drive-by shooting scene in Del Paso."

"Who caught that one?"

"Turner and Shippman got that case, and we were next up in the rotation, so here we are."

John turned onto Garden Highway—more of a high-banked levee road than a highway. A cluster of black-and-white patrol cars blocked a lane of the road, and an officer waved them through on the shoulder, to the ire of stacked-up morning commuters. One hundred feet from the road closure, Garden Highway dipped into a sweeping curve lined with tall grass at the base of the levee. A lone older-model Toyota Corolla sat on the edge of the asphalt.

"An isolated spot for a breakdown," Paula said.

John parked the Crown Vic behind a patrol car at the edge of the road. Yellow crime scene tape ran from the patrol car to a thicket of blackberries across the highway. John and Paula approached an officer at the tape, who had them sign in before entering the crime scene. He lifted the tape for them, and the detectives ducked under.

A uniformed officer stood off, watching one of the medical examiner's people snap photos of the Toyota and the man sitting alongside.

"Where's our witness?" Paula asked.

"She's over there. Kinda shaken up." The officer pointed to a silver Honda Accord parked on the opposite side of the road.

Paula strode over to the Honda, and John walked closer to the Toyota and the dead man. From a distance, the man looked like he'd fallen asleep outside of his car, but as the detective approached, the cuts on his face and the gash on one cheek told another story.

A crime scene investigator was in the car, collecting and cataloging the contents of the glove box. She looked up and smiled. "Hi, Detective."

"Karen, you hear from UC–San Diego yet?"

"They should announce their acceptances this week."

"I like the sound of Dr. Baylor," he said.

"Me too, but until I get in, I'm running from one crime scene to another." She stepped from the car and joined John near the victim.

"Have you finished with him?" John asked.

"Photos and prints. I've bagged his hands." She motioned to the plastic bags attached to each hand to retain any fibers, blood, or particulate matter on the victim's skin.

"Looks like he didn't just cut himself shaving."

"I'm not a pathologist—"

"Yet."

Karen's nose wrinkled for a moment before she went back into professional-mode. "From the lacerations on his face and the way his jaw is hanging—he was beaten and beaten hard."

John got down on one knee and inspected the facial damage. "These look like he was slashed with a straight razor."

"There's too much bruising around the point of impact for that. Oh, and take a look at this . . ." Karen switched on a small flashlight and propped open the victim's mouth.

"What am I looking at? Plastic?"

"Won't know for certain until Dr. Kelly does her thing, but yeah, it looks like a plastic bag is caught in his throat."

Paula joined her partner at the Toyota. "Hi, Karen."

"Good to see you, Detective."

"We have any identification for the guy or registration from the vehicle?" Paula asked.

"Officer Miller has the vehicle registration. The guy's wallet is missing."

Miller overheard his name and said, "The Toyota has expired tags, but it's registered to a Lawrence Burger with an address in North Highlands."

Paula turned to the victim and stared at the dead man's face. "Burger—Burger. I know that name from somewhere."

"Look familiar?" John asked.

"No—wait." She got down closer to the victim. "Shit. Larry Burger."

"You know him?"

"Sort of. He was an informant on an old case."

"Drug dealer?" John said.

"No. He was a cop involved in an investigation when I was in IA."

"This guy was a cop? I don't remember him."

"From Solano County, on a task force, if I remember, but he got a couple of our guys dirty. He called me last week."

"Really? What'd he want?"

"I don't know," she said.

"You might want to take a look at this, guys," Karen said. She cast the beam of her flashlight under the car.

Oil and other caustic-smelling vehicle fluids cast a sheen on the mangled undercarriage and shredded tires.

"He didn't stop here because he wanted to," John said.

Paula knelt near the passenger-side door, donned a pair of gloves, and pulled at a chunk of metal impaled in the floorboard. A piece of the black steel clanged to the gravel.

"You find what he ran over?"

Paula yanked the twisted length of metal from under the car, tugging it from the tangled undercarriage. "Yeah, and it wasn't random roadside debris." She tossed the object in front of the car.

"That's a spike strip," John said.

"Yeah, it is. That property tag says it's one of ours. And what are the chances that any of our patrol units were out here stopping a high-speed chase?"

"Slim to none," John said.

"I'm going with none," Paula replied.

THREE

With Burger's corpse loaded in the back of a white van and Karen Baylor directing the broken shell of a Toyota onto a flatbed tow truck, the crime scene looked sterile to John's eye. A dead car and dead body aside, there was nothing else that marked this bend in the road as a terminal place.

A few paces down the road, in the direction Burger had last traveled from, John noticed gouge marks in the asphalt where the tips of the spike strip dug into the surface. Designed to rip open the tires of fleeing felons, they'd worked exactly as intended, stopping Burger's Toyota in its tracks.

"John, over here," Paula called. She stood at the edge of the road in a flattened section of weeds. The overgrowth stood as waist-high evidence of budget cuts. The city couldn't afford the annual weed abatement needed to clear the fire hazard.

Paula pointed at a trampled patch of weeds next to the pavement. "You think our killer waited here for Burger to drive by?"

"Could be. It's hidden by the tall grass. He could watch the headlights as they approached. Kinda begs the question—was Burger the intended target, or was it random?"

Paula circled around the trodden grass. "Nothing is ever really random. Life finds a way of getting payback."

"Karma."

"Payback. Karma leaves too much up to mystical shit. Payback is real and direct," Paula said. A moment later, she stopped pacing and looked at the blades of trampled vegetation. "Blood trail."

Smears of red had begun to congeal on the grass. The blood wasn't cast off into neat droplets; it was smudged, as if wiped off from someone trampling through the grass. The detectives followed the blood trail across a small meadow, and it became more and more faint by the time the path ended at a dirt road. A last smudge of blood on an oak leaf next to fresh tire tracks in soft red dust marked the end of the trail.

"Know where this road goes?" Paula asked.

John shook his head. "Could be a fire access road. I'll check with Cal Fire and see if it's one of theirs."

Paula walked to the far edge of the dirt road, and the dust clung to her black pants. Thick brush and spindly oak trees lined the thoroughfare, but through the natural barrier, a bright patch of blue shown through. Paula pushed her way into the brush, and the dried branches snapped and cracked as she moved them out of her path.

The vegetation opened into a small clearing, dotted with makeshift shelters. The blue object Paula noticed from the dirt road was a plastic tarp covering a ratty yellowed mattress. There were a dozen tents and cardboard condos set up in the camp.

"Code Enforcement hasn't found this place yet. These people have been here for a while," John said. He pointed out an elaborate table lashed together from mismatched scraps of lumber and discarded nylon rope.

Two men stretched a black plastic sheet over a pile of small branches and stacked firewood. A woman tended a dented black coffeepot suspended over a small fire. The men straightened when the detectives entered the camp. The closest one wore a sleeveless plaid shirt and jeans and had sun-damaged skin. "We don't want no trouble."

"We didn't bring any," John said.

The other man pursed his toothless mouth and pulled down the sleeves on his sweat-stained thermal. The faded street gang tattoos disappeared under the worn fabric.

John pulled the badge from his belt and identified himself.

"That supposed to make me feel better?" the man in the soiled plaid shirt said.

"We just want to ask you guys some questions," Paula said.

"That's how it always starts," the man in plaid said.

A twitch from the toothless man gave him away. He bounced into the brush behind him; the crash of dry twigs marked his path.

John barreled after the man. The homeless man's thin build let him dodge in and out of the brush like a rabbit. Jagged wooden spears snagged John's arms, leaving bright welts. The dense vegetation slowed his pursuit. The homeless man pulled ahead and disappeared in the thicket. Highway noise covered the crash of broken tree limbs and crushed branches in his escape.

When John returned to the camp, Paula had the man in plaid and the woman sitting on a log. The man saw his friend had evaded them, and he smiled. "Yeah, you go, Bullet."

"We just wanna talk," John said.

"What if we don't wanna?" the man asked.

"Then we bring some of our friends down here and go through everything," Paula responded.

The woman looked up through a shock of greasy black-and-gray hair. "Say what you gotta say and leave us be. We ain't bothering nobody."

"What's your name?" John asked.

"Dottie."

"You hear anything unusual before dawn this morning, Dottie?"

"What's unusual?" Dottie said.

"Like a car parked on the road up here? An accident on the highway maybe?" John offered.

"Someone parking on the fire road ain't that different. The first and third Wednesday of the month you can find whores and drug dealers up there looking to take our benefit money."

"Today isn't Wednesday," Paula said.

"No, it ain't," Dottie said.

"So what'd you hear?" John asked. He sat on a stump and rubbed his knee. It had been a while since he'd chased someone. He tried to leave that to the younger officers.

Dottie paused.

"Don't say nothing to them," the man in the plaid shirt said.

"What's got your panties in a twist?" Paula said.

"Bullet didn't have nothing to do with that."

"Bullet, the guy who gave me the slip in the brush? What did he *not* have something to do with?"

"Man, just leave him alone."

"He kinda ran out of here quick for a guy having nothing to hide," Paula countered.

John pulled his cell phone from his pocket. "Do I have to call Code Enforcement to rip down this camp?"

Dottie smiled. "You gotta know we don't have cell reception out here."

John looked at the display on his cell, and it read "No signal." "Nice, Dottie." He pocketed the phone.

The man dressed in plaid flannel rocked back on the log. "Man. That ain't right. You don't gotta hassle Bullet. He didn't do nothing."

"I'd still like to hear it from him," John said.

Dottie looked at John. "Bullet was up on the road last night."

"Dammit, Dottie," the plaid man said.

"He came back early this morning, said he saw somebody on the road. He said it was someone he knew."

"Did he say who?" John asked.

"Naw. But he's been shook up all morning."

"Where would he go?" Paula asked.

"Food pantry on North C Street," she said.

"Shit, Dottie, why you spillin' on Bullet?"

"Whatever Bullet got hisself caught up in ain't no good for the rest of us."

"If Bullet turns up, just let him know we want to talk to him—that's all," John said.

John and Paula retraced their steps back out of the encampment to the dirt road. Paula used her cell to take photos of the tire tracks and the smudge of blood.

"If Karen's still here, let's get her to take more photos and samples of the blood before it's lost to the elements," Paula said.

When they returned to the highway where they'd left their car, Karen was taking samples of the blood trail near the road. It seemed she'd found the trail too. Chances were it was the victim's blood, but if the killer cut themselves on whatever they used to slice open Burger, it could blow the case open. Karen left nothing to chance.

Traffic now flowed into the city as if nothing had happened out here on this lonely stretch of pavement. Commuters passed the spot without a glance. It wasn't like Larry Burger mattered to them. But the killer had gone to a lot of trouble for someone who didn't matter.

FOUR

The detective bureau of the Sacramento Police Department on Freeport Boulevard was already humming with activity by the time John and Paula returned from their crime scene. Robbery detectives gathered around a monitor where camera footage of a convenience store holdup played out in grainy gray-and-white tones.

Detectives Turner and Shippman sat at their desks, tapping out reports from the drive-by shooting in Del Paso Heights. Turner nodded at John as he and Paula reached their desks. "What'd you guys catch?" Turner asked. "Ours was a bust. Gang-on-gang and nobody saw anything other than gang colors."

"What flavor?" John asked.

"Looks like Crip on Blood. One victim. He's at the med center. Doctor says he's gonna be fine."

Lieutenant Tim Barnes crossed the floor and didn't break stride when he said, "Penley, we need to talk. You and Newberry in my office."

Paula tossed a file on the top of her desk, and it cascaded into a paper avalanche, dropping photos and reports from three cases onto the floor behind her desk. "Shit." She bent to gather them up.

"Get that later. My office," the lieutenant barked.

Paula dropped the paper back to the floor and glanced over at her partner. John shrugged and tipped his head toward the lieutenant's office.

The pair hadn't yet cleared the threshold when Barnes said, "Get the door."

Lieutenant Barnes sat heavily in his chair and sighed. "Where do I start? I got a call from the district attorney this morning. Not a deputy DA, but the elected one herself."

"I take it the call wasn't about your parking tickets?" John said.

"I wish. She's got an interest in your case."

"Which one?"

"This morning's junkie you found out on Garden Highway."

"Larry Burger?" Paula said.

Barnes nodded. "The DA seems to believe that it wasn't an overdose."

"She'd be right. But why the interest?" John said.

"He was a witness in a case she's got coming up."

"Burger was into painkillers the last time I ran across him. He went to rehab as part of his plea agreement. So I guess he turned into a career snitch or something?" Paula asked.

Barnes's eyes flashed when Paula mentioned her last involvement with the dead man. "When was the last time you saw him?"

"Um, I guess, three—three and a half—years ago."

"He was originally out of the Solano County Sheriff's Office, assigned to SSPNET." The Solano Sacramento Placer Narcotics Enforcement Team was a joint task force of law enforcement agencies along the Interstate 80 drug corridor from the Bay Area to the Nevada state line.

"Before he got caught with his hand in the cookie jar," she said.

"A cool million in meth and heroin is a tempting cookie jar," Barnes replied.

"He wasn't the only one caught in that honey trap."

"That's what has the DA interested in Burger. Remember Sherman, Charles Sherman?"

"He got ten years for witness intimidation, assault, and possession," Paula said.

"Burger was the primary witness in the case that got him put away," Barnes replied.

"Madam DA said Burger was supposed to cooperate with the feds in the federal prosecution of Sherman and the others. They were up on racketeering, corruption, and civil rights violations worth up to fifty years additional prison time."

"Good," John said. "Except, let me guess—without Burger, the case goes away."

"And even though the DA wasn't prosecuting the new federal case, she was supposed to keep all the witnesses lined up—"

"And alive," John finished.

"Yeah, always a plus when it comes to witness testimony. So, Paula, what do you recall about Sherman?"

Paula leaned against a bookshelf and tipped her head back. "He was a piece of shit. Physically a big guy and used his size to bully his way around. He was a thug—but smart. Burger was our best witness; without him, we'd never have been able to put a case together on Sherman."

"What do you mean?" John asked.

She shuffled a bit. "How do I say this delicately? Sherman was slick. He'd cover his trail and leave someone else to take the fall. But he was an opportunist, and he got greedy. All that money and the illegal drugs were too tempting for him. It was always about what was in it for him."

"That's high-risk behavior," Barnes said.

"High risk, high reward. And Burger's testimony against him, along with my IA investigation, nailed him for it."

Barnes stood and rubbed the back of his head to ward off a growing tension headache. "Suffice it to say, there will be all kinds of interest in your homicide. Make sure everything is documented, and chase down every lead."

"Boss, we've done this a time or two. We have it covered," John said.

"I know, I know. There will be Monday morning quarterbacks questioning our every move on this investigation."

"Understood. We'll keep you posted," John said.

John and Paula headed back to their desks on the other side of the detective bureau. Paula knelt to collect the files she spilled earlier.

"I need to get a look at the IA files on Burger and Sherman and get a refresher on their connections. It's been a couple of years since I've even thought about those assholes," she said.

"Good idea. I'll get in touch with SSPNET and see if they can shed any light on Burger and whether he's been on their radar at all recently."

A thick file folder sat in the center of John's desk. A Post-it note identified it as being from Karen Baylor. John thumbed it open. "Karen left us copies of her photos from the crime scene this morning."

John snatched up a few phone messages and handed most of them to Paula. No one dared to leave a message on the toxic waste storage pond that was her desktop. One misplaced message slip could trigger a FEMA-worthy disaster.

His single message slip was from his wife. He looked at it with a bit of trepidation because Melissa didn't usually call him at work.

He dialed Melissa's cell, and she picked up immediately—never a good sign.

"We have to do something about Kari," Melissa said.

"What's up?"

"The school called and said Kari and another girl got into it in between classes."

"Got into it?"

"A fight, John. They're suspending Kari for three days."

"What was the fight about?"

"I don't know. She wouldn't talk about it."

"She okay?"

"Yeah, they're both fine—it was a girl fight," Melissa sighed.

John didn't respond with some of the gory details of "girl fights" he'd seen over the years that included bloody razorblade-slashing attacks, disfigured faces, and bitten-off earlobes. Girls didn't always fight fair, and grudges sometimes collected compound interest that would make a Wall Street banker jealous.

"What did the school say?" John said.

"They have a zero-tolerance policy for on-campus violence, and if it happens again, Kari will have to go to another school. First the smoking, now this."

"Who was the fight with?"

"Lanette."

"Isn't that one of her friends?"

"Yes." A tired sigh came from Melissa's end of the connection. "We need to figure out a way to get through to her . . ."

John thumbed through the photos Karen left for him as he listened. "Uh-huh."

"She's disrespectful, and she's setting herself up for failure."

"She's sixteen, Mel. It's kinda what they do."

He shuffled to another crime scene photo.

"You aren't taking this seriously, John, and I can't be the bad guy all the time."

"What do you expect me to do?"

"I expect you to give a shit and be a parent." The connection went dead.

The words sounded venomous over the phone. John felt the strain in Melissa's voice. It wasn't anger, exactly—it was a burden borne from guilt. And it had nothing to do with Kari.

Melissa was still regretting a desperate deal she'd made a year ago with a black-market organ dealer for their son, Tommy. He'd been passed up so many times on the transplant list that she'd lost hope. She couldn't have known that a killer had manipulated the wait list and delivered a diseased and decaying kidney for the boy. Tommy nearly died from a botched procedure, and she had never forgiven herself. That guilt bubbled up whenever Melissa felt stressed—and John was more often on the receiving end.

John looked at his phone. "Woah."

"Trouble on the home front?" Paula asked.

"Kari's been pulling the whole-rebel-without-a-clue thing since Tommy got his kidney transplant. Apparently, she came to blows with a girl at school."

"Girl probably had it coming. Besides, Kari's a good kid. She's just jealous of all the attention her brother got after his ordeal," Paula said.

Ordeal was an understatement. Tommy was still a fragile kid after the killer had kidnapped him. John unconsciously rubbed the surgical scar from his kidney donation. That was another bone of contention with Melissa—that John was able to save his son, whereas she had nearly killed him.

Paula held a photo of the spike strip that had disabled Burger's car. "I was able to run this down from our property tag."

"Great. Someone's got some explaining to do."

Paula looked sour, and her jaw clenched.

"Who signed for it?"

"I did."

FIVE

Within an hour of accessing the department's property records and finding her name on the log, Paula sat across from Sergeant Larry Lassiter of internal affairs. John asked to accompany Paula as her representative—officers were entitled to representation under the Peace Officer's Bill of Rights. Paula waved him off.

Larry Lassiter—or "LL," as Paula called him—was an investigator who set a torch to all the tired internal affairs television stereotypes. Lassiter wasn't hated among the rank and file, he wasn't a hard-ass, and he hadn't taken the IA assignment to collect scalps—he took it to accommodate his childcare schedule.

"I don't miss this," Paula said.

"What? Spending quality time with me?" Lassiter asked.

"The whole investigating-other-cops deal."

"You did a good job when you were here."

"Still, with a few exceptions, it was soul-sucking."

"The SSPNET takedown was important work, and you were central in that case."

She nodded. "Didn't take long for your bosses to get wind of Burger getting himself killed."

Lassiter bit his lower lip, a tell that would make him a perpetual loser at a poker table. "My bosses are the same as yours—and yeah, there's a hell of a lot of interest in how he ended up dead before he could testify. Let's do this. You ready?"

"Let's get it over with."

Lassiter clicked the red button on a small recorder and slid it on the table between them. "I'm Sergeant Larry Lassiter, internal affairs division, interviewing Detective Paula Newberry on April twenty-third at eleven ten AM concerning the circumstances surrounding the death of Lawrence Burger."

Paula knew she'd been summoned because of the property records, but to be questioned by IA in connection with Burger's death was still unsettling.

"You've waived your seventy-two-hour notice and representation for today's interview. Is that correct, Detective?"

"Yes."

"Did you know Larry Burger?"

"I did."

"When did you first meet him?"

Paula closed her eyes and searched for the memory of coming across the dirty cop from Solano County. "Approximately three years ago while conducting an internal affairs inquiry concerning criminal activity within the SSPNET task force."

"Was Burger one of the subjects in that investigation?"

"Yes, he was."

"Have you had any contact with him since that investigation closed?" Lassiter asked.

"No. None."

"As I understand it, you discovered his car was disabled by means of a Sacramento Police Department–issued spike strip?"

"No."

"No?"

"I didn't discover it at the crime scene. That was crime scene tech Karen Baylor. I retrieved the spike strip from beneath Burger's vehicle."

"Who was there when you retrieved the spike strip?"

"My partner, Detective John Penley, and Karen Baylor were present."

"Who was present when you checked out the spike strip from the department's inventory?" A slight grin crossed Lassiter's face.

"I don't have any knowledge of how the spike strip came from property, or how it ended up under that assho . . . Burger's vehicle. It wasn't issued to me."

Lassiter passed a document across the table. "I am providing Detective Newberry with a copy of the property log in question. You've seen this document?"

"I have. I'm the one who reported it."

"It shows that you received a spike strip from the department's property storage a month ago."

"I didn't."

"How can you explain this entry?" He tapped a finger on the line with her name.

"I can't. Someone made a mistake; that doesn't even come close to my signature."

"No, it doesn't. That's your badge number, right?"

"Not exactly secret information. Like I said, someone made a mistake."

"Any idea who'd want to make that kind of mistake? Burger wasn't exactly voted most popular."

"Neither was I. And no."

"That concludes this interview." Lassiter clicked off the recorder. He pocketed the device and leaned back. "Paula, you know this is the kind of case that makes the brass see shadows in bright sunlight."

Paula stood and tucked her hands in her pants pockets. "Yeah, I get it, but was all of this really necessary? Someone's got their butt all puckered up because they lost a witness. Wasn't the first and won't be the last."

"No one should give you any grief because of this."

"Thanks, LL."

Lassiter shook her hand and held it a bit too long. "That being said, watch your ass, Paula. Politics make people lose their minds."

John waited in the hallway, popping up from the wall he leaned against when she came out.

"How'd it go? You should have let me come in with you. How did they know about this so fast? Did they tell you—"

"Jesus H. Christ, Penley—is this how you treat your daughter when she comes home from a date? Breathe."

"Kari doesn't date."

"I can see why. Come on and buy me a coffee. Talking with LL gave me an idea."

They walked outside to one of the roving coffee trucks that kept the office caffeinated. They took their two coffees and walked to the far end of the parking lot, away from the line of cops that had appeared from inside the building.

She took a sip. "Who stands to gain if Burger doesn't testify?"

"Potentially any of the SSPNET officers who got scooped up in the initial takedown."

"And people who were on the fringes of that investigation. His testimony could have identified more dirt."

"Nobody connected with that case would want him to talk."

"Politically, the city wouldn't want it known that they have more dirty cops on their police force. If the case goes away, no one questions their management," she said.

John looked into his cup and tossed the bitter coffee in a trash can. "The DA hasn't been on the chief's Christmas card list ever since . . ."

"She had to dismiss a dozen cases after Carson got caught selling dope out of the evidence room. I remember; that was the case that got me the boot from IA."

"You have to admit, you colored a bit outside the lines on that one. An unauthorized surveillance of another cop caught the chief's office by surprise."

"Don't go pretending that Carson didn't get what he deserved. He was dirty, and the old boys' club closed ranks around him and all but blamed his shit on me."

"Paula, I don't like this. They were too damn quick to pull you in and sweat you. You're a common thread between the SSPNET and Carson case. You dealt with both of them while you were in IA."

"There has to be more to it than that. LL didn't even ask me about Carson. It was all about the spike strip and Burger."

John's cell chirped.

"Penley."

He listened and said, "Yeah, she's here with me." He paused. "We'll be right over." He disconnected the call and shoved the phone in his pocket.

"Patrol units in Del Paso found Bullet rummaging in a dumpster."

Paula cocked her head. "How'd they know to call you?"

"Actually, he's asking for you."

SIX

John parked the Crown Vic behind a dollar store at the corner of Harris and Norwood. The store was the nicest place at the intersection, which also boasted a burned-out fast-food joint and a check-cashing business. The vacant lot across the street was a well-used pickup spot for hookers and drugs for long-haul truckers. Easy access to Interstate 80 let the truckers get back on the road quickly, topped off with grass and ass.

Bullet sat on a concrete parking bumper with his hands cuffed behind his back. A pair of uniformed officers stood nearby. The foot traffic paid no attention to the action as they went in and out of the dollar store, testifying that police activity here was a frequent occurrence. Bullet was shirtless; his sweat-stained thermal was tucked in his lap. He had welts on his face and chest from his escape through the brush. The oil-stained denim jeans were held up around Bullet's thin hips with a pair of elastic bungee cords.

When John and Paula got out of their car, the older of the two officers stepped toward them. His nameplate identified him as Stark, but John could've identified him by the self-important swagger alone.

"This one belong to you, Penley?" Stark yelled from halfway across the parking lot.

"Now I know why he called you instead of me," Paula whispered.

"I'm tellin' you, Penley, that broad is gonna be your undoin'," Stark said.

"That's enough, Stark," Penley said.

"You know she'll sell you off to IA in a hot minute."

Stark hitched up his utility belt and closed the distance.

"Stark's an asshole. Don't let him get to you," Penley said.

When Stark reached them, Paula asked, "He asked for me?"

Stark's jaw tightened. "You stoop to using toothless junkies to rat out cops now?"

Paula squared up. "I don't know this guy. You're the one saying he wants to talk to me."

Stark ignored Paula. "Penley, you got this? We got real police work to do."

"Yeah, you need me to swap out cuffs?"

"Nah, he's in flex cuffs. Do what you wanna do with the shit-stain." Stark walked back to his patrol car and signaled his uniformed partner to leave Bullet.

Paula noticed a change in Bullet's posture. He tensed his legs, and his eyes opened wide. "Don't even think about it. Sit." Paula pointed at the pavement. Bullet relaxed and slumped forward.

"Why did you want to see me?" Paula asked.

Bullet screwed up his face and looked up at her. "Who the hell are you?"

"Detective Newberry."

Bullet tilted his head and looked like a confused hound dog. "You're Newberry?"

"Why did you tell Officer Stark you wanted to talk to me?"

"I didn't tell that redneck I wanted to talk to you. I said I heard your name is all."

John stepped forward, and Bullet flinched. John slowly lowered himself down onto one knee so that he was eye to eye with Bullet. The homeless man's pupils were wide, and they danced back and forth. Bullet was high.

"Look at me, Bullet. Where did you hear Detective Newberry's name?" John asked.

"Look, I'm sorry I said anything to that cop. I won't say nothing. Just let me go, and you'll never see me again."

"Say nothing about what?"

"Man, I don't wanna get involved."

Paula towered over Bullet. "You are involved. This have anything to do with what you saw last night on Garden Highway?"

Bullet started to sway back and forth. "Man, man, man, I don't know nothing—please."

"What's got you all worked up Bullet?"

"You know, or you wouldn't be here."

"Tell me, and I'll cut you loose," John said.

Bullet's expression changed as he weighed the risk in trusting a cop's word. His head bowed in acceptance. "All right, all right. I heard the guy who got killed last night say the name Newberry."

"You sure? What did he say, exactly?"

Bullet closed his eyes and searched for the memory in the cobweb of his broken and burnt brain cells. "The big dude was asking him who he been talking to. And he said Newberry."

"Larry Burger said he's been talking to me?" Paula asked.

"If the dead guy's Burger, then yeah," Bullet said.

"Did you know the guy asking the questions? The big dude?" John asked.

He shook his head. "No, I just heard him and followed him back to the dirt road after."

"Why'd you follow him?" John continued.

"I just seen what he did, and he was heading toward our camp."

"Did he see you?"

Bullet nodded. "When he got to the road, there was someone parked down there. I heard some voices, and the big dude musta heard me because he turned around and saw me. I ran, but he saw me."

"What'd he look like—other than big?" John said.

"White dude, bald and yoked."

"What about the car? Make? Model? Color?"

"Old blue van with some kinda sticker on the back panel—it was dark."

"You said you heard voices? Did you see who he was with?"

"I never saw no one else. Musta stayed in the van," Bullet said.

"Anything else you can remember?"

"I don't know who the dude is, but the voice and what he looked like—I know I seen him before. I don't know where." Bullet pressed his eyes shut. "I can't remember."

John pulled a folding knife from his belt and cut the nylon flex cuffs. He handed Bullet a business card and said, "Get outta here and keep your head down. You see that guy again, you get in touch with me. Got it?"

"Yeah man, I got it."

"You want us to take you to the Effort, get you some detox treatment?"

"No, man, I'm cool."

Bullet rubbed his wrists, stood from the concrete parking bumper, and snatched his dingy thermal shirt. Penley's card went into a sagging pants pocket, and Bullet left the front of the dollar store, cutting through the vacant lot. He looked back, and he slowed his pace once he was certain he wasn't being followed.

Paula kicked at a water bottle cap. "I don't get it. Burger hasn't been talking to me. What was that about?"

"You sure? I mean, the guy's getting the crap knocked out of him, why would he say he's talking with you? Makes him sound like a CI."

"I know. But Burger wasn't one of my current informants, confidential or otherwise." She took another kick at the bottle cap, and it rolled under their car. "I don't get it."

"Maybe Bullet didn't hear it right. I mean, the guy's a mess," John said.

"I haven't talked to Burger since that IA investigation a couple years back. He left me a phone message. I never returned his call. Whoever he's been talking to, it wasn't me. Might be worth pulling the old file and going over what he said back then. I mean, it's the only thing I can think of that links me and Burger."

"Burger was coming home from work out at the truck stop, right? Let's swing by there and see if they can shine a little light on what he's been up to. We gotta reconstruct his last few days and see if we can find another intersection between him and you."

Paula tipped her head and let out a sigh. "I'm getting a bad feeling about what Bullet claims he watched happen out there. It sounds like an interrogation and execution."

"It does, doesn't it? What could Burger have that was that important? I get that the DA wanted him to testify, but that's old news, really. Sounds a bit desperate if your entire case comes down to the word of one junkie."

Paula opened the passenger door and rested her elbows on the roof, looking across at her partner. "Unless he was going to give up new names."

"If he was gonna do that, the DA would have already gotten a statement from him to prepare for putting it on the record in open court." John got in and started the sedan. Paula took a last look around the dollar-store parking lot. A light-colored object near the dumpster caught her attention.

"Hang on one second."

She trotted to the dumpster and found a wrinkled sandwich bag containing a dozen pills. She snagged a latex glove from her pocket and picked up the bag by a corner. She held it up for John and then turned the glove inside out wrapping the baggy inside. Paula returned to the car with the contraband.

"Didn't your old buddy Stark say they caught Bullet rummaging through the dumpster?" she said.

"Yeah, so how did he not see that?"

"Maybe he did. I mean, Stark is big and bald."

"Whoa, Stark's been an asshole since he graduated from the academy, but that doesn't make him our guy. He's a sloppy cop maybe, but I don't see him being a killer."

She held the baggie between them. "Burger had plastic shoved down his throat. We saw that this morning. If Bullet—"

"Let's not get too far with this. We can try to twist Bullet for what he knows about the pills. But we didn't see him with them, and Stark missed it. It's uncontrolled contraband."

"I'll see if Karen Baylor can pull prints from the plastic. It's a long shot, but what isn't in this case?"

John pulled the gearshift and left the parking lot, headed toward the Interstate 80 on-ramp. They passed a parked eighteen-wheeler with a woman climbing down from the cab. Purple hot pants and a yellow tube top couldn't hide the jagged pink scar that ran from her waist to somewhere under the clingy fabric. Another survivor of life's grind-you-down plan.

SEVEN

The truck stop on Highway 99 hadn't seen a paintbrush in a decade. The peeling, faded red siding was now more the orange hue of a construction cone. Appropriate, since the parking lot was a rough crumble of asphalt and gravel-filled potholes. There was enough space for twenty eighteen-wheelers, but commerce mostly bypassed this section of south Sacramento, and only four truckers rested their rigs outside.

John and Paula entered the main door, walking toward a man in a brown uniform shirt similar to the one Larry Burger died in. The attendant was a skinny black man who could have passed for twenty years old from a distance. His close-trimmed hair held a few speckles of gray up close. He sat on a stool behind a laminate counter worn by years of keys and coins passed across the surface.

John identified himself and Paula to the attendant.

"How can I help you? I'm Brian, Brian Watters."

"Do you know Larry Burger? He worked the night shift here," John said.

Brian narrowed his eyes. "You say 'worked,' like he's not coming back."

"He was killed last night. We think he was on his way home from work," John said.

"Huh. You mind if I get the owner up here? He should hear this."

"Yeah, sure. He working today?"

"He's here." *He didn't say "working,"* John noted.

Brian got on the intercom and called, "Mr. Benton, up front, please."

Paula nosed around the office area and peeked down a hallway. One side of the passage was lined with lockers where truckers locked up their personal items while they rinsed off the road dirt in one of the truck stop's showers. The first few lockers had names written on masking tape: Benton, Watters, Smith, and Burger.

"You have a key for these?" she asked.

"Depends on who's asking," a voice from behind Paula called out.

"Mr. Benton, these police officers have something you need to hear." The way Brian spoke, the words were carefully chosen to direct the owner's attention to the fact that the police were here and to not escalate the situation with a short temper.

"Cops, huh? Mind if I see some ID?" Benton was an oaf of a man: short, round, and balding. He wore the same uniform shirt as Brian, but truck grease had left permanent stains. He rubbed an oil-laden towel in his hands.

Benton nodded at the identification offered and tossed the dirty towel on the floor. "What do you need?"

"Was Larry Burger working last night?" John asked.

"Yeah, why?"

"What time did he leave?"

Benton shrugged. "I don't know; I'd have to check his time card."

"Anyone unusual hanging out last night?"

"Have you looked around? All we got here is unusual."

"We believe Burger was killed on his way home after work," John said.

The corner of Benton's mouth turned up. "I'm not surprised."

"Why's that?" Paula asked, stepping closer to the man.

"He was gonna self-destruct one of these days. Kinda surprised it didn't happen way before now."

Brian shook his head.

"Is that what you came to tell me? I've got a transmission to put back together."

"Larry Burger was murdered," John said.

An arched eyebrow was the sole reaction from his former employer.

"Can you tell us what happened?" It was Brian who broke the uncomfortable silence.

"Looks like his car was disabled and someone beat him to death," John said.

"Damn. He was already gone by the time I got here this morning. At six thirty," Brian said.

"Whatever he got himself into, it's got nothing to do with me," Benton said and turned to leave.

Paula spied a surveillance camera above the main door pointing at the counter and cash register where Brian stood. "That work?" she asked, pointing at the camera.

"Yeah," Benton said. "Records for five days."

"Can we take a look at the recording from last night?" Paula said.

Benton shrugged again. "Why not? Come with me."

The owner led them to a small office past the lockers and showers. He pulled out a knot of keys on a retractable keychain attached to what John assumed was a belt. Whatever it connected to was concealed by a beer belly. The office was more of a storage room. Excess cleaning supplies, parts catalogs, and cartons of toilet paper everywhere.

Benton caught John surveying the supplies. "I gotta keep this stuff locked up, or it seems to walk away." He moved a box of urinal cakes off the desk and uncovered a small twenty-inch monitor that displayed the front of the store. Brian was behind the counter, and the date and time were arranged on the bottom of the picture.

"Can you back this up to last night?" John said.

"Sure. Let me find the remote." Benton patted a lump of paper towels, opened a drawer, and fished around before he found what he was looking for. He pressed the rewind button, and the screen replayed a jittery version of events, including their arrival at the truck stop. The lighting changed, indicating the angle of the sun had moved down, toward sunrise. Brian appeared, and moments earlier, Larry Burger appeared.

In the rewound frames, Larry walked backward, leaving at the end of his shift. Benton was going to press the stop button. "Let it rewind and see if Burger had any contact with anyone during his shift," John said.

A trucker came, paid for an energy drink and a shower. Three times, Burger left the counter and appeared to look around before heading to his locker in the hallway. He'd opened the locker and taken something from it each time. The locker door hid the contents from the camera.

The shadow of another body came into view. Even in the small grainy picture, Burger looked nervous. A twitchy, anxious response to whomever this new customer was. A moment later, they saw why. A uniformed Sacramento sheriff's deputy approached the counter and seemed to argue with Burger.

John took the remote and hit the stop button, then pressed play. The deputy was having a heated discussion with Burger, pointing his finger in the man's face. At one point, he grabbed Burger by his collar to make his point.

The deputy pulled Burger to the bank of employee lockers and threw the smaller man against the metal doors. He jabbed a finger at Burger, which must have been a demand to open the locker, because Burger quickly unlocked it and stepped aside.

Burger's eyes were cast downward as the deputy searched the locker and withdrew an envelope. The big man's shoulders tensed as he asked Burger something. He opened the envelope and withdrew the contents, which looked like three or four handwritten pages.

Burger looked like he was trying to explain, but the deputy shoved him in the chest and walked out of the store.

Paula looked over at John, tilted her head, and mouthed, "What the hell?"

At that point, John stopped the playback. "I'm gonna need this recording."

"I figured as much." Benton hit eject and handed a tape cartridge to the detective.

When Benton locked the office, Paula said, "Mind if we take a look in that locker—the one Burger kept going to?"

"Don't you need a warrant for something like that?"

"The coroner's office gives us the authority to take possession of the deceased person's property," Paula said.

John craned his neck around Benton, looking at his partner. "Bullshit," he mouthed behind Benton's back with a smile.

The owner selected another key from his collection and opened Burger's locker.

Paula pushed in front of Benton and peered inside. The locker was empty except for a 750 milliliter bottle of vodka and an envelope. Two-thirds of the cheap spirit was gone. The camera video showed Burger going to his locker for a drink throughout his shift. She donned a pair of latex gloves, opened the envelope, and confirmed it was empty. But the handwritten address on the front turned her blood cold.

It was addressed to *Detective Paula Newberry, Sacramento Police Department.*

EIGHT

Paula reread the envelope for the sixth time on the drive back to the office. "What's this supposed to mean? What the hell was in here? I don't know anything about this," she said. She slid it into a plastic evidence bag.

"It's gonna be tough to get a handwriting analysis on this to prove Burger actually wrote it, him being dead and all," John said.

"First we have Bullet saying that Burger mentioned my name before he was killed and now this. I'm starting to get a little paranoid."

"You sure he didn't try to get in touch?"

She shook her head. "He left that message to call him, but nothing more. But I can't dwell on it too much. I want to find out who that deputy was. Him arguing with Burger a few hours before Burger gets offed has to be connected somehow."

John's cell phone rang, and he handed it to Paula while he drove. She looked at the display screen.

"It's the lieutenant." She answered, "Detective Newberry." She listened for a moment. John heard the low rumble of the lieutenant's voice. He couldn't make out what was said, but the pace of his speech marked it at urgent or frustrated.

"We're ten minutes out," she said before disconnecting.

"What's up?"

"The lieutenant wants us in his office. He said it has something to do with Larry Burger's testimony and the DA's office. It didn't sound like we're going in for a warm and fuzzy chat."

"With Burger unable to testify, the Fed's new case just went down the tubes along with the DA's news-grabbing headlines for her reelection campaign."

When John and Paula reached Lieutenant Barnes's office, he wasn't alone. District Attorney Linda Clarke stood next to his desk. John didn't exactly know what a "power suit" was, but he was certain the attorney wore one. Tight, tailored, and red.

Barnes gestured to the chairs in front of his desk. Linda Clarke was having none of it. She crossed her arms and glared at the detectives. The opposite of the image she portrayed in front of the camera. Confident, sure, and calculating marked her public persona. Out of the camera's eye, in the lieutenant's office, she fumed. The tight-lipped tension added five years to her face.

"Ms. Clarke has just delivered a bombshell. She hasn't gone public yet and wanted to give us a courtesy heads-up—" Barnes started.

"Courtesy, my ass! You've burned my case to the ground. Without Burger, we have nothing," Clarke said.

"We've burned? What are you talking about? What case about Burger?" Paula asked.

Clarke squared up and looked Paula straight in the eye. "The court might grant Charles Sherman a new trial. Without Burger, the entire SSPNET case goes up in smoke."

"Wait, what case are we talking about?" John asked.

"The original prosecution of Sherman, Burger, and the SSPNET officers," Barnes added.

"So what if the court orders a new trial? Re-try them and be done with it," Paula said.

"I can't. We don't have a credible witness."

"We have the IA investigation. We can read Burger's testimony into the record. I can testify again," Paula said.

"It's not enough. The court will toss Burger's testimony based on the appearance of prosecutorial misconduct," Clarke said.

"Misconduct?" John asked.

"Sherman's attorney received an affidavit from Larry Burger claiming he was paid to testify."

"That's bullshit! Who was supposed to have paid him off?" Paula said.

"You," Clarke said looking at Paula.

Paula shot from her chair. "That's absurd. No one paid that piece of shit to testify."

"The attorney for the petitioner filed copies of two city checks issued to Burger, totaling five thousand dollars."

"What? No frickin' way."

"We're following up on the check issuance now," Barnes said.

"Good," Paula followed. "Still, we have enough to keep Sherman in prison."

"I don't think we do," Clarke said. "Unless we get new evidence, the convictions of Sherman and the others will likely be set aside. He'll get a new trial—a trial with very little evidence to present."

"How long do we have?" John said.

"I'd say a week at most before the court orders a new trial because of the alleged misconduct."

John stood. "Then we'd best get started. Lieutenant, can you have IA give us access to the files and notes on Sherman and the others? The IA folks get a bit squirrelly about turning over their case files."

"I'll make the call," Barnes said.

"I should demand that you be suspended pending a full investigation, Detective," Clarke addressed Paula directly. "This is your one shot to clean this up, or you'll go down in flames. Someone's getting nailed for this mess, and I don't really care who. You or Sherman. I have a nice warm vacation coming up, and I want this wrapped up before I leave." Clarke turned to the lieutenant. "I expect regular updates." Then she strode from the office.

"Well shit," Paula said as she collapsed into the chair. "Why has this become my cross to bear?"

"I don't know what to make of the court's review of an appeal from Sherman. Convicts appeal everything from broken cookies in their lunch bag to the size of their prison cell. Why is this one so different?" John said.

"For the DA, it's political. A huge case she prosecuted turns to shit and there is no way she can distance herself from it. The whole thing stinks. If the case against Sherman and the others gets tossed, the taint of corruption will hang over the department for years.

The city will pay out thousands for civil claims to the imprisoned SSPNET cops. Hell, they might even get their jobs back. If that happens—"

"I'm toast," Paula said.

"Let's not let that happen, shall we? Any ideas where to start on this mess?" Barnes said.

"I want to take a look at the IA files to get the lay of the land. Paula has that background, but I'm a few steps behind," John said.

"I need to look into this new affidavit from Sherman's attorney. And I wanna know who the hell cut city checks in my name."

Barnes shook his head. "You can't get involved in the check issuance matter—IA will handle that. You need to steer clear. Get your old case files and see if they make anything bubble up for you. If you look into Burger-Sherman connection, just know that the DA is watching, and she needs a scapegoat."

NINE

The detectives hadn't stepped ten feet outside the lieutenant's office when John's phone rang.

"Penley here."

"Detective, it's Karen Baylor. I found something you need to take a look at. Can you swing by the office?"

"We're in the building now. What do you have?"

"Blood—and it's not from our victim."

"The killer left his blood at the scene?" Penley said so his partner could follow. He tipped his head toward the hallway that led to Karen's workspace.

"Could be," Karen replied. "But there's something not quite right. That's why I'd like you to take a look at what I've got here."

Karen's workspace was part lab, part machine shop, with a bit of mad-scientist decor thrown in for ambiance. When John and Paula arrived, the crime scene investigator was bent over a microscope. She glanced up. "Come here." She pushed back from the instrument. "Take a look."

Paula stepped forward and looked through the eyepiece. "What am I looking at? It looks like strawberry jam."

"I scraped that from our victim's clothing. I took a small sample after I ran a test with Tetramethylbenzidine. It's blood."

"Why don't you sound convinced about that?" John said.

Karen went to a worktable, took a glass microscope slide from a tray, and set it up on another scope next to Paula. "This is the blood from our victim. Check it out."

Paula scooted over to the microscope. "Okay. Red, flaky, powdery stuff—so?"

John looked at the first sample. "The first one you had me look at is darker and 'thicker,' I guess is the word I'm looking for." He swung over to the second scope. "Yeah, the vic's is definitely lighter in color."

"So what's this mean?" Paula said.

"If you have blood at a crime scene, and it's from the victim or the killer, you assume that it happened at nearly the same time, right? A killer cuts himself while stabbing the victim. Happens all the time. The blood left behind dries at the same rate—or should."

"But these look different," John said.

"Are you saying that they were left at different times?" Paula followed.

"Yes and no. But you've hit upon the right question." Karen returned to the worktable with a swatch of material cut from the victim's clothing. She put this on a lit surface and swung a magnification panel over the fabric. A projection of the image appeared on a whiteboard behind Paula. "The darker, thicker blood is on top of the victim's blood."

"So the blood splattered after our victim's blood?" John said.

"You would think . . ."

"But?" John said.

Karen switched off the viewer. "The darker blood is older than the blood underneath. I'm still testing some ideas, but the moisture content of the blood is lower, meaning it's been drying longer. It shouldn't be on top of the more recent blood."

"What would explain that?" Paula asked.

"I'm not sure, and it's pissing me off," Karen said.

"You're certain it's not our victim's blood?"

Karen shook her head. "I did a quick blood type test, and the victim was O positive. The older, darker blood doesn't match. Different types, different sources. I have the Department of Justice running the DNA, but that might take a while."

"Any medical reason that would explain the blood drying at different rates? Like hemophilia, or anemia?" John asked.

"I don't know. The viscosity of the blood could correlate with what we're seeing. But it's more than drying and evaporation. It has to do with the age of the samples. I'm going to rerun all these again in case I screwed something up. But the DNA profile is our best bet right now."

"What are the chances it came from someone already in CAL-DNA?" John asked.

"There are two and a half million DNA profiles in the system, collected in the last thirteen years. Even if we get a hit on our sample, it could take some time to track it down," Karen said.

John nodded. "Keep us posted?"

"You know I will. Have you heard anything from the medical examiner on the autopsy on your victim?"

"Nothing yet. With the budget cuts over there, probably won't get anything going until tomorrow," John said. "Why?"

"I don't know. Maybe Dr. Kelly will find something during her autopsy that will explain the differing blood profiles. I'm kinda stumped, and I don't like that feeling."

"I don't like anything about this case. There's some weird shit going on," Paula said.

Paula's cell phone chirped—literally, as she had the ringtone set to sound like a field of crickets.

"Newberry."

"Detective Newberry, this is Amanda Farney over at the *Sacramento Bee*." Amanda was a mostly fair reporter at the local newspaper, one that hit up Paula from time to time for an exclusive.

Paula clenched her jaw. "Amanda, how'd you get this number?"

"A girl's got her sources."

Probably bought the watch commander a drink after work. "I'm kinda tied up right now. Why don't you call my office line and leave a message—"

"I just need a quick response about the court looking into Charles Sherman's request for a new trial."

"You should call the department's public information officer," Paula said.

"I have a source indicating the court may grant the appeal. Do you have a response for me?"

"Not that you can print, Amanda. I think that's a bit premature. I doubt the court will put much weight in anything Sherman has to say."

"I'm looking at a copy of the appeal. He's making claims that you set him up."

"Fuck him!"

"I can't print that."

"I told you," Paula said and disconnected the call. "Shit, shit, shit!"

"Your mom set you up on another blind date?"

"Amanda Farney over at the *Bee* is going to run a piece on Charles Sherman's appeal."

"You had to figure the press was gonna get ahold of that at some point."

"I've got to get my hands on a copy of the appeal. Amanda made it sound like the court's buying into his bullshit that he was set up," she said.

"You think there's any coincidence that the press got this leak right after the DA had her little visit with us?"

"It would be just like that bitch to spin this to make it look like this is all someone else's—my—fault."

John gestured down the hallway. "I bet the lieutenant can get us a copy of the appeal. You can enjoy some light fiction while I drive out to the prison. Time to get something right from the horse's mouth. Let's see what Sherman has to say."

She shrugged. "Aren't we supposed to call his attorney before we talk to him about his appeal?"

"*If* we were going to talk about the appeal. Our interview is in regard to a person of interest in the Burger case. If he happens to mention that appeal—well, that's on him."

TEN

The California State Prison–Sacramento was a maximum-security prison tucked in the foothills next to the historic Folsom Prison. Unlike its 1880s counterpart, CSP-SAC was a modern facility designed to house the most dangerous and violent prisoners in the system. Slightly more than three thousand convicts called the place home, and most would never see the outside world again.

By the time they pulled into an empty parking space in front of the administration building, Paula had gotten worked up, throwing the copy of Sherman's appeal on the floorboards.

"How can anyone believe this shit?"

John knew to keep his mouth shut and let her vent. Stay out of the blast radius.

"The only thing missing in this conspiracy story is that I shot JFK. Break out the tinfoil hats for everyone. Jesus!" She hit the dashboard with a fist.

"That good, huh?"

"There is no way Sherman could have prepared this on his own. City accounting records, personnel file details, IA interview transcripts—all stitched together with enough paranoia to make it sound real."

"That's what his attorney is supposed to do."

She kicked the document on the floorboard. "Mission accomplished."

"How would Sherman's attorney get IA interview transcripts?"

"Beats me. They weren't used in Sherman's trial, and they weren't part of the discovery given to the defense attorney. How did they even know my interview with Burger existed?"

"Someone leaked it." John put the car in park and shut off the engine.

"Out of context, it makes it sound like I forced Burger to rat out his SSPNET buddies. Follow that with a city paycheck, and it even makes *me* wonder what he was being paid for. I don't like this one damn bit."

"Like I said, that's the appeal attorney's job—to punch holes in the case."

They got out of the car, Paula slamming her door a little harder than she needed to.

"Feel better?" he asked.

"Not in the least." She glanced at the wire-and-concrete prison complex. A stark and imposing place, complete with a lethal electric perimeter fence. "How long has Sherman been here? I didn't keep tabs on him after he went to the reception center at Tracy."

They walked toward the administration building and passed through an entrance gate where they showed their identification and stored their weapons before entering the prison.

"I spoke with the chief deputy warden, a guy by the name of Griggson. He said Sherman transferred here about a year ago for treatment."

"Treatment? They have treatment to de-asshole-ify someone?"

"He didn't get into details and said he'd explain more when he met with us. That's him waiting by the door."

"You know him?"

"I met him when he was a sergeant on the old prison's security squad. Helped us get the convictions of a few guys back then for trying to smuggle weapons into the courthouse while they testified in a Mexican Mafia murder trial."

"Penley, good to see you again," Griggson said as he shook the detective's hand.

"This is my partner, Detective Paula Newberry."

"Detective," he said with a nod.

"So what treatment is Charles Sherman getting here?" she asked.

"I can fill you in. You mind going for a walk?"

A half-mile trek through gates, doors, and multiple sally ports brought them to a bunker marked "A Facility Control." A last check of identification and the detectives followed Griggson down a concrete-lined hallway with a steel door at its terminus. A tall window set into the door looked out to the main yard. A handful of blue-denim-clothed prisoners could be seen walking in the distance. When they reached the door, an electric lock popped, and Griggson pushed the door open.

There were thirty inmates roaming about, and at first glance, it looked like it could be any one of a hundred prison exercise yards. A few convicts played basketball, and others spent their time in the sunlight consumed in solitary activities. What set this apart from the other prison yards John had seen was that the inmates held heated conversations with imaginary adversaries, ducked and dodged from unseen insects, and one even mimicked awkward kung fu movements. A large enclosed cluster of metal cages took up a third of what looked like a soccer field. The individual cages held one inmate; some worked out, others paced, and some just sat against the expanded metal screen.

"What's that?" Paula asked. She'd stopped at the collection of pens.

"Those are walk alone yards for the PSU," Griggson said. When he saw the confused look on Paula's face, he continued, "The Psychiatric Services Unit houses inmates who require mental health care for severe issues: extreme psychosis, schizophrenia, or other debilitating psychiatric disorders. These men also can't be housed in the general population because they've killed a cellmate, assaulted one of our staff, or violated other rules. If they didn't have the mental health condition, they'd be in a security housing unit at Corcoran or Pelican Bay."

"Is Sherman in the PSU?" John asked.

Griggson nodded. "He's in group. I'll show you." The chief deputy warden approached a white steel door set into the concrete wall with "Treatment Center" stenciled above the threshold. He tapped a button on a speaker. "Yard door."

The electric lock popped, and Griggson pulled it open and gestured John and Paula forward. As opposed to the stark concrete in the yard, the treatment center was modern and polished, an ambiance that had earned it the nickname "Taj Mahal" from prison insiders. The space offered individual treatment and clinical space for the doctors and psychiatric techs working with the mentally ill inmates. As a reminder that this wasn't a typical community treatment facility, holding cells for disruptive inmate-patients were included in the design.

Griggson asked a correctional officer at a podium to locate Charles Sherman, and the officer consulted a roster and directed them to one of the group rooms.

A short distance down the hallway, windows exposed the group treatment rooms for the PSU inmates. Like other group counseling settings, the patients were arranged in circles while a group leader—a psychologist, according to his identification card—directed the discussion. In this prison-based counseling, each inmate was enclosed in an individual cage, roughly three foot by three foot, and the psychologist wore a stab-resistant vest.

Paula saw him before they entered the room. Charles Sherman sat in his cage, seemingly unengaged in the lesson plan for the day. He'd aged since she'd seen him last. Close-cropped gray-and-black hair, dark circles under his eyes, and he looked heavier.

All faces turned to the door when they entered. The group leader nodded and tried to continue the discussion, which was on the subject of empathy. Selling salvation to the soulless.

"You FBI?" a man in the closest cage called out.

"Johnson, we were talking about how your victims felt," the psychologist said.

"Man, fuck them. They had it coming."

Sherman's eyes locked on to Paula and followed the detective as she moved through the room.

When John and Paula got to his cage, Sherman stood. What Paula saw wasn't a prison version of the freshman fifteen. Sherman had packed on at least twenty pounds of muscle, most of it in his shoulders and chest.

"We need to talk to you, Sherman," John said.

"This is my treatment time. Come back later."

Paula made the sign of the cross in front of his cage. "There, you're cured."

The man in the next cage stuck his nose to the wire mesh and sniffed the air.

Griggson signaled to two correctional officers to pull Sherman from the cage. A ritual of attaching handcuffs and waist chains occurred before the cage door opened. Sherman was walked backward from the cage, a correctional officer on each arm. They led him to a private room used for individual patient treatment. Sherman was directed to a chair, and the correctional officers backed off and leaned against the wall behind the inmate.

The chief deputy warden excused himself, saying he'd arrange for an escort out when they were done with Sherman.

John sat in a chair opposite Sherman while Paula hovered behind.

"You remember Larry Burger, don't you?" John said.

Sherman rolled his neck and remained silent.

"He was responsible for you ending up in here, wasn't he?"

Stoic, the prisoner showed no reaction or indication that he'd heard or understood John's question.

"What did Sherman do to earn a PSU bed?" John asked the correctional officers.

"Other than being batshit crazy? He killed his cellie."

"Really? Still winning friends everywhere you go, Sherman?"

"He said he wanted a single cell, and when they tried to house someone in with him, he beat the guy into a coma."

"Is that right? Well, Larry Burger got himself beat to death too," John said.

A flicker of a grin shone from Sherman's thin lips at the mention of Burger's demise.

"Did you have anything to do with that? You have anyone on the outside carrying a torch for you?"

Paula slammed her palms on the table. Sherman didn't react to the loud slap of skin against the surface. "I guess you didn't count on getting another conviction for the murder of your cellmate, did you?"

Sherman turned his head so that he faced Paula. "They didn't prosecute. Turns out I'm too crazy to be held accountable."

"Where's the justice in that?" Paula seethed.

Sherman leaned forward. "Who are you to talk about justice?" he said in an icy voice.

"I know you had Burger killed," Paula said.

Sherman raised his shackled wrists. "I have the ultimate alibi. Do you?"

Sherman stood. "Take me back to the house." The correctional officers escorted him from the room. He stopped at the doorway while inmate traffic was cleared from the passage. He looked over his shoulder. "I'll be seeing you soon."

Back in the administration building, John and Paula looked in on the chief deputy warden.

"Get what you needed from him?" Griggson asked.

"Not really," John said.

"How easy is it to play crazy?" Paula asked.

"You think Sherman is a malingerer? There are easier ways to game the system than getting yourself into the PSU."

"One of your officers mentioned Sherman assaulted another inmate," John said.

"Beat a cellmate to death, if I recall. That happened a little more than a year ago over at Old Folsom."

"Did you decide not to file on that case? Sounded like a solid felony."

"We file on all of them. The decision to prosecute isn't ours."

"What happened with Sherman's case?" Paula asked.

Griggson picked up a phone and dialed a number. "Nora, get the DA determination on Charles Sherman and bring it to my office, please."

Moments later, a lieutenant entered with a small file in hand.

"Lieutenant Nora Carrozo, our litigation coordinator."

She handed the file to Griggson. He opened it and scanned the topmost document. He handed it to Paula.

"As I remember it, we filed for murder and assault with great bodily injury. The case was rejected for prosecution. There's a note that says, 'The accused's mental status diminishes the likelihood of conviction.' I've had cases go forward with less evidence. That happens sometimes."

Paula tapped a finger on the page and showed it to her partner. The decision not to prosecute was personally signed by Linda Clarke, the district attorney herself.

ELEVEN

"You think Sherman is faking it?" Paula asked as they returned downtown from the prison.

"He could be, but like the prison staff said, why? Seems like a hard way to do his time."

Paula reached down and snagged the wrinkled pages of Sherman's appeal from the floorboard. "This doesn't mention anything about his current mental health status or that he'd killed another inmate. Isn't that a bit odd?"

"Anything that happened in prison after Sherman's conviction doesn't have anything to do with the original trial and verdict. I think the whole thing smells, but the court is gonna look at the facts in the appeal, nothing else."

"Facts, my ass. Sherman is gaming the system. He always had an angle, and I know he does here too. You heard him back there; as soon as the shrink was out of earshot, he dropped the silent act and started talking," she said.

John swung the car into Paula's driveway. He shifted into park but didn't shut off the engine. "We're on call tonight. Why don't you try to get Sherman's game out of your head? He's trying to get you rattled. Whatever the court decides to do with him is out of our hands."

"You make it sound like a twelve-step meeting, all that powerless-over-my-addiction noise. I'm telling you, he's got a plan, and I want to be there when it comes undone." Paula got out and made the trek to her door. Her pace mirrored her anger—quick, tense, and hot.

John waited until Paula closed the door, then he backed out and went back to the office. He found Lieutenant Barnes in his office going over a stack of reports. The lieutenant glanced up and wagged a report at John.

"Did we forget to teach report writing at the academy? Or how about using spell check? It's not like they have to handwrite these damn things anymore. If we had the budget, I'd send Shippman back for a GED."

John sat heavily in a chair across from Barnes. He took the report and scanned the pages. "Shippman tends to take shortcuts when he thinks no one cares about the case." John looked at the first page, which identified the victim, suspect, and location of the crime. "This is that drive-by shooting out in Del Paso. He probably figured if no one wanted to come forward, then he wouldn't bust a grape on the investigation." John tossed the report back on the desk.

Barnes tapped a finger on the file. "This isn't how we work. Every case gets worked. Justice matters. We start picking and choosing which cases get investigated . . . hell, that's profiling, and we know where that leads."

"I don't think Shippman was profiling so much as he was being lazy. Want me to talk to him?"

Barnes pinched the bridge of his nose. "If you can, otherwise I might end up in a city-sponsored anger-management program."

"Speaking of anger, we went to visit Charles Sherman out at the prison this afternoon."

"Sherman still pissed at the department for flushing him away?"

"Did you know he's in a locked mental health unit?"

"Huh. No, that's news to me."

"Killed a cellmate."

"No shit? That should buy him—and us—some time before we have to worry about his appeal," Barnes said.

"You'd think, but no. The DA declined to prosecute him for the crime."

"Really? What rookie deputy DA made that screening rejection?"

John sat back. "I had the same reaction. But the rejection was made by the DA herself."

"Why would she pass on a slam dunk like that?"

"I don't know, and after her tirade here this morning, I don't know what to make of it."

"I hate it when politics get in the way of common sense," Barnes sighed.

"We're still following up on Burger, but the threads are getting harder to find." John stood and paused. "I'm worried about Paula. She's feeling the heat on this one, and getting blamed for Sherman's appeal is getting under her skin. She's a good cop and has learned to follow her instincts. I don't want her to fall apart because of one asshole."

Barnes remained silent.

"What?"

"IA is going forward with an investigation into the allegation of paying Burger for his testimony."

John's shoulders slumped. "You gotta be kidding me."

"I wish I was. With the DA's interest in this Sherman appeal, the brass decided to cover their asses."

"At Paula's expense."

"She'll get through it. IA will give her notice of the investigation tomorrow. You might want to be around when they do their drive-by."

John nodded. He didn't like the feeling growing in the pit of his stomach, and that feeling took a sour turn when he arrived home. Melissa pounced before he had a chance to close the front door.

"What are we going to do about Kari? She's out of control." His wife stood with her hands on her hips. Her eyes betrayed that she'd been crying.

"I'll talk to her."

"Talk to her? This needs more than a talking-to, John. This is serious."

"Jesus, Mel, what do you want me to do, string her up by her thumbs?"

Melissa's cheeks bloomed with heat. "She's gotten suspended from school this time. You can't act like that's no big deal. We should think about a private school. She needs more structure and counseling."

The mention of counseling flashed John to the PSU with patients arranged in their little caged circle.

"Let's not get too far ahead here. Let me have a minute, and I'll try to talk to her."

Melissa huffed in frustration and walked away.

John unclipped his weapon and holster and placed them in a safe mounted in the entry closet.

A glow from the office flickered, and John expected to find Kari venting parental unfairness to the interwebs on Facebook, Snapchat, or whatever social media platform was in with the cool crowd. Instead, his son, Tommy, pecked away at the computer keyboard.

"Hi, Dad."

"Hey, kiddo. What's up?"

Tommy raised his eyebrows. "I figured it would be best if I stayed out here, away from Mom and Kari. They're being mean."

John sat on a corner of the desk and glanced at the screen. "American history paper?"

Tommy nodded.

"Sorry, I can't help you with that one."

"There were only thirteen states when you went to school anyway," Tommy said.

"We called them colonies actually, smart guy. Your sister in her room?"

"Yep. If you're going in there, been nice knowing you." Tommy tapped out a few more words.

John started from the room. When he got to the door, he looked back at Tommy, working away. It wasn't that long ago that the boy survived a difficult kidney transplant. He was still a small boy in size, but the experience forged a painful maturity that an eleven-year-old kid shouldn't carry. Good and evil in the world didn't always balance out, and bad things happened to good people. Tommy's color had improved in recent months, from ashen to pink.

The organ-rejection medications left him with a bit of a puffy face, but he didn't seem to care.

At Kari's door, John rapped a knuckle on the frame.

"Go away!"

John opened the door, and Kari sat on the floor at the foot of her bed, cross-legged, typing out a text on her phone.

Her eyes glistened, but she tried to hold the tough facade together.

John shut the door and sat on the floor next to his daughter. He took the phone from her hand and set it next to him. "So you wanna tell me what's going on?"

"Nothing."

"Nothing if you're Sugar Ray Leonard."

"Who?"

"Never mind. Why the fight with Lanette?"

"Doesn't matter. I'm so done with her."

"I thought Lanette was one of your friends. You've been in the same class since, what, fifth grade?"

"She's—it doesn't matter."

"It mattered enough for you to deck her."

Kari's eyes started to water, and the thick eyeliner smudged when she wiped a teardrop with a knuckle.

"You want to change schools?"

She flicked her eyes in her father's direction. "No." Kari chewed on a chipped black-lacquered thumbnail.

"Apparently the school isn't too keen on you dropping other girls like a bag of rocks. This three-day suspension is supposed to get your attention."

"She started it."

"Doesn't matter. You're both at fault for letting it get this far. What was it about anyway?" John tried to come back to the reason behind the fight again.

"I can't trust her anymore. She . . ." Kari shut down.

"Can we trust you not to go smackdown on anyone you have a problem with?"

She shrugged.

"Well for the next three days, you need to figure out how you're gonna survive without this." John palmed her cell phone and stood.

"Wait. What? That's not fair."

"Who said anything about fair? I asked you to tell me why you thought you needed to get into a fight, you decided you didn't need to talk. So no talking then."

"God. You're all the same. You wouldn't do this to Tommy."

John went into the hallway, and Kari must have gotten up from the floor, because she signaled that her side of the conversation was over with a door slam.

Melissa waited in the kitchen for John's report. "Well?"

"She's hiding something. Kari said she couldn't trust Lanette anymore. I don't know what happened between them. But here, Kari won't be needing this for the next three days." John handed Melissa the confiscated cell phone.

"What about setting up a counseling session?"

"I don't think we need to go that far with this. It's only a fight—"

"*Only?* John, that's bad enough. But with her attitude around here, we have to do something about it. I think we need to get her into therapy."

"If you've already made your mind up about it, why did you even bother asking me?"

"I thought you'd want to do the right thing."

"The right thing? That's rich coming from you." John regretted the words while they were still hot on his lips. Melissa had drained their savings to make a deal for Tommy's black-market kidney—she'd thought that was the right thing to do, but it had only come back to haunt them.

Melissa's cheeks flushed, and she turned on her heels, leaving John alone in a cloud of distrust.

It always came down to trust.

TWELVE

John arrived at the office early so he could give Paula a heads-up about the bombshell she was going to get from internal affairs today. A little forewarning could make the difference in whether Paula would say something she'd regret. John knew a thing or two about saying something he'd regret—like he'd done last night.

When John got to the detective bureau, a computer tech and Larry Lassiter from IA were at Paula's desk. The computer geek lifted a computer box from a rolling equipment cart and started connecting all the cords, plugs, and wires.

"Morning, Double L. Paula's not going to like this."

Lassiter tipped his head. "That's why I'm here now. Otherwise, I'd have a vest and riot shield."

John sat at his desk and reorganized the stapler, phone, and message slips dropped off by the evening shift. "How bad is it?"

"I don't know. There's a ton of pressure from up top. Please, tell Paula to get a rep for this one."

"I'll try, but you know her. You gonna do the interview?"

"It's assigned to Kamakawa."

"Can you push to get it reassigned to you? I'd like to see her get a fair shot."

"I'll see what I can do. Can't promise anything. You know how Kamakawa is, the anointed one. That guy is willing to do anything to get the next promotion. Oh, shit, here she comes."

"What the hell is this, LL?" Paula said.

Her abrupt arrival caused the tech geek to smack his head under her desk.

Lassiter held his palms out. "It's standard protocol. You know, those city checks issued to that lowlife, Burger. We're having IT run your computer to eliminate any link to you and that check request."

"So you have to go sneak in at the crack of dawn?"

"Well, yeah, actually. Because of this right here, Paula. You kinda scare me," LL said. A smirk grew on his face.

She shook her head, and the bluster started to fade. She walked behind her desk and kicked the side panel. "Get out from under there, you little perv."

The tech crawled backward on his hands and knees.

"Go do five minutes of deep breathing or that downward-dog crap, and get your shit together. Kamakawa is supposed to pay you a visit this morning about those checks," John said.

"Sammy? Oh, wonderful. He have you doing his dirty work, LL?"

"Lassiter came by to give us a heads-up that Kamakawa was tapped for this one."

"Did you plant a listening device on my phone now too?" Paula said.

"No, you want me to? Makes message playback much easier," Lassiter said.

She parked in her old wood-framed chair, the one that made her a little taller so she could reach all the stacks of files strewn on her desktop.

"I'm sorry, LL. I shouldn't have taken this out on you. It's not about you."

"What was that? Sorry?"

Paula flipped him off and picked up her phone on the first ring. "Newberry."

She listened and then said, "How is that even possible?" She sank deeper into her chair and slammed the phone down.

"Karen got a match on the blood she found on Burger's clothing," Paula said.

"The bloodstain on top of the victim's blood?" John asked.

She nodded. "It came from Sherman."

"That's not—"

"Possible?" she finished. "No, it isn't, since Sherman's locked up in prison."

"There has to be a mistake. I mean, I love Karen, but she got this one wrong."

LL took a step forward. "How could his blood end up at the crime scene?"

"It can't," Paula answered. "I can't explain it." She looked to her partner. "Did you notice any cuts on Sherman's hands yesterday?"

"I didn't see any, but I wasn't looking for them, either."

"How hard would it be for Sherman to escape from the PSU, a prison within the prison, and kill Burger?"

"And get back inside, sight unseen, after the crime? Not very likely. I'm not saying impossible."

"But his blood was at the scene," Paula said.

"And on top of the victim's blood. From a timeline perspective, it means Sherman's blood transferred last."

"Karen Baylor was certain about the blood matching Sherman?" LL asked.

Paula rubbed the muscle knot that had tightened at the base of her neck. "Sherman was in the CAL-DNA database. It wasn't a blood type match; it was a complete DNA match. That was Sherman's blood at the crime scene."

"How did Sherman's blood get there? I can only imagine what the defense attorney will say about someone's DNA being on the scene when he's already in prison. It's bound to be ugly," Penley said.

"I'm gonna let you detectives deal with this. I'll see if I can run interference with Kamakawa," Lassiter said.

Paula nodded.

John pulled his drawer open and grabbed a notebook. He thumbed to the last page. "The DA is going to go ballistic when she gets wind of this. Shit! This is all I need today."

Paula rested her chin in her hands and looked at her partner. "Trouble in paradise?"

"I shot my mouth off again. Melissa and I are dealing with Kari's latest rebellion, she made a crack about me not doing the right thing, and I bit on it."

"She's still feeling guilty about Tommy. That's not something she's gonna forgive herself for quickly."

"We have trust issues to repair after that. Honestly, I don't know if we can. Kari getting suspended for punching another girl isn't helping."

"I still think the other girl probably had it coming. Go Kari!"

"No. Not 'go Kari.' Suspended Kari. She won't cop to why she got into the fight in the first place."

"It was over a guy," Paula said.

"How can you be so sure?"

"It's always a guy."

"Let's get out of here before Kamakawa shows up," John said.

"Fine by me." Paula grabbed her jacket from the back of her chair.

"I want to go someplace where I'm not gonna get bitched at," John said.

"You have a travel brochure in your desk drawer?"

"Something like that—I'm taking us to a nice quiet hideaway."

THIRTEEN

While not on the beaten path of vacation getaways, the Sacramento County Coroner's Office was a peaceful place. The sandstone veneer gave the impression of a corporate office rather than a temporary depository for earthly remains. As was his practice, John drove to the rear entrance, avoiding the public lobby and waiting area. Mornings were the time that devastated families collected their loved one's personal belongings, made funeral arrangements, and faced the reality of futures lost and lives changed.

Through the loading dock and back hallway, there was a bustle of activity as the coroner's technicians began the prep work for the day's autopsies, transfers, and cadaver storage. The process relied on the efficient use of dwindling resources and space. The lone chief forensic pathologist, Dr. Sandra Kelly, managed more than one thousand autopsies each year and kept everything running with precision.

John and Paula found Dr. Kelly in the hallway outside her office, reviewing a clipboard. When the doctor glanced up, she frowned at the detectives, then she went back to the clipboard.

"I don't have anything on the schedule for you, John, and don't ask me to bump you ahead," the doctor said.

John put his hands up in surrender. "Wouldn't dream of it, Doc. We need to talk with someone with a sound mind."

"You've come to the wrong place. Nobody matching that description here."

"It's more of an I'm-about-to-lose-my-mind situation," Paula said. She shifted weight from one foot to the other. "Can we talk about blood transfer?"

Dr. Kelly's eyes narrowed. "Don't you have crime scene people for that? Karen—Karen Baylor is very good at interpreting blood spatter and velocity."

"Karen already gave us her ideas, and I need more—context, I guess," Paula said.

"Walk with me." Dr. Kelly tucked the clipboard under an arm and began down the hallway. "Okay, lay it out for me."

"Our victim had blood from two different people on his clothing," Paula said.

"Not unusual. The victim and assailant were likely both injured in the course of the struggle. But you know that. What else?"

"Here's where it gets complicated. The blood from the 'alleged' assailant is layered over the victim's blood. Karen rattled off some science-y gobbledygook about the hydration, viscosity, and proteins and which one was older. Basically, the 'alleged' killer's blood is older than the victim's blood. How does that happen?"

Dr. Kelly frowned. "Did she mention the presence of bilirubin, by chance? It's a by-product of extravascular hemolysis—a fancy way of saying recycling. The old blood breaks down, and iron in the form of bilirubin is absorbed into the liver, other proteins are turned into amino acids—that kind of thing. The appearance that blood is broken down by hemolysis is affected by a couple of factors, only one of which is time. The level of hemoglobin can cause blood to lose moisture content. The humidity and heat all affect drying time. That's why we don't rely on bloodstains or clotting to determine the time of death. There are too many variables."

"The blood sample Karen found—there must be an explanation because the 'alleged' killer—"

"You keep saying 'alleged.' What's up with that? If the blood was found at the scene, on the victim, it likely came from the killer."

John sighed. "Except it couldn't this time. The DNA came back to a guy already in prison."

"Well that's a damn good alibi," Dr. Kelly said.

"Kinda," Paula said.

"Now I see why the age of the blood transfer is an issue."

"How can we be sure it came from him?" Paula said.

"If the DNA says it's his blood, then it's his blood," Dr. Kelly answered.

Paula started to respond, but the doctor stopped her. "There are only two ways it happened. Your guy was there, or his blood was transferred from something else. That's it."

"Could the DNA be wrong?" Paula said.

"I know the media makes hay out of DNA evidence being thrown out from time to time. It's usually a collection error—a contamination that taints the sample. It's possible, but I wouldn't bet the farm on it. I'd find an explanation for how your suspect got to the crime scene from prison," Dr. Kelly said. "Or how his blood did."

"If our suspect's blood showed signs of hemo-sa-whatsit—"

"Hemolysis," Dr. Kelly said.

"That—how would it get layered over more recent bloodstains at the crime scene?" John asked.

"That is a detective question, Detective. Now if you don't mind, I need to get started. What's your victim's name? I'll let you know when I'm ready for his postmortem."

John gave Dr. Kelly the information on Burger, and she jotted a note in the margin of her schedule.

On the way back to their car, they passed the usual morgue hall-way traffic of draped gurneys being rolled into place in the autopsy suite. Each lumped form represented unfinished stories and interrupted dreams. John often heard people talk about closure and the need for answers. But detectives know that sometimes the answers made things worse.

"Wanna go grab a cup? I don't need the office politics this morning," John said.

"God yes."

He found a parking spot near Naked Coffee on Fifteenth and put in their order while Paula lurked over a table until two women felt uncomfortable enough to leave. John brought two cups to the table, an Americano for himself and a black coffee for her.

Paula wrapped her hands around the paper cup. "Since we know Sherman wasn't on a work furlough release from the prison, where did his blood come from?"

"I kinda doubt Sherman is a blood donor. When you donate blood, they always ask if you've been incarcerated over the past year because of the high rate of blood-borne pathogens in prison, like hep C and HIV. Even if the blood bank had his blood, who would have access to get to it and have reason to kill Larry Burger?"

"The Department of Justice had blood and saliva for the CAL-DNA. We didn't take any because Sherman wasn't arrested for a violent crime. So we wouldn't have anything in the evidence room hanging around."

"Which reminds me, we need to find out where Karen is on that baggie of pills we found."

A thin, tattooed barista approached their table. "How was your Brazilian?"

"Excuse me?" Paula said.

"Your Brazilian Blue Pearl coffee. Would you like a refill?"

"Oh, no. No thanks."

"I'm good too," John said, although the barista was more interested in his partner.

Once the young man went to another table to collect empty cups, John whispered, "You thought the guy was asking about your Brazilian wax job, didn't you?"

"Who asks, 'How was your Brazilian?' for shit's sake?"

"I thought you were gonna choke him out."

Paula's cell chirped. "Newberry." She rolled her eyes. "Yeah, yeah. I'll be there in a bit." She ended the call and tossed the cell on the tabletop. "Speaking of choking someone out, that was LL. He said Kamakawa will be waiting for me in the lieutenant's office."

"LL was going to try to get Kamakawa to let him take this one. I guess that didn't happen," John said.

"LL said Sammy just left the chief's office with the DA," she said.

"Oh, wonderful. Let's get more politics in the middle of this."

"This is nothing but politics." She pushed her coffee cup to the center of the table. "No sense in putting this off any longer. Still wanna be my rep?"

FOURTEEN

Yard time for inmates in the PSU was regulated by federal court mandate. Most convicts locked in the unit would agree to anything to get a few extra minutes in the dog runs. Each caged "walk alone" yard allowed an inmate to get their hour of exercise time without getting involved in a melee with other mentally ill inmates. The arrangement was safer for everyone. Even the inmates who collected a dozen different voices in their minds would rather sit in the sun than grow moss in their cells.

Charles Sherman wasn't like the others. Sherman had refused yard time on every occasion since his placement in PSU a year ago. The caseworkers wearing the required stab-resistant vests came to his cell door and asked why. They never came away with an answer. Sherman would sit motionless on his bunk and ignore them. He was compliant with custody staff and not among those who "gassed" the officers when they delivered food, tossing urine and feces out the food port at them. Sherman never understood what that was supposed to accomplish, other than earning a good ass-kicking.

Today, Sherman's refusal to attend treatment sessions and yard time brought a visit from a caseworker, Viki Mendoza. Inmates peered out cell windows when Mendoza entered the dayroom. The unit was quiet until the electric door clanged shut, eliminating any chance that she could come and go unnoticed. Catcalls and demands for attention echoed in the cellblock. She ignored them and walked to Sherman's cell, 8121.

"Sherman, you declined yard again?"

He didn't respond.

"You've been missing group sessions. That's something we need to work on."

Sherman swiveled his head and stared at Mendoza through the cell window. Her hair was pulled back in a tight ponytail, and a bulky green protective vest largely concealed her white blouse. Even with the vest, Sherman thought she would be attractive to most. He turned away, without a response, and stared at the expanse of gray cell wall opposite his bunk.

"Dr. Lewis has you set up for a one-on-one with him this afternoon," she said.

He exhaled a deep breath. "Tell him not to bother; I won't be here."

Playing along with the fantasies of psychotic inmates was a dangerous line—encouraging the delusional thought framework was a game of psychic Jenga. One misstep and the entire structure could crash down. "Where will you be?" Mendoza asked.

"Free."

"What will you be free from?"

The cellblock door opened, and a pair of correctional officers entered the unit. They approached Sherman's cell door. Like the caseworker, they wore the bulky stab-resistant vests, and in addition, they also wore Plexiglas shields to prevent inmates from spitting in their faces.

The shorter of the two hung his hands from the vest's shoulder straps to relieve a little of the weight. The other asked, "You about done with Sherman? We gotta move him."

"Yeah, I'm finished. Where are you taking him?" Mendoza asked.

"Court," the officer said.

Sherman locked eyes with Mendoza, and a slight smile split his lips. The caseworker left the cell front, a little ill at ease from the conversation with Sherman. More notes for an already thick mental health record.

The shorter officer called through the gap at the side of the door, "Sherman, you got court again. Strip and come to the door."

The officer directed him through an unclothed body search and passed an orange jumpsuit through the food port. A minute later

Sherman was in handcuffs, leg-irons, and a waist chain that secured his hands in front of him.

A ten-minute shuffle from the PSU to the prison's receiving-and-release unit and Sherman was turned over to a transport detail from the Sacramento County Sheriff's Department. Each county was responsible for its own court transportation, and Sacramento County had sent a single deputy in the county's black uniform to claim Sherman. The gold sergeant stripes and the chevrons down his arm testified that this man had been on the job for a long while. He was a heavily muscled, a serious-looking specimen. Not a deputy with whom a prisoner would risk a confrontation.

They loaded Sherman in the Sacramento County van and processed him out of the facility for another court appearance.

The two officers who had escorted Sherman watched the van pull away. The shorter one looked toward the blacked-out windows and said, "That is one strange dude."

"Anyone who doesn't smear shit all over themselves is okay in my book."

"Really? That's all it takes to make you happy?"

"Most days, that's enough. What you think of that transportation sergeant? He strike you as a little odd too?"

The officers walked back toward the PSU for the next escort on their list. The short officer shrugged. "Didn't notice. He didn't try talking to Sherman like most of them do."

"Whatever. Who's next?"

The officer pulled a paper from the zipper of his vest. "Johnson in 8220 to the infirmary. Oh, man."

"See, I told you. He's gonna cover himself in his own filth, and we get to do the old cellblock slip and slide."

"Let's pick up a spit hood to toss over his head and a couple of biohazard suits for us on the way."

"Great."

When the pair entered the cellblock, the floor officer assigned to the unit was finishing up a search of Sherman's cell. "Hey guys, come here for a sec, would ya?"

They leaned on the open cell door, and the taller one said, "I'm gonna go roust Johnson. How's he doing today?"

The floor officer flipped Sherman's mattress and checked for broken seams indicating hidden contraband. "He's been quiet today, been taking his meds. Don't go winding him up."

The shorter officer pointed at the wall opposite the bunk. "I didn't know Sherman was the artsy type."

A pencil drawing of a woman, appearing to be in her thirties, easily four times life-size, gazed back at the officer: dark shoulder-length hair, deep dark eyes, and a serious expression on full lips.

"Well that's new," the floor officer said. He released his grasp on the mattress and stared at the wall art.

"Not bad. She's a looker."

"And imaginary."

The officers left the cell and signaled for the control booth to slide the door closed. The shadow of the sliding door sank down over the woman's portrait, over Paula Newberry's likeness.

FIFTEEN

Lieutenant Barnes sat at his desk trying his best to ignore Sammy Kamakawa pacing across the width of the office. The rail-thin IA man stopped every time someone entered the detective bureau. When Paula and John finally arrived, Kamakawa waved them over like an impatient schoolmarm.

"Finally. You've deliberately kept me waiting," the IA man said.

John ignored Kamakawa and pressed past him to the lieutenant. "We heard back on the blood samples. There was a DNA match. Charles Sherman."

Barnes pushed back from his desk. "How is that possible? Sherman is in prison."

"One of our forensic people confirmed that Sherman's blood was on the victim," John said.

Barnes rubbed a tense spot on his temple. "Is it worth sending the blood sample out to the Department of Justice labs?"

"That's where she got the results. She called in a favor and got the fastest turnaround I've ever seen on a DNA sample. Karen Baylor knows her stuff. If she says it belongs to Sherman, then it does. I can't get to the how is all, with him sitting in a prison psych ward."

"Excuse me. I need to begin my interview with Detective Newberry," Kamakawa interjected.

"I'm sorry if real police work is getting in your way," Barnes said.

"Lieutenant Barnes let me use his office as a courtesy to Newberry," Kamakawa said, directing his attention at Paula.

"Because you're all about courtesy, Sammy," John replied.

Barnes stood and gathered an armful of reports. "Don't measure the drapes yet, Sammy. Get this done quickly. I need Newberry back on the Burger investigation."

John remained standing.

Kamakawa nodded to the door.

"I'm staying. I'm her rep on this one."

Paula sat in one of the office chairs and grabbed another with the heel of her boot, pulled it closer, and crossed her feet on it.

"John, I don't need a rep on this. I'll see what Sammy has to say and be done with it."

"We talked about this."

"No, I don't need you trying to fix up something that doesn't need fixing. I'm better on my own. I can handle this."

John paused. "Paula—"

"I appreciate the offer, but I've got this."

John nodded and left Paula with Kamakawa in the lieutenant's office. The IA officer closed the door, took a seat, and began his interview.

Barnes sat at a side chair pulled next to John's desk, the pile of reports in his lap. John dropped his notebook on his desktop and sat.

"Is she taking this seriously?" the lieutenant asked.

John leaned back, and the old desk chair creaked. He stared at a chipped ceiling tile above his desk. "I sure as hell hope so. I don't like her going in there without a rep."

"She should be careful. We both know that Kamakawa has his sights set on bigger things. He wants to be the chief someday, and he'll do anything to get there."

"And sacrifice anyone in the process," John finished.

An officer piloted a dolly loaded with file boxes to the desk. One wheel had a flat spot that gave off a muffled thump on each rotation. "I have case files for Detective Newberry," the officer said.

John shot a glance at the four file boxes and caught the case name written on the side, "SSPNET Sherman, et al." "Park them over there." John pointed to Newberry's desk.

The officer looked at Paula's wasteland of a desk—with empty paper coffee cups, an overstuffed in-box, and a pile of sweat shirts and jackets on the floor behind her chair—and turned back to John. "Someone works there? I thought it was a crime scene training tool."

"Just stack them next to the desk."

The officer dumped the files near Newberry's desk and looked around to see if he was the target of some practical joke.

"Thanks," John said.

"No problem," the officer replied as the dolly wheel thumped away.

The lieutenant's cell phone sounded. He looked up to see if it was Kamakawa saying he was through, but the IA man and Newberry were still holed up inside the office.

"Lieutenant Barnes," he answered.

He dropped the file he was reading on the top of the pile. John saw a flush run up his boss's collar. The lieutenant saw John watching and slowly shook his head. Whatever this was, it wasn't good.

"I'll put Penley on it." A pause, then, "He will, Chief." The call ended.

"What did you sign me up for?"

"You remember Bobby Wing?"

"Wingnut? Sure, who'd forget that crazy ass. He had to hold the record for the most use-of-force complaints. I thought he went out on disability last year."

"Well, he may have started one too many fights. His body was just found in Southside Park."

"No shit? That was one of his old hangouts. He'd meet informants by the lake."

"According to the first on scene, a kid chased a soccer ball to the edge of the lake and saw him facedown in the weeds."

John stood, pulled his jacket on, and grabbed a fresh notebook from his bottom drawer. "So what did you promise the chief that I 'will' do?"

"The chief knows your track record and trusts you to keep a lid on this one. You have to handle it solo. Paula needs to sit this one out," Barnes said in a low voice.

"And the chief is going to let them nail Paula for the DA's case going to hell?"

"He's pushing back as much as he can; the IA investigation will determine the outcome. The chief is taking a wait-and-see approach. But with Kamakawa on the IA side of things, the scales might be a bit uneven."

"I get that, but why pull her from this new case? Wing's got nothing to do with the Burger investigation."

Barnes rubbed the bridge of his nose. "Wing and Burger were partners on the SSPNET task force."

"Oh, shit."

"Very deep 'oh, shit.'"

Barnes glanced at Paula through the office window. She was explaining some point with her hands. She only became animated like that when she was upset.

"Is the chief ordering you to put her on admin leave?"

"Not yet. She's gonna be riding a desk in the office until we get this cleaned up."

"I'm gonna head out to Southside Park. I'll call you with an update. I don't want to be here when you tell Paula she's grounded."

"You can tell her; it'd be good practice for you as a parent of a teenaged girl," Barnes said.

"That's why you're the lieutenant and get the big bucks." John headed out. Paula saw him leave without her from the lieutenant's office. She stiffened and tried to give him a nod, but it ended up looking like an abandoned child watching hope leave.

John gestured with his palms down: Relax, it'll be okay. He hoped it would, for Paula's sake.

SIXTEEN

Southside Park, once a hotspot for hookers and the drug trade, was still resisting all gentrification efforts and boasted an annual "floater" in the lake, as a reminder to the city fathers that building condos wasn't the answer for everything.

John pulled his sedan into an empty slot on the east side of the park along Fifteenth Street. A body turning up in the park was so common that the joggers on the trails that encircled the nineteen-acre green space kept their pace in spite of the police activity. The big network television outlets rarely bothered covering crimes in the park because it wasn't news—it was simply a regular day in the park.

Yellow crime tape staked out a twenty-yard swath of green from a bocce ball court to the water's edge. Vegetation at the shoreline was a foot tall but not enough to conceal the outline of a potbellied man on his back. A crime scene technician lugged a set of screens to hide the body from view and protect what was left of the victim's dignity.

John immediately spotted Karen Baylor on a knee, taking a photo near the body. After he had signed in on the crime scene log, he ducked under the tape and circled around the bocce ball court to a storage building, keeping a wide berth of Karen and the body. Behind the building, four numbered yellow markers on the ground identified blood spatter and a possible weapon: a yellow-handled hammer. The "possible" disappeared upon a closer inspection. The hammer's handle was half-covered with blood, and a chunk of flesh clung to the claw end of the tool.

"Did you know Sergeant Wing?" Karen said from behind him.

"Some. Never actually worked with him."

"Looks like a smash-and-grab—literally. Bashed him with that hammer and took his wallet," she said.

John and Karen walked to the spot where Wing ended his existence on earth. They followed along a trail of bent grass and blood. The ex-cop had crawled to the water's edge after he was attacked.

"Was he faceup like that when he was found?" John asked. A ragged divot in Wing's forehead was a match for the claw end of the hammer. The skin at the bottom of the wound was lifted and torn from the blow.

"He was facedown according to the kid who found him. Officer Tucker has the boy and his mom over by the picnic tables. He figured you'd want to get a statement from them."

"He figured right," John said. "So facedown, crawling away from his attacker?"

"Looks like it. The front of his pants are covered in grass and mud, and he crawled to where you see him."

"The first hammer strike didn't put him down. Wing was an obstinate bugger. Second wound?"

Karen nodded. "Back of his head. A round wound, probably from the hammer again. Dr. Kelly will tell you it's a depressed fracture of the anterior cranium."

"Any word on that med school admission?"

"Not yet. I'm getting kinda stressed that I might not make it through the process. It's so competitive."

"Don't worry yet. If you don't get in, Dr. Kelly and I will both go pay the dean of admissions a little house call."

Karen smiled. Then back to business. "My takeaway from this is he was attacked behind the storage shed, hit a second time here, and the killer tossed the hammer back up to the shed."

"Why toss it there when you have a nice deep lake three feet away?" John asked.

She shrugged. "That's what the physical evidence says."

"Send me your photos when you can?"

"Always do."

Karen went about documenting the crime scene, and John crouched down near Wing's body. Granted, it was a few years since he'd last seen the man, but the year off from the police force had not been kind. Wing's face was puffy and blotched from too much time in the sun. A scraggly growth of gray-and-red chin hair gave him the look of a crack-addicted garden gnome. The clothes were worn but serviceable—definitely not new.

"What brought you out here?" John said.

The dead man's pockets were turned inside out, a sign that someone—perhaps the killer—had targeted him for a quick score.

John sat back on his haunches, and a glimmer of something in the water a few feet away took his attention. He rose, went to the waterline, and whatever it was glinted in the sunlight. Karen was halfway back to her van with her equipment, so John pulled out his cell phone and snapped off a few photographs of the object in the water.

He retrieved a wide-mouthed net from the storage shed and scooped up the shiny thing, dropping the object at his feet. John didn't need to clean the leaves and moss off of it to identify what it was. Wing's Sacramento Police Department badge and wallet lay on the ground. Credit cards and cash were visible in the creases of the black leather bifold.

Who would kill and rob a man and leave this behind? If this was about robbery, they wouldn't.

John went to the picnic table where Officer Tucker sat with a Latino boy who held a soccer ball in his lap, tossing and catching it. He looked to be about nine years old. A woman in her midthirties in bulging yoga pants and an oversized T-shirt stood nearby. She shifted her weight from foot to foot, her patience obviously having worn thin.

"Officer Tucker, who do we have here?" John said.

"This is Mario Luna and his mom, Antonia."

John sat on the bench with Mario. "I understand you were playing soccer and saw something unusual."

The boy shrugged.

"The man near the water," John prompted.

"Yeah. I seen him."

"Did you notice anyone around when you were playing?"

Mario shook his head.

"You come here a lot to play?"

"Sometimes."

"You ever see him here before?"

"I think so." Mario dropped his soccer ball, and his mom gathered it in her arms.

"Is this gonna take much longer?" the boy's mother asked.

"Mario, I need you to remember the last time you saw him. What was he doing?"

The boy's face scrunched up in concentration. "Day before yesterday, I think. He was talking to another man. He seemed mad."

"Who was mad?"

"That man." Mario pointed in the direction of the dead man. "He was yelling loud about not wanting to do something."

"What didn't he want to do?"

The boy shrugged.

John tried a different angle. "What did the guy look like? The one he was arguing with?"

"He was tall, big, and shaved his head. A white dude. He was like you."

"Had you ever seen this other guy before?"

Mario shook his head.

"I gotta get my boy to his *tia's* so I can get to work on time," Antonia said.

"I understand. Officer Tucker took your contact information?"

Tucker nodded.

"Mario, if you can think of anything else, I'd like you to call me, okay?" John handed the boy one of his business cards and a second one went to his mom.

"I don't know what else I can think of. He was just like you."

"Come on, *mijo*," she said. The boy hopped off the bench and followed his mother out of the park. John noticed the mother snatch the business card from the boy's hand.

"I think that's going to be a dead end," Tucker said.

"You heard what he told me. You pick up anything else from them before I got here?"

"Nope, other than the kid comes here almost every day after school before his mom has to head off to work."

John leaned back on the bench and watched as the medical examiner's crew began loading up Wing's body. "You notice anyone showing up at the crime scene who looked out of place?"

"How so?"

"Wing was one of us at one time," John added.

"There were a couple of units that did a drive-by and wanted a look-see. Stark and his new partner for one."

"Stark keeps showing up. He say anything?"

"He's always saying something. But no, now that you mention it, he didn't say a damn thing. That's unusual behavior, wouldn't you say?"

SEVENTEEN

The receiving-and-release unit at the prison was the central control point for all prisoners coming in and out of the maximum-security institution. Charles Sherman returned from his OTC—out to court transport—and stepped down from the caged van. The same sheriff's sergeant who picked him up signed the paper work returning him to state custody, reported no issues with the prisoner, and didn't want to stick around and swap stories with the R&R staff like most other transport details did. Once again, Sherman was the only inmate in the transport van.

The evening meal was almost ready, the smell wafting from the central kitchen, two facilities to the north. It didn't matter what was on the menu; everything held the same cloying odor and every prison kitchen smelled the same. Sherman was hungry on the drive back to the prison, but the sergeant didn't stop for food like some do. Luckily the starchy, potted-meat smell quelled his hunger pangs.

"How'd you hurt your hand?" one of the R&R officers asked.

Sherman's right palm bore a fresh cut. It had stopped bleeding, but it was a ragged gash. Sherman didn't answer.

"Just like those county cops to drop someone off and leave us the paper work. I'll get in a request for a medical technical assistant to check him out." The officer typed in a message into the prison-wide computer system noting the injury to the inmate's hand.

The officers got the usual nonverbal but compliant response from Sherman. He didn't resist during his escort back to his cell. The housing unit was louder than normal, with most of the noise coming from a cell on the second tier. The cell directly above his had flooded; its occupant had been stuffing his toilet with his sheet again. A cascade of water fell from the tier and pooled on the dayroom floor. The inmate kicked the cell door, and the blaring, rhythmic sound echoed in the enclosed unit.

"Someone's gonna have a headache later," one of Sherman's escort officers said.

Sherman got to the cell front, and the control booth officer pressed the button to open his door. At the same time, a cell extraction team entered the dayroom: a half dozen officers assembled with helmets, pepper spray, and large Plexiglas shields. Another officer carried a video camera to document the process and ensure that all use-of-force policies were followed.

"Lock up your prisoner," a lieutenant with the extraction team said to Sherman's escorts.

Sherman stepped inside, and the door slid shut. The officers removed his handcuffs and waist chain through the food port.

"Let's get out of here before we end up writing reports on this," one of the escorts said.

Inside his cell, Sherman went to his bunk, sat, and faced his pencil-drawn image of Paula Newberry. He glanced out his cell window, waiting until all the officers in the cell extraction team were occupied with the disruptive prisoner above on the second tier. Sherman stood and fished a hand down his jumpsuit, around behind, and found a short piece of string and pulled, grunting. He lifted his hand out and stepped to his stainless-steel sink and rinsed the shit off of the plastic-wrapped bundle he'd just pulled from his rectum.

Sherman untied the string and unwrapped the plastic from around a brass key, freshly cut based on the brightness of the metal on the business end. At the rear of the cell, Sherman pried up a piece of caulking from the window. The key went into the space behind the caulk, and Sherman rubbed the flexible material back into the gap, the broken seam almost invisible.

He sat back on his bunk once more, smiling at Paula's image while a symphony of metal batons on human bone rang from above.

EIGHTEEN

"Kari wasn't home when I got back from picking up Tommy after school." Melissa pounced before John had a chance to take off his jacket and lock his service weapon in a gun locker inside the entry closet.

John glanced at his watch. "It's after six."

"She's not taking my calls; she's letting them go to voice mail," Melissa said.

"We took her phone last night, remember? It's in the desk drawer."

Melissa huffed to the office, opened, and slammed drawers.

"Bottom drawer," John called out from where he stood at the front door. He hung up his jacket and went to the kitchen. He thought about a tall gin with a splash of tonic but decided he didn't need the ration of crap he'd get from Mel.

Melissa returned with the cell phone listing her missed calls to her daughter. All ten of them.

"She's never done this before. Getting suspended, then she doesn't come home. What's going on with her?" Melissa said.

"You tried calling any of her friends?"

"They acted like they were covering for her. I've known these girls since they were in diapers, and I know when they're lying."

"Why would they need to cover for her?" John said.

"Because she's changing. She's not the Kari we used to have."

Tommy came down the hallway with a math book. "Hey, I'm having a problem understanding this—could you?"

"I can try," John said. "This Common Core stuff makes no common sense to me. Hey, where do you think your sister is?"

"I don't want to get her mad at me," Tommy said.

"Did she tell you where she went?" Melissa asked.

The boy shook his head. "She didn't tell me."

"Dammit," Melissa muttered.

"But I kinda overheard what she was doing."

"And," his father prompted.

"Kari was gonna go meet some friends after school and hang out. The mall, I think."

"Mall, which mall?" Melissa said.

Tommy shrugged.

A rustle at the front door drew everyone's attention. Kari opened the door and tossed her purse on the sofa. She raised her chin and gave a defiant stare to her mother. "What?"

"Where have you been?" Melissa asked.

"Out."

"Out where?"

Kari rolled her eyes. "What does it matter?"

"It matters because you're sixteen."

"I'm sixteen, and I can be with my friends."

"I never said you couldn't! The courtesy of a call to let me know isn't asking too much."

"You took my phone! How was I supposed to call?"

Tommy slithered back to his room and closed the door.

"What's his name?" John asked.

Kari's face flushed. "What?"

"What?" Melissa echoed, turning toward him.

"His name, Kari. Who's the guy?"

Kari pursed her lips.

"Spill it, Kari," John pressed.

"Cameron. His name is Cameron, all right?"

"Does Cameron have a last name?"

"Meadows."

Melissa started to speak, but John put up his hand. "Does he go to your school?"

"Uh-hum."

"Is that a yes?"

"Yes."

"Is this why you got into a fight with Lanette?"

"She tried to come between us—" Kari said.

"You fought with your friend over a boy?" her mother asked, cutting her off.

"You don't understand."

"If this Cameron is thoughtless enough to let you and Lanette come to blows over him, then he's an insecure ass who doesn't deserve your attention," John said.

"Can I go to my room now?"

"We're not done with this—" Melissa started.

"Go," John said.

Kari put her head down, grabbed her backpack, and stormed down to her room.

After Kari's door slammed, Melissa turned on John. "How dare you undermine me in front of her. It's bad enough trying to parent by myself."

"There was nothing more to gain from bitching at her." As soon as the words left his mouth, he regretted them—again.

"Bitching? Really? You're going to make this my fault? Don't you think we need to know where our daughter is and who she's with?"

"I didn't say it was your fault. And she told you. She has a boyfriend—Cameron. Maybe if she didn't think you'd jump down her throat, she'd have told us sooner."

"You're an asshole."

"I'm getting that a lot lately." John went for the gin bottle after all. He poured himself a double.

Another door slammed, and John found himself all alone. He carried his drink out to the patio and pulled out his cell phone. He hit Paula's number and sat in a lounge chair.

Paula must have looked at the caller ID because she answered, "How's your supersecret Bobby Wing case going?"

"Nothing secret about it. Even Stark showed up to pay his lack of respects."

"Stark?"

"Uh-huh. He keeps showing up, and it's not from a desire to do a crackerjack job of his police work." John took a sip of his drink. "How'd it go with Kamakawa?"

A sigh from Paula's end of the connection. "That man is infuriating. I mean, I get it. He has a job to do. Believe me, I get that. But he doesn't have to be an absolute prick about it."

"I'd worry if he wasn't."

"So his big deal was someone signed for a check requisition for five grand for a payment to Burger," she said.

"That much we already knew. The DA told us that much."

"Apparently, I submitted the request. At least that's what the paper trail shows. Just like the spike strip, someone signed my name."

"No shit? Why you?"

"That was Sammy's unending question. The signatures didn't match each other and certainly didn't come close to looking like mine. Sammy said that could have been deliberate on my part."

"We need to come at this like we're working a case. Who'd want to drag you through the shit?"

"Really?"

John could visualize Paula's incredulous expression, head tilt, and scowl. "Who jumps to the top of that list, then?"

"I can't think of anyone I've arrested who would have enough access to departmental resources to pull something like this off. Which, as shitty as it sounds, means it's someone from inside the department."

"Someone with a history with Burger and Bobby Wing. The SSPNET files came in today—four boxes of them. We add the Sherman connection to the mix, and we'll find the key to this mess."

"Yeah, I don't think I'm gonna get any help from Sammy, that's for sure." She paused. "Thanks."

"For what?"

"You never asked if I paid Burger to testify."

"Never crossed my mind. Threatened him perhaps, but not pay him."

Paula laughed. "You're an asshole."

"So I hear—repeatedly. See you first thing in the morning, and we'll start going over the SSPNET files."

"Yeah, I'll be a few minutes late. I have to replace the lock on my garage. I'm not sure when, but someone tried to break in and messed up the dead bolt on the side door. I want to say kids, but with all the shit going on, I'm feeling a bit paranoid."

"Need me to come over?" John offered.

"No—I've got this. I'm sure it was nothing. I shouldn't have said anything. See you tomorrow."

They hung up, and John settled back into the patio chair. He felt a twinge from the surgical scar on his side. The pain was good. It reminded him of what was really important. Every new case began as a faceless paper file, another in an endless line of victims. There would always be another one. But he only had one family, and it was falling apart around him.

John tossed the last inch of his drink on the lawn and went back inside. Kari was in the kitchen, getting a bottle of water from the refrigerator and looking like she was hoping to avoid parental contact.

"How long have you been seeing Cameron?" John rinsed his glass in the sink and placed it in the dishwasher.

"A couple of weeks maybe."

"You like him? Never mind that; you do or you wouldn't be smacking Lanette around for trying to poach him." John leaned back against the counter.

"Yeah, I guess."

"You gonna bring him around here so we can meet him?"

"Are you kidding? You and mom will act all weird and freak out."

"Why? Does he have a tail or something?"

"You just will."

John pushed away from the counter and gave Kari a hug. She was a little stiff at first but then hugged him back. "Do me a favor. Give your mom a break, okay?"

"She treats me like a little kid. I'm not five anymore." Although the pout on her face would say differently.

"Give her some respect; she deserves that much. You act differently, and she might treat you differently."

"I guess."

"But you do need to let us know when you're going somewhere. Parents worry enough without throwing that into the mix. Okay?"

Kari nodded. She hugged her father once more and took her water bottle back to her room.

John grabbed two glasses of water and took them to the master bedroom. Melissa was propped up on the bed reading a novel, one of those popular fantasy books with vampires. She glanced up and gave a bit of a smirk.

"Truce?" John said.

"You ply me with water?"

That was one of the things John loved about her. When Melissa angered, she burned hot and didn't pull her punches, but then it was over. Rarely a grudge or resentment held. He held the water out for her and pulled it away when she reached for it. "Truce?"

"Give me the water, and we'll talk about it."

"Jesus, more talk?"

She grabbed him by the shirt collar and pulled him down. "You really are an asshole."

He handed over the water and propped up on a pillow beside her. "I think Kari is afraid of how we'll react to her little friend."

"She's ashamed of us—what teenager isn't?"

"Probably just you; I'm the cool parent," he said.

Melissa slapped him on the thigh.

"How did you know she had a boyfriend?"

"My keen parental awareness."

"Bullshit."

"Paula told me her fight with Lanette was probably about a guy. Turns out she was right."

John's cell phone rang.

Melissa tried to grab it. "No."

"Penley."

He listened for a moment and then said, "Where?" He rubbed the back of his neck. "I'll pick up Paula—" He shook his head and bit his lip. "All right, Lieutenant."

John tossed the phone on the bed.

"What's the matter?"

"Something turned up with a connection to a case we're working. I'm flying solo until IA stops screwing over Paula."

"Why would they do that?"

"They need a sacrificial lamb, and it looks like it's gonna be her."

NINETEEN

John pulled up to the midtown Victorian home a few seconds after Lieutenant Barnes.

"You sure we need to do this?" John asked.

"Better coming from you and me than one of the asshats in city hall," Barnes said.

They walked up the sidewalk toward the front door and heard a noise come from the side of the building, the high-pitched whir of an electric drill. The pair went to the source of the sound, on the side of the detached garage, and found Paula repairing the door.

She drove three-inch screws into the doorframe around the strike plate for the dead bolt. A surprised look appeared when she noticed their approach, one that went from a smile to concern in seconds.

"Gentlemen? I know SPD doesn't make home repair house calls . . ."

"I thought you were gonna do this in the morning," John said.

She finished driving in the last screw and dropped the drill into a tool bag at her feet. "I was, but then I thought that leaving it unlocked overnight might invite problems."

"Was anything taken?" the lieutenant asked.

"No, why?" she countered.

"Are you certain?" he asked.

"I mean, I didn't take an inventory, if that's what you're asking, but some expensive power tools and my road bikes weren't touched."

Barnes had a brown paper bag at his side, one that Paula didn't seem to notice until he started to open it.

"Does this look familiar?" Barnes said.

"It's a hammer. I have one like that."

"Where do you keep yours?" John asked.

She glanced at the door with the repaired lock, then to the tool bag at her feet. She kicked it toward her partner.

The zippered top was already open, and John snapped on a latex glove and parted the opening. Yellow-handled tools were strewn on the bottom of the bag under the drill. Four screwdrivers, a small yellow pry bar, and a set of matching wrenches, but no hammer. "Could it be on a workbench inside or something?" John asked.

"No, it was in there," Paula said.

"This one," the lieutenant hefted the bagged hammer, "has your prints on it. Could it be yours?"

She tucked a wayward strand of hair behind her ear and leaned closer to the bag. "It's the same brand as mine."

"Was your tool bag in the garage when the lock was broken?" John asked.

She nodded.

"You didn't report it when you noticed it?" John asked.

"Why? Nothing was taken." Then she glanced back at the hammer in the bag. "I didn't think anything was. It would have been one of those pain-in-the-ass over-the-phone crime reports. There wasn't a point."

"When was the break-in?" John asked.

"Sometime in the last couple of days. I found it about an hour, hour and a half ago."

"That's in our window," Barnes said.

"Window? What window? What's this about?"

"This hammer, your hammer, was used in a homicide," the lieutenant said.

The color drained from Paula's face, and she leaned against the garage wall. "Well, shit. Who was killed?"

"Bobby Wing," John answered.

"Another SSPNET connection. Son of a bitch. Lieutenant, you gotta know I didn't have anything to do with this. I keep getting pulled into this river of shit. Sherman wants me to go down for these killings."

Barnes placed the hammer back into the brown paper bag. "I know you didn't—couldn't—but someone is going through a hell of a lot of work to make you look really bad on this one."

"I'll nail down the timeline for both killings, and it will prove you had nothing to do with them," John said.

"Not to sound like I'm paranoid, but why me?"

"You are the common denominator. Wing, Burger, and Sherman were all connected with your SSPNET investigation. If your credibility is undermined, what happens to the case?" Barnes said.

She nodded. "It goes down the toilet with me."

"The DA made a point of saying either you or Sherman will burn for her case falling apart. We need to find another source to testify against Sherman, what with Burger out of the equation now."

"Bobby Wing would've," Paula said.

"Wingnut was Burger's partner. You think that means he was ready to back Burger against Sherman?"

"I think so. Bobby was willing to look the other way on a lot of things, but he didn't think much of Sherman and his cowboy attitude."

"Who else in the SSPNET would back Burger's original testimony regarding Sherman?" Barnes asked.

Paula tipped her head back and shut her eyes tight. "Burger was the focus. Once we turned him, everything fell into place against Sherman and the others. I'd have to go over my notes, but there could be one or two who might testify in exchange for a reduced sentence."

"So we aren't talking about upstanding citizens, are we?" Barnes said.

"Not so much. It's bad when character witnesses are all dirty cops moonlighting as meth dealers. Shit, what am I gonna do?"

John rolled a pebble under his shoe, and his sole kept catching on it—it wouldn't go away. A spark of a lingering thought ignited. "Where was Stark when the SSPNET stuff was going down?"

"Stark's been on patrol his entire career. There's no way he'd get picked for a task force assignment," Barnes said.

"Wait." Paula stood taller. "Stark went to the academy with Carson—"

"The cop who got busted selling dope out of the evidence room?" John asked. "What does he have to do with—?"

"—and Carson and Stark were patrol partners when I started," she finished.

"They were. I remember that," Barnes said.

"You think Carson told his old partner what was going on in the SSPNET?" John asked.

"Maybe?" she responded. "You think Carson and the SSPNET guys had a deal for a cut of whatever they confiscated? A piece of the action for Carson on what he was able to move out of the evidence room?"

"Holy shit. Not this again. That evidence room bust was a disaster. Cases dismissed because the evidence went missing, our investigations questioned by every defense attorney. When the chief gets wind of this, he'll have a stroke," Barnes said.

"Wait a sec," Penley said. "Let's not jump headfirst here. Stark is a waste of space. I think we can all agree on that. I can't see him as a great mastermind, pulling all this elaborate setup together to make Paula look guilty. He doesn't have it in him. But he knows something."

"IA won't let you investigate another cop," Barnes said. He turned to the street, where a van pulled up. "I asked for a crime scene tech to come and see if we can pull prints or fiber from your break-in."

"Great," Paula said.

John recognized the small silhouette in the street. "Karen will handle this quietly."

"The old lock and strike plate are in the garbage can. It's gonna have my prints all over it."

"We're covering all the bases here, Paula," Lieutenant Barnes said.

"I know. I don't have to like it though."

"I think I can get Stark talking," John said.

"How's that?" Barnes asked.

"You've already put her on desk duty. Now reassign or suspend her."

"Wait? What? Do I get a say in this?" Paula said.

"I think I see where you're going with this." Then to Paula, Barnes said, "Detective Newberry, report to the armory at zero eight hundred tomorrow morning."

TWENTY

"Well, well, well, what do we have here?" Stark said. His throaty voice carried in the small confines of the armory.

Paula ignored the question and marked off shotgun serial numbers on a clipboard. She was in uniform, a clear signal to her peers that her time in the limelight as a detective had come to an abrupt end.

"Hey, Princess, I can't tell you how much this warms my heart."

"Don't you have someplace to be?" Paula said without taking her eyes off the inventory on her clipboard.

Stark leaned against the gun cage where the department's weapons were stored and repaired. "It was only a matter of time until your lies bit you on your pretty little ass."

"Thank you. I didn't think you noticed."

He slapped the metal of the gun cage with an open hand, the loud sound finally drawing Paula's eye up to him.

"They put you in a cage for a reason. Get used to the view, or do us all a favor and kiss the end of one of those shotguns."

Paula stiffened and tossed the clipboard on a nearby desk.

"That's enough, Stark," John's voice sounded from the hallway.

Stark turned and nodded at John. "Me and your old partner were catching up. Happy to see you didn't get dragged down with her. Like I told you before, she's ruined careers of good cops with her bullshit."

"You're running late for shift briefing. I'll walk with you." Stark and John turned away, and John glanced over a shoulder at

Paula. He couldn't hide a smile as he said, "She's gonna have to live with what she's done."

"Ain't that the truth," Stark said.

Paula narrowed her eyes and flipped John off.

Once out of earshot, John leaned to Stark. "What are they saying about Paula? About her getting the boot? Any scuttlebutt about me getting pulled into her mess?"

Stark loved being the center of the station gossip universe. If there were a departmental equivalent to the *National Inquirer*, Stark would be it, always digging up who's sleeping with whom and which cops were lazy. Somehow, though, Stark never put himself on his own list.

"It's great. I knew you shouldn't have been saddled with that baggage, and she finally got hers. Far as everyone goes, you're golden."

"You really think she had something to do with getting Burger killed?"

Stark's jawline tensed for a split second. "She paid him to lie about what went on in the task force. That was enough to get him killed."

"How do you know she paid him?"

"Burger told me."

The watch sergeant's voice sounded from the briefing room.

"Hey, I gotta go," Stark said and headed into the briefing.

John backtracked to the armory, where Paula sat at one of the desks inside the gun cage, not going over weapon repair orders as noted on the binder in front of her, but the SSPNET internal affairs files she had tucked away inside.

"He knows something. I asked him straight-up if he thought you had something to do with Burger and his response was weird."

"Consider the source," she said.

"True, but he thinks you paid Burger to lie about the task force and that was enough to get him killed. Not that you killed him or a drug deal went bad. Ratting out the task force is what ended him."

"Snitches get stitches."

"Something like that. I didn't get to press him about Wing or Sherman."

Paula tore off a scrap of paper and slid it through the wire mesh. John took it and unfolded it. "What's this?"

"Those are three more cops who went down because of the Sherman case. They stand to gain if the DA tosses the case. One is still inside, doing time at a fire camp down south, the other two are back out on the streets, both local."

He tucked the note into his shirt pocket. "I'll check it out. I've got a name for you to run down. Cameron Meadows."

Paula jotted the name down. "How's he figure in?"

"He doesn't. That's Kari's new friend."

"I knew it."

"She's afraid to let Mel and I meet him."

"Smart girl."

"Just see if he has a juvenile record, would you?" John said.

Paula opened another IA file. "I will. And I'll keep at this. I know there's something in here that will keep Sherman in prison for the rest of his term."

"I'll get back to you on what I find out about these." John tapped his shirt pocket.

At his desk in the detective bureau, John started to look up the names Paula had supplied when a loud voice from one of the other detectives said, "Turn that up."

A television breaking news alert came across the screen of the TV set tucked on top of a file cabinet. The banner at the bottom of the screen said, "Accused Cop May Get New Trial."

A news anchor with thin shoulders and a receding gray hairline announced, "Sources within the district attorney's office revealed that the court will rule today on the appeal of former cop Charles Sherman. Sherman was found guilty of multiple accounts of fraud, corruption, and possession of controlled substances, all stemming from his participation in a multiagency drug task force. The ex-cop appealed on the grounds that his conviction was secured by means of coerced testimony and prosecutorial misconduct. If the court grants Sherman's appeal, he could be re-tried on the charges. District Attorney Linda Clarke will provide a statement after the court issues its ruling."

The talking head went onto another story dealing with water restrictions during the drought before someone in the squad room turned the volume back down. "Sherman's guardian angels must be looking out for him," a voice said from one of the desks.

"Guardian angel, my ass," John muttered.

He unfolded the note Paula gave him with the names of two ex-cops who threw their careers and pensions away for Sherman. Both were former sheriff's deputies from adjoining counties but listed residences in Natomas, on the northern edge of the city.

John typed in their information in LEADS—the Law Enforcement Automated Data System designed for local law enforcement to manage parolees in the community. The first name, George McDaniel, wasn't under parole supervision. He had been discharged without parole because of the nonviolent offense that brought him to prison. A prison mugshot showed the ex-cop looked more like a skinhead gang member now: shaved head, defiant glare at the camera, and a recent prison-issue white pride tattoo on the side of his neck. *If you can't beat 'em, join 'em,* John figured.

The second man was Joseph Ronland. The system reported he did his time in county jail and never made it to state prison. Ronland was African American and sentenced to three years' probation, which meant John could search the man's residence without a warrant. John printed his mugshot.

Ronland worked at a car wash downtown, a place popular with ex-cons. The car wash wasn't far from the office, so John decided he'd drive by and see if Ronland was working. Ronland had gotten himself tagged on a possession-for-sales charge, and his place of employment put him in the mix with addicts, hustlers, and dope runners. Time to see how reformed the ex-cop had become.

TWENTY-ONE

Bob's Car Wash took up an entire corner on L Street in midtown. Faded art deco—era signs from when motoring was a pastime rather than a necessity gave the business a lost-in-time feel. It might have seemed a bit desperate if not for the six cars in line for a handwash.

John pulled in front of the combination office and waiting room, where customers could get out of the elements and watch their cars get a going-over—or a going through, based on the proclivities and drug withdrawals of the workers at the time.

The owner, Bob Sunshine, tipped back a Mountain Dew and watched an SUV being attended to on the line through the window. Sunshine wasn't his real name, but people called him that because he blew sunshine and rainbows up the skirt of any parole or probation officer who checked on his employees. His expression faltered when John entered. The man's ruddy complexion darkened, and his shoulders tensed—that what-did-they-do-now? look.

"Detective, finally get tired of the inmates doing a half-assed job on your car?"

"Business looks decent, Bob."

He tipped his soda can to the heavens. "Thank God for the drought and dust."

John handed him the printout with Joseph Ronland's mug shot. "He working today?"

"Yeah; what'd he do?"

"Nothing. I just want to talk to him."

"That's what all you guys say before you Taser them and have them carted away. He's been a good worker. Joe shows up on time, doesn't cause drama with the other guys, and keeps his mouth shut. You sure you have to do this here?"

"Could you call him over for me?" John put the printout back in his jacket pocket.

"Fine." Bob rapped a knuckle on the window, and his workers knew that was a signal. All of them stopped and looked to the window at their boss. Bob pointed to Ronland and crooked his finger, ordering him to the office.

Ronland nodded and glanced over at John. He stared for a moment until Bob knocked on the window once more. He dropped a wheel brush in a bucket and walked to the office door.

The others went back to work but kept an eye on the office to see if Ronland got "rolled up"—slang for getting sent back to jail.

Bob gestured out front. "There's a picnic table you guys can use." In other words, take this confrontation out of my office and away from paying customers.

John followed Ronland outside, where the worker sat at the picnic table with his back resting against the tabletop. He kept the car wash and the other workers behind him as well. John got the message: sit next to him to appear less adversarial. Years of watching cops on the streets, in prisons, and in jails made the men who worked here experts at reading body language. Facing away from them took that out of the equation.

"What brings you here today? I don't think it was for the fine customer service experience at Bob's Urban Car Wash." Ronland fished a pack of cigarettes from his pocket and offered one to John.

"No, thanks. I quit last year. You remember Charles Sherman?"

"Huh, how could I not?" Ronland blew a perfect smoke ring.

"How about Bobby Wing and Larry Burger?"

"Yeah. What is this, a walk down memory lane? Listen, I got involved in stupid shit with those guys. I cooperated, did my time, and I'm done with them. I haven't seen them, talked to them, or 'associated' with them." He used his fingers to air-quote "association," which would be a technical violation of his probation.

"I hope not, 'cause they're dead," John said.

Ronland dropped his cigarette. "What?"

"Your old road dogs are dead, and Sherman might get a new trial because of it."

Ronland stomped on the smoldering cigarette. "Larry and Bob—both?"

"Uh-huh."

Ronland fidgeted with his menthol pack and tossed it on the table. "We knew that was always a possibility. I mean, going up against a dude like Sherman—he's got friends. But when he got sent up, we thought that was gonna be the end of it, ya know?"

"Why is it that you got county time instead of prison?" John asked.

"We all cooperated with the DA in the prosecution. Burger agreed to testify, but Wing and me didn't have to raise our hands and swear in open court. We were on the witness list, but Burger wanted to be the one to do that. We got county time, Burger got a suspended sentence."

"Kinda leaves you as the last man standing, doesn't it?"

"Looks that way. You know who killed them?"

"Working on that. When's the last time you saw either of them?"

"Man, that would have been . . . three—no, two weeks ago."

John expected Ronland to say he hadn't seen either of the dead men since the trial. "How did you manage to catch up with Burger and Wing? An ex-cop reunion?"

Ronland glanced over at John. "Dude, you guys need to talk to each other. We all got called into the district attorney's office once Sherman filed his appeal. Met with Madame District Attorney herself to go over testimony in case the court granted the defense motion for a new trial."

John's gut tightened. "How'd that go?"

"Let's just say DA Clarke wasn't too thrilled to see her star witness coming down the backside of a three-day pill binge."

"Burger?"

Ronland nodded. "That left Wing and me to carry the weight. We agreed to testify again, and she promised to get our convictions set aside, for what that's worth. Can't give me back the time I spent in jail."

"Has anyone from the DA's office gotten in touch with you since Burger died?"

"I didn't know either of them were dead until now."

"Any idea who Sherman would use to take out Burger and Wing?"

"Man, it could be anyone. That guy had his hands in more shit than any cop I've ever seen. It wouldn't surprise me if he had them killed."

"Where does McDaniel figure in this?" John brought up the other local SSPNET man on the street.

"He's a piece of work. A real Aryan Warrior, that one."

"Could he be Sherman's man on the outside?"

Ronland shrugged. "It wouldn't be totally out of character."

John stood. "Thanks. You keep your head down with what's been going on. If you can swing it with your PO, you might want to get out of the city for a while."

"I'm fine. I'm living at my sister's place in Natomas. I'm no threat to anybody."

"I'll arrange for a car to sit out front of your house for a while."

"I hear ya. But I'll take my chances." Ronland got up and stuffed his cigarettes back in his pocket.

John started to leave, then stopped and turned back. "You ever hear anyone mention Detective Paula Newberry?"

"Oh, that one. The IA cop who brought the task force down. Yeah, everyone talked shit about her."

"Like?"

"Hey, I get it now. She was doing her job. At the time I got caught with my hands in the proverbial cookie jar, not so much. I thought she had it out for us. Maybe did some things she wasn't supposed to do in her investigation. Searches, wires, that kind of thing."

"You ever hear any talk about her paying you guys to testify?"

He shook his head. "Nah. By the time the trial came around, we all agreed to do what we needed to do. Sherman was a cancer, and we had to make sure he didn't spread any further."

"Who'd want to get back at Detective Newberry?"

"Sherman, no doubt. He was obsessed with her and talked about how he was gonna get even someday. Just kinda wrote it off as Sherman pissing in the wind."

"Thanks, man."

Ronland went back to his place in the car wash line and grabbed his wheel brush.

John sat in his car, closed the door against the noise of the car exhaust and water hoses. Ronland didn't know anything about the payoff to Burger. Sherman's attorney would argue Ronland wouldn't have known about the money. If he could get McDaniel to corroborate the idea that there was no payoff, it would go a long way to clearing Paula from this mess.

He started the engine and pulled out of the car wash, glancing at the Natomas address for George McDaniel. The address was familiar, but John couldn't put a finger on why.

TWENTY-TWO

Once John turned on Elverta, he remembered this address. A line of motorcycles filled the driveway and spilled out onto the brown lawn. From a half block away, you could hear the loud, heavy metal music blaring from inside the house. He and Paula hit this place last year after a tip from a confidential informant who swore there was a meth lab operating out of the house. They didn't find any drug operation, but it turned out to be an Aryan Brotherhood flophouse. Nothing technically illegal about that housing arrangement, but nothing good could come of it either.

John pulled up to the curb and counted eleven bikes in the driveway. The garage door was open, and two guys worked on another ride in the shade. George McDaniel was one of the men. Still sporting his shaved head, the ex-cop had added a little muscle to his frame while in the joint. Like most prison bodies, all the added bulk was in his shoulders and chest, above skinny chicken legs. Killing a cellmate or fending off an attack didn't require lower body strength.

Both of the bikers put down their wrenches when John got out of the car. One disappeared inside while McDaniel stood and stayed near one of the bikes. The former cop was a little unsteady on his feet, and the pile of empty beer cans and a wisp of smoke rising from a two-foot-tall bong said the bikes weren't the only things getting a tune-up.

"Hey, George. I'm Detective Penley, Sac PD. I'd like to ask you a couple quick questions."

"What's this about?"

John leaned on a corner of the garage so he could watch the front and keep engaged with McDaniel. "How long you been out?"

"A couple months. I'm not on parole, so don't get all wound up about me having a few beers."

"And some weed."

"What if I was? It's legit now. 'Sides, I got a card. A medical condition."

"I'm sure you do. Have you been in touch with any of your old SSPNET crew?"

"Not since court. Why?"

"What do you know about Wing, Ronland, and Burger?"

A flash of beer-buzzed anger flashed at the mention of the names. "Those cheese-eaters? They'd sell out their own mothers if they got something out of it."

"You seen any of them lately?"

McDaniel spread his arms. "We don't exactly run in the same social circles anymore."

"How about Charles Sherman?"

McDaniel started turning a motorcycle handlebar. "What about him? He's still inside, isn't he?"

"He is. Have any contact with him?"

"Me? No. Why you asking about Sherm?"

"So Sherman didn't ask you to kill Larry Burger and Bobby Wing?"

"Those two rats are dead? Good deal." McDaniel looked content with the demise of his former teammates. "What about Ronland? They get to him yet?"

"Who's they, George?"

"I dunno. Whoever took out Burger and Wing. Let 'em know I want to buy 'em a beer. Those two got exactly what they had coming."

John noticed the handlebar moved every time he did. The black plastic cap on the end looked new, and the tube was discolored. Purple-and-black streaks ran up from the grip, evidence of intense heat. He took a step to the side and pulled his weapon.

"Step away from the bike, now," John said.

McDaniel put up his hands and backed away as he was told.

"That your bike?"

"No."

John approached the bike and kept his weapon trained on McDaniel. With a free hand, John pried off the plastic cap, and it revealed a 12-gauge shotgun shell hidden in the handlebar. A small button released the shell, sending it tumbling out to the floor. Somewhere up the handlebar, another spring-loaded switch would serve as a trigger. John didn't want to take his eyes off McDaniel to find out.

"Turn around and keep your hands behind your head."

The biker followed the instructions and was in handcuffs moments later. John walked him to the curb, away from the weaponized motorcycles.

He pulled McDaniel to the cement curb and ordered him to sit. "Even if you're not on parole, an ex-felon with a firearm charge is gonna sting a bit."

McDaniel looked up, his eyes yellow from an obvious case of hepatitis. "You can't prove that was mine, or that I even knew it was there."

John nodded to the house. A pair of long-haired men wearing T-shirts with cutoff sleeves stood in the garage watching. "Your new friends know about you being an ex-cop?"

"Yeah."

"They trust you?"

"With their lives. I've done my bit to earn their respect."

"So if I tell them you just ratted them out—"

"They won't buy it. Now, you better let me go," McDaniel said.

Three more of McDaniel's "brothers" stepped into the garage; one of them held a shotgun to his side.

The sound of a fast-moving vehicle drew John's attention, and not a second too soon. An older Ford van tore into view, and the driver held a rifle out of the window. The weapon spit out rounds at a high rate, and a quick glance revealed a one-hundred-round drum magazine in the rifle.

John pulled McDaniel behind his car, and the bikers in the garage dove for cover.

The driver slowed and continued to fire until the magazine was empty, then he accelerated away. John caught a muzzle flash to his right as one of the Aryan bikers fired a shotgun blast at the van. The buckshot scored the back doors of the fleeing van.

"Nice neighborhood you have here, McDaniel," John said.

Sensing that the gunshots would bring more cops than they cared to handle, the bikers began leaving the house like a swarm of angry bees. Bike after bike roared to life and poured out onto the road. The swarm followed the path of bullet shells left by the Ford van.

"Looks like your brothers left you behind."

George lay motionless next to the car, his wife-beater T-shirt now blossomed red from two gunshot wounds to the chest.

"George!" John knelt by the man and felt for a pulse. Faint, but the wounded man's heart still pushed blood through his shocked system. John opened the trunk and grabbed two trauma pads from his first aid kit. He pressed them into the wounds and called 9-1-1.

McDaniel didn't respond when paramedics loaded him into the ambulance, and his color faded from gray to stone. John waited for the detectives who worked gang cases to arrive. They would want to take a good look at all the hardware left in the house when the bikers fled. He wouldn't be able to tell them much about the shooter; the driver wore a black hood to hide his identity. Rival gang shootouts were not an uncommon occurrence out here.

John looked at all the bullet holes in the house behind him. Most were high on the wall—head height, or above. Stray and random gunfire. Hell, his car didn't even have a scratch. The only one hit in the melee was McDaniel.

A hundred rounds fired and ninety-eight of them miss?

The two gunshot wounds were tightly grouped, within four inches of each other. That wasn't accidental. McDaniel was the target, and all the rest was distraction and cover.

The paramedics cut off McDaniel's shirt to hook him up to a heart monitor. John gathered it into an evidence bag to make sure it didn't get left behind. Underneath the soiled shirt was a bloodstained envelope. It must have fallen out of McDaniel's back pocket when the paramedics worked on him.

The letter was folded in half and addressed to McDaniel at this address. John turned the envelope over in a gloved hand and saw the return address: Charles Sherman AY-2981, California State Prison–Sacramento.

TWENTY-THREE

Sherman went to the rear of his cell, sat on his bunk, and took in his drawing of Detective Newberry. Her hair was shorter now. He'd have to change his drawing if he were going to be here much longer.

He needed to be there when it all came crashing down on Newberry. She had caused him so much pain, but what he wanted to do to her promised to destroy her. It was worth everything he'd gone through, even subjecting himself to these daily mental health treatment sessions. As if they had the power to change him—the doctors and tight-faced counselors didn't have a clue. Sherman had manipulated his placement into the high-security mental health unit for the extra attention. The very thing most convicts sought to avoid. Now it was time to see if it paid off.

After the sounds of the cell extraction on the tier above his died out, Sherman pried up the caulking and removed the key he'd secreted in the hidden space. He popped it in his mouth and tucked it along his lower jaw, between his teeth and cheek. He could have left it tucked up in his ass, but the metal detectors would have caught that.

He stripped off his bed linen, threaded one end through the vent in his cell, and tied the end off against the vent cover. A few loops and Sherman fashioned a noose. He turned off his cell light and waited for the sound that would tell him it was time.

Five minutes later, the section door opened, and the nurse with the pill cart rolled to the end of the first tier. The routine was numbing but also so predictable. Sherman wrapped the bed sheet noose around his neck and pulled it taut. The front of the pill cart appeared at his window.

Sherman let go and went limp, his legs splayed out with his full weight on the noose. He heard his heartbeat hammer in his temples. Sherman's vision started to blur. This was happening too fast. A thread of panic set in, and he kicked his feet, but the thin layer of soapy water he had splashed on the floor kept him from purchase.

"Man down 121!"—a shout from the pill pusher outside the cell door.

A shrill electronic alarm sounded inside the unit. The responding staff made their way to the unit.

"Throw me the cut-down kit," the floor officer yelled.

A team assembled to enter the cell and cut the bedsheet noose and secure Sherman in handcuffs. Protocol was maintained—the very protocol that Sherman now counted upon. There were scores of fake suicide attempts to lure responding staff into cells only to get their throats slashed.

A cutting tool came out while a team secured Sherman and lifted him against the pressure of the noose. The razor edge of the cutting tool made quick work of the linen hangman's noose.

Sherman coughed and spit as his lungs pulled air in. His face was red, and a bruise had already begun to set in where the noose had cut off the blood flow to his brain.

Sherman was laid out on a gurney and the same team that cut him down rolled him to the infirmary. A doctor loomed over him and placed a stethoscope on both sides of his neck. He wasn't regaining a rhythm to his breathing, and the state doctor wasn't willing to take any risk with a patient dying in custody on his shift. A neck brace went on and Sherman went limp.

"Let's get him to Folsom Mercy. I want an ultrasound on his neck and airway."

After a rush of administrative approvals, a maximum-security inmate's transport to a local community hospital was authorized.

Two correctional officers were assigned to accompany Sherman, one in the ambulance and one in a chase car. Both were armed with 9-millimeter side arms.

A triage team went into action at the hospital. IV lines were placed, and oxygen was administered. Sherman was breathing, but his airway seemed obstructed. He went into a locked unit set aside for the medical needs of inmates from the prison while an ultrasound was arranged. The federal court took a dim view of inmate deaths, especially suicides, and Sherman knew the protocol, having witnessed other men taking a "self-parole" from prison.

"I want a phone call," Sherman said, his jaw stiffened by the neck brace.

"Look who's awake and looking for attention," one of his escort officers said.

"If he wants attention, let's put him on the list for a colonoscopy," the second officer responded.

"Let me have a phone call."

"No calls and no visitors. That's the rules."

"Then you get on the phone and call your watch commander. You tell him I need to talk to the district attorney," Sherman said.

"And why would the watch commander do that?"

"Because I have information the DA needs on two murders. I know who did it, and I will turn her over to the DA and only the DA."

TWENTY-FOUR

John gave Lieutenant Barnes a briefing of the McDaniel drive-by shooting. Even though John didn't fire his weapon, too many shots rang out to go unnoticed by local media. That likely meant press coverage about the uptick in violent crime in the city, which would lead to questions about city council leadership, which caused phone calls to the chief's office demanding answers. Answers John didn't have.

When is a drive-by not a drive-by? When it's an assassination. John kept coming back to that conclusion every time he ran the events through his mind. But who would waste time and a hundred rifle rounds on a lowlife like McDaniel?

The biker crash pad held the barest precursors to a small-time meth lab in a bathroom, but McDaniel was no central player in a drug operation, and the residue in the place wasn't enough to get on the DEA radar. But if the white supremacists pushed their product in the wrong neighborhood, the delicate balance of Sacramento drug commerce that made the Trans-Pacific Partnership look simple would unravel in a violent fashion. Still, if someone wanted to leave a message, a Molotov cocktail would have been more effective. All those bikers in the driveway to shoot at and McDaniel was the only victim.

John understood the need for payback the bikers had after an attack that left one of their number bloody in the gutter. But these guys were usually more disciplined and left security behind to keep their home base safe. This time they'd all taken off after the shooter. They were more interested in getting away than taking care of business.

John picked up his desk phone and dialed Karen Baylor's extension. The call went to voice mail after a half dozen rings. John glanced at his watch. Karen was gone for the day. He left a message for her to call him whenever she got in.

As soon as he hung up, his phone rang. He grabbed it, noting the internal extension on the caller ID. "That was quick, Karen."

"It's Paula. You hear?"

"What's up? You mean about George McDaniel getting shot? Yeah, I was there. It's strange, though—"

"Sherman's in the hospital. He tried to off himself."

"What? How?" John said. A jolt shot down his spine. "When was this?"

"He and a security detail got to Folsom Mercy Hospital about a half hour ago."

The timing of the suicide attempt wouldn't put Sherman at the McDaniel shooting. John shook the image away—the man was still in prison custody. "Why would he try to check out when the court was leaning toward a new trial?"

"You saw him. Hell, sound reasoning wasn't his strong suit," Paula said.

"Granted, but even he had to have a glimmer of the consequence of this kind of a move when his appeal was moving forward."

"If that asshole cared about consequences, he wouldn't have been in prison in the first place."

John leaned back in his chair and rubbed his temple with his free hand. A tension headache was blossoming fast. "The hospital has him under wraps, right? They have the new security unit for prisoners. It would be just like him to fake a suicide as a means of escape."

"The prison has security on him. But you're right. I wouldn't put it past him to try something desperate. This might have been a trial run. Maybe we should take a look at all of his prior addresses and associates. Anyone who visited, corresponded—"

"Shit!" John fumbled with his notebook and grabbed the plastic evidence bag with the letter from Sherman he'd collected after the McDaniel shooting.

"What?" Paula asked.

"Correspondence reminded me. Sherman was writing George McDaniel. I found a letter sent from the prison. Let me open it." John pulled on a pair of latex gloves and laid down a piece of blank paper. He took the letter from the plastic bag and placed it on the center of the paper.

"It's already open." John slid the letter out and unfolded it. "It's a bunch of numbers. Just random bullshit numbers. 18567, 16583, 14127—"

"Wait. Say that last one again," Paula said.

"14127."

"That's my badge number—14127."

"The others must be too. Let me run this by personnel—"

"Read them off again. I can run them against the armory records here in the gun cage."

John read off the first number, and he heard keyboard clicking in the background.

"No. Nothing."

After reading off the second number, Paula confirmed it as Bobby Wing's badge number. Paula's number was next on the list. The fourth number didn't register as a Sac PD badge number.

"Hang on for a second," Paula said.

John heard her flip through a file, the paper making a snap with each brisk page turn.

"That last one was Joseph Ronland's badge number. He wasn't one of ours, so it didn't pop on our database. Give me that first one again."

John read off the number.

"Larry Burger. What is McDaniel doing with a list of SSPNET badge numbers?" John said.

"And mine. I'm more concerned about where they came from. Sherman. That guy is one brain cell away from needing a drool bib, and he sends out a hit list to McDaniel?" Paula said.

"Sherman sees everyone on the list as playing a role in his downfall. Burger and Wing are dead. That leaves you and Ronland left."

"Even if McDaniel wore one of his old Sheriff's uniforms, that wasn't him in the truck stop video. He wasn't the one who got tough with Burger. McDaniel doesn't match the description Bullet gave us of the person at the Burger crime scene. And I can't see him as Sherman's bagman, can you?" she said.

"McDaniel got shot a couple of hours ago. That happened before Sherman went to the hospital."

"McDaniel was hardcore back in the day. He wouldn't have testified against Sherman. He was one of those 'I'm not gonna rat on my brothers' guys, even though Sherman was the reason he got nabbed."

"Okay, so let's say, for the sake of argument, that McDaniel got the list of badge numbers from Sherman. What was he supposed to do with them? I mean, how would he know who those numbers represented?" John asked.

"He'd have to do what we did. Someone would have to run the numbers for him. And who'd do that for a dirtbag like McDaniel?"

John tapped on the letter once more. "Sherman couldn't have committed this to memory. He had to copy this from somewhere. Feel like a ride out to the prison in the morning? I'd like to go through his personal effects and see what he's got. If he had an appeal going, the court filings might have had the badge numbers of the officers involved."

"Makes sense. If McDaniel was subpoenaed as a witness, he might have used the appeal as a key to unlock the hit list from Sherman."

"Until then, I'm gonna have a patrol unit sit on Ronland's place and make sure Sherman doesn't try and bust out of the hospital to take a shot at someone. And you need to stay away from your place for the night. Wanna stay with Mel and me?"

"I'm not gonna let a shit stain like Sherman keep me out of my own house. If he comes, I'll be ready. Come by and pick me up in the morning."

Paula hung up, but John had an uneasy feeling leaving his partner out in the open, like tethering a sheep outside for the tiger.

TWENTY-FIVE

Paula was sitting in an Adirondack deck chair with a mug of coffee when John arrived at her place. After he'd parked, John strode up the walkway and noticed her service weapon on the table next to a coffee press. The glass cylinder was empty, but the condensation on the inside meant that it hadn't been that way for long.

A second cup with steam lofting up from the rim sat on the other side of the table. She motioned him to the cup and the other wooden chair.

John took the coffee and drew a sip. Paula let the silence pass. She looked worn. The dark circles under her eyes betrayed that sleep hadn't come easy last night.

"Could I have been wrong?" she said.

"Narrow that down a bit for me."

She put her mug on the table. "All this. Did I get everything wrong about Sherman? What if they're right and he's innocent?" She sat on her hands and hunched her shoulders forward. It made her look small and fragile.

"Why would you even ask? Worse yet, why would you lose sleep over Sherman? He's a low-life piece of—"

"He tried to kill himself because of me. If I really caused that—I don't know. I've never really thought about what happens after we close an investigation. Old cases go away, and new ones pile up. An unending supply of misery and pain. What if I got it wrong?"

"You didn't."

She hung her head. "Someone thinks I'm to blame. Bobby Wing was killed with my hammer, for God's sake. Checks were issued to Burger under my name. All because I should have let it go."

John took a sip from his mug. "This isn't bad. I've gotten used to that swill we have at the office." He tried to change the downward spiral of the conversation. When she didn't respond, he put his mug down next to her weapon. "What's this for? Keepin' solar-panel salesmen away?"

She glanced over. "If Sherman's guardian angels wanted to pay me a visit, I thought I'd meet them halfway. Yeah, I've heard the guardian angel talk."

"You stay out here all night?"

She nodded. "Except to make you coffee. It's Brazilian, by the way."

"Brazilian? You see your coffee shop friend?"

A hint of a smile graced her face.

"I withdraw the question," John said.

Paula grew serious again, and the wisp of something positive evaporated. "I'm not afraid of Sherman's avenging angels. If they want to bring it—fine."

"What are you afraid of then?"

The question took her by surprise. She sat forward and tensed. "If I fucked up the case, that's one thing; I'll take my lumps."

"But—"

"That's why I asked you if I was wrong. I'm afraid that I'm gonna lose the one thing that I can do: be a cop. If they take that away from me . . ."

"Who are 'they'?"

"The district attorney, the chief, the lieutenant. You heard the DA. If the Sherman case falls apart, she wants my ass on a platter."

"Clarke is a politician and a blowhard. We have to keep plugging on the Burger murder, and that will collapse this mess right on Sherman. He had a hand in those two murders—we even have DNA on Burger's body."

"You're forgetting about his ultimate alibi—he's already in prison."

"Except for right now. He's in the hospital," John said.

Paula stiffened. "Yeah, he is. If he manipulated his move to the hospital, then it's part of his grand plan to screw me. How well guarded are those wards in a local hospital?"

He shrugged. "You're talking about a rescue? Someone busting in and breaking him out? I don't know. Why do something that desperate when his appeal might do the same thing without the risk?"

"I still think we should go out to the prison. I want to get a look at anything he has in his cell that might have referenced those badge numbers he sent out to McDaniel," she said.

"I'm sure the chief deputy warden will help us get a peek at his property. I'd like to see what they have to say about his correspondence with McDaniel too."

Paula got up and worked the stiffness from her knees, holstered her weapon, and told John she'd be right back. She gathered the mugs and the coffee press and locked them up in the house.

John tossed her the keys. "You drive while I give Griggson a call and let him know we'd like to take a look around his prison."

Twenty minutes later, thanks to light traffic, they pulled into the prison entrance gate, signed in, and locked up their weapons. Griggson left a message with the gate officer to have them park and take the shuttle to the A/B sally port.

Lieutenant Amber Rendon met them at the sally port and guided them through the multiple layers of security fencing, gates, doors, and control rooms to the bunker that controlled the facility, to housing unit 8, the psychiatric services unit.

"Is it always this busy?" John asked. There were clinical staff moving about the unit, officers collecting food trays, and inmates in holding cages awaiting movement to some other part of the prison. "I've seen other units here, but this is different."

"It's always active here. The mission of this unit is mental health treatment for inmates with the highest need coupled with a risk to themselves or a danger to the prison. If they weren't mentally ill, they would be at Pelican Bay or Corcoran SHU." The lieutenant pronounced it "shoe."

She must have recognized the confusion on Paula's face. "SHU means 'security housing unit.' It's like a prison within a prison. The

PSU gives them the best chance of treatment in a high-security safe setting," Lieutenant Rendon said.

"It's louder than I thought it would be," Paula said. The cries and catcalls from the cells were punctuated with moaning and pleas against unseen torment.

The lieutenant turned and surveyed the activity in the unit. She shrugged. "You get used to it."

An inmate banged on his cell door, pale from the lack of sunlight, eyes wide and wild. "The bugs! Get them off me!"

Lieutenant Rendon asked the floor officer, "You call in a psych tech yet?"

The officer nodded. "Yeah, we're on hold while they handle a cell extraction over in the CTC."

"Let me know if you need another S&E to sit on him."

"CTC, S&E? You guys have your own language," John said.

Rendon laughed. "I guess it sounds like that. It makes for easy communication with staff and eliminates any confusion. CTC is the correctional treatment center. It's more of an intensive clinical setting where we manage inmates after suicide attempts or those who refuse medication. S&E is a search and escort officer—kind of a utility officer we can redirect to cover the staffing needs."

"I've seen cell extractions when a guy refuses to come out of his cell or won't give up a food tray, but what would cause the need for an extraction in the CTC?" John asked.

"Some inmates are extreme. If they stop taking their meds, they completely fall apart. They'll rub feces on themselves, set fires, attempt suicide. Granted the CTC limits their ability to cause that kind of problem, but they still try."

"Man, what a screwed-up place to work," Paula said.

"Better for them and us."

An officer stepped over to Rendon. "Lieutenant, you wanted a printout of inmate Sherman's movement history and approved correspondence?"

She took the manila envelope and handed it to John. "This should give you what you were looking for." Then to the control booth officer, "Pop 121!"

The cell numbers were painted onto steel doors, and 8121 was on the lower of two tiers. The door slid back, driven by an electric motor.

The lieutenant gestured at the cell. "That's your boy's house. Take your time, and we'll have the control booth officer secure the rest of the section. Just give him a shout when you're done."

John and Paula entered the concrete box where Sherman lived. The ten-by-six-foot cell had a single bunk, a table, and a combination sink/toilet. Tall, thin rectangular windows at the back and a glass panel in the cell door were the only sources of outside light that spilled into the concrete cavern.

The mattress was bare, which seemed unusual until John put together the fact that Sherman had used his bed sheets to hang himself. He turned to the door and found the vent opening over the toilet. One of the metal grates bowed outward, bent from Sherman's body weight.

A lidless cardboard box sat under the metal bunk. Paula pulled it out and laid it on the mattress. She wasn't about to sit on the bunk where Sherman slept, so she stood and flipped through the papers in the box.

"Hey, Paula?"

"Yeah."

"You're gonna want to take a look at this," John said.

She turned and came face-to-face with her own image drawn on the cell wall.

"I think you made an impression," John said.

Paula centered herself with the drawing, crossed her arms, and tilted her head. "It's so . . ."

"Angry?" John followed.

"I was about to say 'big.' Do I look like that when I'm angry?"

"I'm gonna take the fifth on that one, partner."

"That's intense."

A voice from the cell door said, "It's you."

A correctional officer at the opening looked at Paula and then back to the drawing. "Wow, I thought it was a girlfriend from the outside. You're not—"

Paula cut him off. "Oh, hell no! How long has this been here?"

"I first saw it about three to four days ago. He's been assigned to this cell for about six months. They aren't supposed to deface the walls, but it was pretty good, and that was the least of his problems."

"How so?" Paula said.

"I'm not saying it's art therapy or nothing. But if an inmate's occupying his time drawing, then he isn't gassing us."

John moved to the box of paper work on the bunk while Paula spoke with the officer. Most of the contents looked like trial transcripts; the pages where Burger testified were dog-eared and worn. Letters from attorneys, turning down his request for representation on his appeal, and handwritten pages of Sherman's summary of his own case stuffed the cardboard container. Technically, there was an attorney-client privilege for an inmate's legal work, but they weren't reading any of the man's legal briefs—they were looking for something that didn't belong. He dumped the box on the mattress and pulled out the cardboard square from the bottom of the box. It was supposed to support the weight in the box, but it was also a place to hide a few documents.

In the bottom was a photo of Paula in the same pose as the drawing on the wall. It was a photo from when she'd testified at Sherman's trial. The small letters on the bottom said it was from the *Sacramento Bee*. Another folded scrap of paper was a prosecution witness list, with the names of Paula, Burger, Wing, Ronland, and McDaniel typed out along with their badge numbers.

A witness list wasn't that unique, but the bold lines drawn through the names of Burger, Wing, and McDaniel were unsettling. A shiver shot up his spine when he noticed the small print at the bottom of the page.

It was Paula's address followed by a single comment: "Burn it."

TWENTY-SIX

The level of noise in the cellblock amped up suddenly. Most of the inmates were at their cell doors, yelling and banging the steel fronts. John stepped from Sherman's cell, anticipating a riot like some episode of *Prison Break*. There was nothing in the dayroom. The disturbance came from behind secured steel doors. The faces locked on to something behind John, and a few inmates joined in with the loud protest because the others did. A sympathetic display—solidarity of the broken.

John glanced over his shoulder and found the magnet that had attracted the inmates' attention. A television mounted on the dayroom wall broadcast a local station with the closed caption feature activated. Charles Sherman's prison mugshot filled half the screen, with the other side dominated by a live shot of a press conference. District Attorney Linda Clarke took up the podium and adjusted the microphone.

"Hey! Can you turn this up?" John asked the officer in the control booth.

The officer nodded, picked up a remote, and raised the volume until it started to reverberate off the concrete and steel of the dayroom.

The DA opened a folder and glanced down at the prepared statement. "The Ninth Circuit Court has ruled on the appeal of former law enforcement officer Charles Sherman. The court has ordered his conviction set aside and that he be granted a new trial on the grounds of prosecutorial misconduct in the form of 'possible' coerced false testimony."

"Son of a bitch," Paula said, now standing next to her partner on the dayroom floor.

"The court has reason to believe that a state's witness was paid to give testimony against Sherman and that the witness recanted his statement."

"Burger never recanted," Paula said.

"The change in statement was never provided to the defense, and it prohibited Sherman's legal counsel from providing effective representation.

"As a result, my office has reviewed the likelihood of a conviction following a new trial, and I have decided not to burden the court with a new proceeding that will not serve justice. Witnesses that could have testified against Mr. Sherman are no longer available."

"She's gonna let him walk," Paula hissed.

The assembled media at the news conference began pummeling the DA with questions. No one thread was discernible in the jumbled mass, each shouting for attention. DA Clarke pointed to someone off-camera. "Ron."

The camera swung to the reporter. "Are you saying that Charles Sherman is innocent?"

"No. I'm saying I have no evidence to bring before a jury."

"Does that mean no charges will be filed?"

Clarke looked annoyed at the question but responded slowly like she was teaching a group of first graders. "When you have no evidence, you cannot file charges."

"Will Sherman be released?"

"Yes, he will."

Paula's knees buckled, and she leaned against a stainless-steel table.

Another murmur shot through the crowd. "When will you release him?"

"That is a matter between the court and the state's prison system. I have nothing to do with it."

"Where is Charles Sherman now?"

"As I understand it, Mr. Sherman is recovering in a local hospital following a tragic suicide attempt," Clarke said.

"Yeah, just frickin' tragic," Paula seethed.

"Will he be filing a civil claim against the state?"

"You'd have to ask his attorney, but given he was imprisoned over potentially false testimony and went so far as a suicide attempt, it's safe to assume he will file some sort of civil suit. What I can add is that Mr. Sherman has provided my office with significant information that will likely lead to an arrest for the person responsible for the recent murders of two former law enforcement officers."

"Man, why doesn't she just tee it up for him?" John said.

The television coverage of the press conference ended, but a news anchor came on and continued breaking news coverage. "We bring you now to Folsom Mercy Hospital for a live update."

The video feed switched over to a reporter inside the hospital. "In an unusual turn today, prison officials have allowed us access to Charles Sherman, who is recovering from injuries he received in prison." The camera panned over to Sherman in a hospital bed. A deep-purple bruise showed on his neck, and he made no effort to hide it.

"Mr. Sherman, what are you feeling following today's court ruling?" the report asked, shoving a microphone in his face.

"Relieved and angry, if that makes any sense."

"What are you angry about?"

"I've been locked up based on fabricated evidence. The DA finally saw the truth, but not until I was so desperate that I did this," Sherman said, pointing to his neck. A mist filled his eyes. "I don't blame the district attorney for prosecuting me; she only followed the evidence she was given. Now that witnesses have died—witnesses who could have fully exonerated me—and cannot testify, I will always carry the stink of a man convicted of a crime that he didn't commit." A slight tear fell to Sherman's cheek.

"Man, he's been practicing this monologue," John said.

Paula remained riveted to the screen. The light flickered off her graying face.

"What are you going to do when you're a free man?"

"I want to help the DA bring justice and closure to my illegal confinement. There is one person responsible for this."

"We've learned that Detective Paula Newberry of the Sacramento Police Department was the investigator in charge of the original case against Charles Sherman." A reporter at the scene held a photo of Paula, and a larger copy of the one found in Sherman's cell came up on the screen. "The Sacramento Police Department has yet to comment on this matter."

The news coverage flipped to another story in the cycle.

"I—I gotta get out of here. I need some air," Paula said. She started to wobble but quickly regained balance and rapped a fist on the dayroom door.

John hefted the envelope detailing Sherman's correspondence. He'd planned to have Paula look through it while he drove back, but he decided against that as she pounded on the dayroom door for a second time.

Paula and John gathered their weapons and phones at the entrance gate after retracing their path from the bowels of the maximum-security prison. He tucked the envelope under his arm as they walked.

John glanced at his phone. "Ten missed calls, five from the lieutenant. This can't be good."

Paula had two missed calls, one from Kamakawa of internal affairs and one from the chief's office. "No, this can't be good at all."

John drove this trip while Paula returned the call from the chief's office. Her temper only burned hotter when those calls went unanswered, and they had no way of knowing the level of heat that awaited them when they arrived.

TWENTY-SEVEN

The chief's outer offices were sparse, arranged for convenience rather than adornment, unlike some law enforcement heads, who splashed photos of themselves with prominent politicians and celebrities. This chief only featured photos of the men and women of the department.

Joanne was the gatekeeper and controlled access to the chief and arranged his schedule. She'd served the three chiefs before the current one and showed no sign of slowing down.

When John and Paula arrived, Joanne picked up the phone. "Detectives Newberry and Penley are here." She hung up. "It will be just a moment. John, how's your son?" Joanne asked.

"Good. Tommy's doing really well. How's the mood in there today?" John said pointing to the inner office.

Joanne widened her eyes and shrugged. "It's been busy."

The inner door swung open, and an angry Linda Clarke strode from within. The DA scowled at Paula as she passed. It looked like she wanted to rip into the detectives, but she tightened her jaw and kept walking.

"Detectives," Lieutenant Barnes said from inside the chief's office.

The chief stood at the far side of the room. He usually kept his emotions on a tight rein, but the red blotches on his neck served as a bellwether of what waited for the detectives.

Barnes closed the door behind them and motioned them to a pair of chairs at the chief's desk.

"How was your morning? Mine included calls from the mayor's office, every news outlet in northern California, and a congressman, and a drop-in from one very pissed-off district attorney. The only thing missing is a protest by the West-somewhere Baptist Church," the chief said, "but it's still early."

"Clarke was out of line at her press conference this morning," Barnes interjected.

"Out of line or not, we have a problem," the chief said. He paced back to his desk.

"Chief, I'm sorry," Paula said.

"I don't want to hear that."

"Sir?"

"Saying you're sorry doesn't get us anywhere and isn't going to fix the problem."

Paula buttoned her lip and sat erect in the chair, waiting for the next blow.

"Chief, Sherman's been playing us all along," John said.

"As much as I want to believe that, how is it possible that a mentally ill prisoner in a maximum-security prison had anything to do with the murders of the DA's witnesses?"

"I'm not sure yet," John admitted.

"That's not comforting," the chief responded.

"He could have a connection on the outside carrying out the hits for him. We've all heard the stories about Sherman's guardian angels; maybe there's something to it," John said.

Barnes sat in a vacant chair. "It makes more sense than Sherman teleporting in and out of the prison."

"Is there anything to back that theory up?" the chief asked.

"We're working on it," John said.

The chief glanced over at Paula. "You can imagine the conversation DA Clarke and I just had. We have records of payoffs to a witness, a spike strip at one murder scene, and a murder weapon at another. All with one common denominator: you."

"There are two," Paula said. Her voice quavered.

"Two what?"

"Sherman's blood, his DNA, was at the crime scenes too."

Barnes nodded. "It was. The defense will argue that it was a lab error—or planted deliberately."

"Occam's Razor," John said. Blank looks from the ranking cops in the room came in response. "When given two possible explanations, the one with the fewest assumptions is usually the better option."

"What are you saying, Detective?" the chief asked.

"The blood. The simplest way the blood was at the scenes of our murders is that the suspect—Sherman—was there."

"You're missing the big picture. He was in prison. Talk about the ultimate alibi," the chief said.

"He was there," John said.

"He had to be, Chief," Paula followed.

"I wish I shared your confidence. But we don't have anything to support your story—I won't even call it a theory. But we have to get this case solved and show some progress or the DA will make good on her threats. She claims Sherman can tie you to the crimes."

"He wants to take me down," Paula said. The drawing of her face in Sherman's cell came to mind once more. "He's obsessed."

"And she wants your head on a pike. Why did she get scope lock on you even before the Wing murder?" the chief asked.

"Clarke prosecuted the original Sherman case and rode that reformer bandwagon into her reelection. I know she's taking the case blowing up personally, but she won't be the one to take the blame," Barnes said.

"It stinks," Paula said.

"The bottom line is we don't have long to take action. When Sherman is released and files a claim against the city, we're gonna get zero support from the mayor and city council," the chief said.

"You're gonna suspend me, aren't you?" Paula asked.

The room chilled with the question finally asked.

The chief stared at her. "Let's hope it doesn't come to that. I support my officers until they prove to me that my trust is unfounded. You have my trust. No, Detective, we're not suspending you."

"Thank you, sir," she said. A bit of color returned to her face.

"Don't thank me yet. We have to tie this down, and I hope to Christ on a cracker you can. Clarke reminded me she has a holiday coming up. The city council meets in two days, and if we haven't given the DA two homicide cases wrapped up with pretty ribbons, the suspension issue may be the least of your concerns."

"What are you saying, Chief?" John said.

"Remember Clarke's comments in my office? Either Sherman or you? She's making noise about filing an indictment," Barnes said.

"She can't be serious," John said.

"When she presents the spike strip property log, the city check request, the hammer with Paula's prints all over it, and the connection to the Sherman case, the grand jury will have to take a hard look," Barnes reminded him.

"Grand jury indictment; that's a route the DA's office doesn't use too often," John said.

"She can control the evidence presented, and Paula won't get a chance to refute anything she puts out there. A grand jury would eat up Sherman's testimony," Barnes said.

"Would Clarke really do that to save her political future?" John asked.

"I don't want to find out. So, detectives, you have two days until the city council meets." The chief sat back and put his palms down on his desk. "Forty-eight hours. Go make it count."

TWENTY-EIGHT

Paula nearly collapsed outside of the chief's office. She leaned flat-backed on the wall, head cradled in her hands. "I can't do this."

John put an arm on her shoulder. "You did fine."

"I don't know if the chief believes me."

"He does, but he's only got so long until it's not up to him anymore—"

"Until the DA throws my ass away."

Paula craned her head up, releasing some of the tension that had taken residence while in the chief's office.

John's cell rang.

"Penley." He listened. "I understand," he said. His jaw tightened. "Do we have eyes on him? Let me write that down." He snatched his notebook and jotted something down before he disconnected the call.

"That was the hospital. A Folsom PD cop called with the heads-up. Sherman's out. They released him."

"Christ, the DA didn't waste any time, did she?" Paula asked.

"It had to be in the works before her press conference. A friend came to pick him up. Folsom PD gave me the license number of the guy's truck."

"I can't believe this," Paula said. "Everyone's buying his bullshit and thinking I set him up."

"Not everyone."

"Thanks, but you don't count," she said, trying to make a joke, but then thought better of it. "Actually, you're the only one who counts."

John called the watch commander and gave him the information for a newer-model silver Ford F-150 pickup truck as described by the Folsom cop.

"While they're running that for us, any guess to where Sherman will hit up straight out of prison?"

"I hope he goes to an all-you-can-eat buffet and swallows his own tongue," she said.

"I'm saying the biker meth house. He's got unfinished business there."

"You're on."

Less than ten minutes later, a patrol unit spotted the truck, and the newly paroled man's first stop proved them both wrong. Sherman's friend pulled into a fast-food taco joint where the freshly minted free man filled his gut with greasy tacos and acidic packets of salsa. When he came out, he rubbed his belly in satisfaction, and they got back into the truck.

The next stop would have earned John a dinner, but the reception wasn't what the detectives expected.

TWENTY-NINE

John thought Sherman meant to finish the job on McDaniel and his biker brothers. If the detectives saw Sherman threaten the bikers with a gun, furnished by his truck-driving friend, everyone goes to jail—end of story.

The pickup pulled in front of the driveway, blocking the line of bikes from escaping this time. A big man in biker leathers gathered his long greasy hair and tossed it over his shoulder as the truck stopped. He dropped a socket wrench in a toolbox, and it gave a heavy clang when it hit the metal container.

John pulled up a block away, at a corner with a view of the garage.

"Sherman's still in the truck," he said.

Paula pulled a digital camera from a zippered pouch and attached a telephoto lens. She pointed it at the front of the house and rotated the lens until it came into focus.

"You drop that thing, and Karen won't talk to us again," John said.

"Sherman and the driver are still inside the cab. A biker, no, make that two bikers in the garage. One's about six three, two seventy-five, with prison ink on both arms."

She snapped off a dozen photos in quick succession and magnified a shot on each man: the two bikers, Sherman, and his friend.

"Sherman's opening his door. Here we go. The big dude and his buddy are coming toward them."

John rolled his window down, but the voices were caught in the wind going in the other direction. "I can't hear a thing."

Sherman stepped out and faced off with the thick-necked biker.

"I don't see a weapon on either of them," Paula said.

"Keep watching."

With an abrupt movement, the biker threw his arms around Sherman and lifted him off his feet.

"What the—he's hugging him. They're laughing," John said.

The driver got out of the truck cab, walked around the front, and shook hands with the other biker who came out to the drive-way. The bigger biker's embrace ended, and Sherman put his arm around the big man.

"What this hell is this, a family reunion?" Paula said, snapping off more photos.

"I don't get it," John said.

The biker pointed to the front of the house. He trotted to the chipped stucco above the garage and pointed. He smacked the driver on the shoulder, and the man shrugged.

"What's he looking at?"

It took a few seconds to hit. "The bullet holes from the drive-by. He's pointing out the bullet holes from when McDaniel went down."

The biker motioned them into the garage, and they disappeared inside the house.

Paula lowered the camera. "It looks like Sherman knew about the hit. And the smile on his driver's face looked—I don't know, prideful?"

"He could've been the shooter. He wore a mask, so I can't be sure. But how does Sherman figure in with a bunch of white-power meth heads?"

A pair of bikers rode up to the house, and the loud engine noise rattled the windows of the car when they passed. They parked their rides, backing them into the curb behind the truck. One man unstrapped a black nylon satchel the size of a grocery bag from his bike. Both men glanced around as if they expected trouble and headed for the house.

"The one without the bag has a gun. He's got his hand on it. This could get exciting now," Paula said.

The expected gunshots didn't occur. Instead, the two bikers who arrived minutes ago came out without the black bag.

Paula snapped a series of photos of the men as they approached their bikes. "They're relaxed now. No hands on weapons."

"Delivery boys," John said.

Their motorcycles rumbled to life, and the pair charged down the street, setting off a car alarm a block away.

John's cell phone chirped. He rolled up the window so his voice wouldn't carry and alert the bikers. "Penley."

"I have the plate info on the Ford truck for you. Ready?" the watch commander said.

John snagged a notepad from the center console and tucked the phone against his chin. "Go."

"The vehicle is registered to Mark Andrew Wallace. The DMV flagged the record as a restricted plate."

John knew what that restriction meant. He had one of his own. "He's a cop?"

"Sac County Sheriff, according to the DMV records," the watch commander said.

"Is he undercover?" John asked.

"Don't know. That truck is a personal vehicle, for what it's worth."

John took down the residence information for a place in midtown near East Portal Park. "Got it. Thanks." He put the cell on the seat.

"The driver's a cop, eh?" Paula asked.

"Looks like it. Sac County. The name Wallace doesn't ring a bell."

"I know most of the detectives over there, and this guy doesn't look familiar at all. Wait—Wallace works for the sheriff's department. Does he look like the guy in the video with Burger?"

Paula pulled the camera up when she noticed movement in the garage. Sherman, Wallace, and the big biker came out onto the driveway, and Sherman carried the black bag. She captured a good image of Wallace when he took off his sunglasses and wiped his forehead with a forearm. "He looks like the deputy in the video."

"He's about the same size. Man, it's got to be him. Same build, shaved head—even the way he stands," John said.

Sherman and the biker shook hands, a transaction complete.

"God, I wanna know what's in that bag," Paula said.

"Nothing good comes by way of an armed biker delivery."

Wallace and Sherman got back into the truck, and the biker went back to the motorcycle frame.

The Ford pulled away, and John followed at a respectful distance. Wallace made one stop, at a liquor store, before he pulled into the driveway at his Forty-Fifth Street home.

John parked on the opposite side of the street, one house down from the well-kept home in the city's Fab Forties neighborhood. Wallace keyed the front door of an art deco–inspired home and went back to the truck to carry in four dark-amber liquor bottles. Sherman followed with the black bag in one hand and a twelve-pack of beer under the other arm.

"Looks like a welcome home party for Sherman," John said.

Through the gauzy linen curtain in the front, they were able to watch Sherman drain a beer in two long pulls. He popped another, and this one took three swallows.

"Looks like they're gonna tie one on. Should give us some time to find out what Sherman had in that bag," John said.

"Wait until he's passed out drunk and break in? You can't be serious."

John shook his head. "You went right there, didn't you? No, I'm not talking about going in there." John started the car. "We're gonna see a man about a bag."

THIRTY

John parked the sedan in the first spot he could find at the UC Davis Medical Center. The trauma unit was a small plain concrete-faced building in the shadow of the larger hospital tower. Multiple ambulance bays kept the unit fed with trauma victims from all points of the region.

George McDaniel's room was the only one with a Sacramento police officer stationed at the door. After John had flashed his ID for the officer, they entered the patient room. McDaniel was awake, but he could've been mistaken for dead because his complexion was more gray than pink.

McDaniel looked worried at John's entrance, then relaxed as his morphine allowed his mind to register who it was.

"Hey there, Detective." His voice was thin and raspy.

"I gotta admit, I didn't think you were gonna make it for a minute there," John said.

"Lucky for me, I don't remember a whole lot about anything after the gunshots started. I woke up in this place."

"Nothing good would come out of remembering any of that."

"It's funny. All those years of working as a cop, even the sketchy shit we pulled, and I never got shot. And I get caught in some random tweaker drive-by."

Paula plopped in a chair at the foot of McDaniel's bed.

"My partner, Detective Newberry."

"How long you been hanging out with the low-life types like those bikers?"

"They're really not that bad. Besides, not too many people accepted me for what I was—am."

"You hook up with them in prison?" Paula asked.

McDaniel coughed and grabbed his ribs. "Yeah—yeah. They gave me protection from everyone who wanted to make their bones killing a cop."

"What'd you have to do for them?" she asked. "Protection like that ain't free."

He looked down the bed at Paula, who now had her boots resting on the bed rail. "I wasn't a saint. Never claimed to be. I moved weapons, collected rent, and muled shit for them."

"So these friends of yours, why would they be behind you getting shot?"

McDaniel's eyes shot from Paula to John.

"Looks like it," John said.

"No. You're lying."

"You gotta ask yourself, why would they do that?" John repeated.

McDaniel's eye's unfocused for a moment, and John snagged the remote button for the pain medication before McDaniel could check out and avoid the questions.

"Who is the big dude at the house? Over six feet and pushing three hundred with thick greasy hair?"

"That would be Junior. He runs the place and reports directly to the Brand."

"Brand as in 'Aryan Brotherhood'?" John asked.

"He ain't a member or nothing; they let him do pretty much whatever he wants as long as they get their end."

"Would their end include getting you out of the picture?" John asked.

McDaniel shrugged.

"Do Junior and Charles Sherman know one another?" John said.

With a side-eyed glance, McDaniel responded with another question. "Why would you ask that?"

"Because they seemed to hit it off really well earlier today," Paula said.

"Sherman's out?"

"Yep, so where does that leave you in the big picture?" Paula said.

John shifted and moved to the foot of McDaniel's bed. "Let me take a shot at it, and you tell me how close I get. Sherman and your ex-roommates are in business together, and now that Sherman and his task force connections are in play, the Brand doesn't really need you. How'd I do?"

"Closer than you'd think. Sherman has what the Brand wants. He has something that I couldn't give them. I set them up with connections, dealers, and street-level distribution. Sherman has all that juice too, but he has the product too."

"What product?" John asked.

"I want immunity."

"From what? Your ass was already in prison for this shit," Paula said.

"Not for this, I wasn't."

"What's Sherman got? You need to give us something if you expect us to go groveling to the DA with an immunity deal," John said.

"You'll back my play for immunity?"

"It isn't up to me. But I gotta hear what you have that will make my boss and the DA want to give you a deal."

"Sherman. Like I said, he's a major player. He has enough product to flood the city."

"My bullshit meter is ringing loud," Paula said. "Sherman's been in prison. In-car-cer-ated. He's not a player in anything."

"You really don't know, do you?"

Paula got up and gave the bed an inadvertent kick with her boot, causing a wince of pain from McDaniel. "Come on, he's got nothing. Let's pull his protective detail and let Sherman and his Brand buddies clean up their own mess."

"Okay—okay. Try this on. How many years was Sherman working on the SSPNET task force? Like five, six years, right? How many busts and seizures went down in that time? Hundreds."

"Get to it," Paula said.

"Every one of those takedowns was light."

"What are you saying?" John said.

"If we took down ten keys of coke, five got papered and booked."

"Skimming? Sherman was siphoning off evidence?"

"Yeah, and not just him. I did, Ronland, Wing, Burger—all of us," McDaniel said. The man looked scared, and the waves on his monitors confirmed it. His blood pressure went up hard.

"Sherman got busted holding pounds of cocaine, heroin, and meth. That's old news," John said.

"Not this. It's stashed."

"Where?" John said.

"Nuh-uh. Not until I get my deal."

"Is he in business with Junior?" John asked.

"Junior is a middleman. That's all I'm saying until you come through with a deal."

A young black nurse entered the room and checked McDaniel's monitor. She readjusted the blood pressure cuff and manually pumped it for a new reading.

"You might want to call it off for the day; your pressure is higher than we'd like it to be."

McDaniel was flushed and pulled the sheet down, exposing an assortment of racist and white-power tattoos. The uneven color and rough lines gave away where these came from   prison.

The nurse didn't bat an eye and made sure McDaniel was as comfortable as possible. She even handed him the pain medication button.

"Could you send in the white nurse next time?" McDaniel said.

The nurse tilted her head and stared at her patient for a moment before she said, "I'm going to write that off to the morphine talking."

When the nurse left the room, Paula gave the bed frame a hard kick.

"Ow."

"You're an asshole, you know that?" Paula said.

"What?"

"I thought some of your buddies in the Brand must've rubbed off on you. But now I know you've been an asshole your entire life," Paula said.

McDaniel pushed the morphine button. "Fuck you."

THIRTY-ONE

"What do you think about Sherman having a stash of stolen drugs?" John asked as he backed the car from the hospital lot.

"McDaniel knows how bad we want Sherman. The kind of action he was talking about—someone would have noticed that. You can't take half of a drug seizure without someone asking questions. The dealers they arrested would start to squawk about the missing product so they didn't take the fall from their distributors. It doesn't hang together for me."

"It could explain what was in the bag Sherman got from Junior."

"Burger would have known where it came from," Paula said.

John turned on Twenty-First and headed downtown. He glanced at his partner as she bit her lower lip.

"You remember Burger's dead, right?"

"Don't be an ass. I haven't lost my mind, yet," Paula said.

"Just checking. Why bring up Burger at all? How's that gonna help us now?"

"Burger put in dozens of hours prepping for testimony. Drilling for the questions the DA was gonna ask him. The whens, wheres, and whodunits. Clarke and her team handled that. I wasn't there. My part of the case was over. I wanna go over my notes in the files and compare what Burger told me against what came out in his testimony. He might have hinted at how the missing drugs were handled."

"Wouldn't the evidence room records flag missing drugs?"

"If the drugs never hit the evidence room, the records wouldn't show anything. The books would balance out."

"Sherman's off-the-books stash."

Paula shrugged. "Maybe. But the kind of stash McDaniel was going on about wasn't gonna fit in that gym bag Sherman picked up."

The Sacramento Sheriff's Department headquarters building looked like it was designed as a fortress. The long slit windows reminded John of those on the prison cells in the PSU. Nothing remotely welcoming for public access; even press conferences were held outside the building.

"You know Connie Newhouse?" John asked.

"She's the administrative captain, right? I met her once. What does she have to do with Sherman? He was Solano County Sheriff's Department."

"It's his new BFF, Wallace, I'm curious about."

"Really? Is BFF part of your vocabulary now?" Paula said.

John nosed the car into a tight parking space in the garage across the street from the sheriff's building. "Yeah, so? Kari says it all the time. I'm hip."

Paula undid her seat belt. "You're closer to breaking a hip. She's a teenager, and old folks do not say 'BFF.'"

John got out of the car. "You just call me old?"

"You need a hearing aid too? Come on, Gramps; let's see what Captain Newhouse can tell us about Wallace. Or are you gonna file an elder-abuse complaint?"

He shook his head and pretended to be hurt by her comments, but he was actually glad to see Paula loosen up a bit considering the pressure the case and the DA had put on her. Paula was at her best when she was quick, when she kept two steps ahead.

The administrative captain's offices were buried deep in the complex. From there, she managed the department's communications, records, and human resources. Captain Newhouse came out of her office to greet them.

"John, what brings you to the dark side?"

"Just a little interdepartmental cooperation. Some simple background info, that's all."

The captain put her hands on her hips and gave him a stern look. "It's never 'simple' with you."

John shrugged.

"Come on. This way." Then to Paula, "Detective Newberry, isn't it?"

Paula shook Newhouse's hand.

"I'm sorry for your burden," Newhouse said.

"Sorry?"

In the captain's office Newhouse continued, "John didn't tell you? He and I used to be partners back in the day, before I transferred to the county."

Paula glanced at her partner. "No, he didn't tell me that."

"I'm painfully aware of what it's like to have a partner who is moody, keeps things to himself, and likes coloring outside the lines." Newhouse grinned when she was done.

"But you made it out alive!" Paula said.

"Come on, Connie, it wasn't that bad," John said.

"He must have mellowed a bit since then," Newhouse added.

"If you say so," Paula said.

Newhouse sat behind her desk, which was piled with paper work. "What can I do for you?"

"One of your deputies is involved with a suspect," John said.

"Okay. Isn't that more of a matter for our detectives or internal affairs division?"

"That's not what I'm after. That kind of inquiry would trigger a formal request from our chief to your sheriff, and everyone would get their boxers in a twist. I'd like to keep this low key. I'm only interested in this guy and his connection to our suspect."

Newhouse put on a pair of reading glasses and pulled her computer keyboard in front of her. "Let me have it."

"Wallace. Mark Andrew Wallace," John said.

Newhouse typed in the employee's information. "Yep, got him here. Sergeant Mark Wallace." She turned the screen to show the photo displayed on the screen. "This look like the guy you're interested in?"

The man's face was unmistakable—he was a bit thinner now, but the pinched expression and tight jaw gave him a presence that could only be described as "cruel."

"That's the one," Paula said.

Newhouse swung the screen around. "Now quid pro quo, why you looking at him?"

"He's an associate of a man connected to a couple of homicides," John said.

"Associate of—connected to? Pretty thin to go around poking at another law enforcement officer."

"He picked up our suspect from prison and drove him to a meth house connected with the Aryan Brotherhood," John said.

"Go on."

"We think he's the sheriff's deputy we caught on tape with Larry Burger a few hours before Burger was found beaten to death."

"Anything else?"

"That's all. I want to know if there is any connection between Wallace and our suspect. Something to explain why a sheriff's sergeant would be so willing to pal around with a freshly released prison inmate." John decided to keep Wallace's possible role in the McDaniel shooting to himself at this point. An allegation like that would draw in the detectives or internal affairs and spook Wallace altogether.

"Who's your suspect?"

John paused a moment. "Charles Sherman."

Newhouse pushed back from her desk. "That Sherman? The one who's been all over the news?"

John nodded.

"I need to turn this over to internal affairs."

"Connie, I'm asking you to hold off for a bit. Let us put a case together."

"What do you need?"

"Give us two days to wrap this up, and I'll make sure you know when we have anything solid on Wallace."

Newhouse shook her head. She scrolled into Wallace's information. "Huh."

"What?"

"When did Sherman go down for that task force bullshit?"

"About three years ago."

"Wallace transferred to Sac County three years ago. His prior work history includes sergeant in the Solano County Sheriff's Department. Also SSPNET task force supervisor."

"Son of a bitch," Paula said.

"He must have gotten out of Dodge before the task force blew up," John added.

"That's our connection," Paula said. She was excited now. Her foot started to bounce.

THIRTY-TWO

The moment they returned to the detective bureau, John grabbed the envelope from his desk, the one they'd picked up with Sherman's prison records. With the winds changing after Sherman's release, prison records seemed irrelevant, so he tossed them back in a drawer. He tore the envelope open and scanned through the prison movement records. While Sherman was continuously housed at the prison for the better part of a year, and at Folsom Prison a year before that, the detailed movement history recorded every cell change, assignment to the PSU, and court appearance.

"Paula, call the court clerk in department 140 and see if they can provide a list of all court dates for Sherman in the last year. He's got at least a dozen in the prison records."

Paula dialed the main superior court information line.

John looked through the prison records and made note of the date of each court pickup. Every single transport was released to the custody of the Sacramento County Sheriff's Department. The last two dates on the list stood out. John knew these dates. The same dates as the Larry Burger and Bobby Wing killings.

"Son of a bitch," John said while he leaned back in his chair. He flipped to a page where the prison staff had attached visiting and correspondence approvals on file. The visiting record was almost empty. Three visits by his attorney, and one other visit, over a year ago: Mark Wallace.

Wallace wasn't among those listed for approved correspondence. None of his former SSPNET colleagues were there either.

Crime partners were usually prohibited from writing one another while inside. That didn't explain how Sherman's letter ended up with McDaniel.

None of the five names listed on the approved correspondence looked familiar at all. John ran his finger down the list of outgoing mail sent by Sherman, and one address kept reappearing, every two weeks like clockwork. And usually, within four days, a letter from that address would come in addressed to Sherman.

Paula hung up. "We got us a situation. According to the court, there is no record of any appearance by Charles Sherman in department 140. You sure they got that right?"

John flipped the pages over and tapped on the printout. "Yeah, it says 140. Hang on." John flipped through the bundle of papers. "Here is a minute order from the superior court, county of Sacramento, issued from department 140, ordering Sherman to appear for court proceedings."

"He never appeared in any department 140 proceeding. It's fake."

"Sherman went out for nonexistent court dates the same days Burger and Wing were killed."

"We got him! His DNA was at the crime scenes, and now his alibi is shot to shit!"

Heads turned in the detective bureau.

"Easy now. The court dates were faked, but we need more to give DA Clarke a reason to back off."

Paula tossed a pencil across the bureau. "Dammit. No alibi and his DNA at the crime scene; what more could she want? The DA's never shied away from a case with less than that."

John's phone rang.

"Penley."

He listened and signed off with a curt, "No, sit tight and let me know if he moves."

"I asked a patrol unit to cruise past Wallace's place every fifteen minutes, and they just spotted him leaving. He was dressed for work—in a sheriff's uniform."

"Sherman?" she asked.

"Wallace is alone. I asked the unit to watch the place and call us if Sherman makes a move."

Paula's cell sounded. She recognized the number on the screen. "Dammit. It's Mrs. Conner, my neighbor." She jammed her finger on the okay button and started in. "Mrs. Conner, I don't have time for this right now."

The blush of anger drained from her face. She disconnected the call without responding.

"What's she need?"

"The fire department. My house. She called to tell me my house was on fire."

THIRTY-THREE

Wisps of acrid steam wafted from the front door. Two fire trucks clogged the street, and while the flames had died out, the crews poured water on hot spots that smoldered inside. Water coursed out of Paula's front door, down the steps, and trailed to the street, leaving ash and charred bits behind.

Paula stood as close as the fire crews permitted on the sidewalk, helpless as strangers tromped in and out of her home. John knew how she felt, the place she dumped all her overtime checks into had been violated; all the time she'd spent restoring and refinishing was wasted. When a smoldering sofa landed on the front lawn with an unceremonious thump, she looked like she wanted to throw up.

John gave her some space while he talked with the fire captain, who manned the first truck on the scene. John knew his partner had a deep, personal connection to this place. It was an expression and an extension of herself. The damage had been done to more than plaster, wood, and paint; it was a rip in her soul.

He joined Paula on the sidewalk a few minutes later and stepped through a river of wastewater pumping from her home.

"Your neighbor called nine-one-one when she saw smoke coming under the front door."

Paula remained silent.

"By the time the fire department got here, the flames were starting to build, and the smoke alarms were going off. The fire damage was limited to the living room."

"They say what started it?"

"Not yet; they have a fire marshal in there now. It began on the sofa," John said.

"You know this was Sherman, right?"

"Maybe he thought you were home."

"He knew—somehow he knew how important this place was to me. Sherman did this because he knew how much it would hurt."

A man in a fire department uniform came outside and looked at the smoldering remains of the sofa in the yard. He pulled up a cushion and tossed it aside. The bottom fabric was black, charred, and fell out in clumps. He pulled off his gloves and took a small digital camera from his turnout coat, snapping a series of photos.

The fire marshal said something to a group of firemen nearby, and one of them paused rolling up a three-inch fire hose and pointed at Paula.

The fire marshal came over to them. "I understand you're the property owners."

"I am," Paula said.

"As a fire marshal, it's my responsibility to determine the cause and origin of a fire like you've had here."

"When can I get inside?" Paula asked.

"We'll get to that in a moment. Were you on the premises when the fire started?"

"No."

"Do you smoke?"

"No. Why?"

"There are cigarette burns on the sofa cushions."

"I don't smoke, and there were no burn marks on the sofa when I left this morning."

"What time was that?"

"Six forty-five."

"Who has keys to the place, other than yourself?"

"Why?"

"The doors were locked when we arrived. A fire like that can smolder for hours before it catches hold. You certain that you, or someone you know, didn't leave a cigarette unattended?"

"I'm sure. There was no one here when I locked up."

"You have insurance coverage for the place?"

"Of course."

"I've got to ask, are you behind on mortgage payments or anything?"

"You think I torched my own place?"

John held his arm out in front of Paula, in case she grabbed the fire marshal by the jacket collar. He didn't need to though, because she was preoccupied with the damage to her home.

"We think we know who started it," John said.

"Yeah?" the fire marshal questioned.

John showed his ID. "A murder suspect has threatened Detective Newberry. In fact, he said she was gonna 'burn.' His words."

"No shit?" the fire marshal said.

"No shit," John answered.

"Let me show you something." He took them to the sofa, and the smell of hot, fetid water and burnt fabric was worse the closer they got to the house.

The fire marshal kicked the cushion with the toe of his boot. "Did the cushion have this rip on the bottom?"

"No. The sofa was reupholstered less than six months ago."

"The cushion was sliced open, and the stuffing pulled out. Everything points to a cigarette or two left burning in a pile of the stuffing."

"Like a slow-burning fuse?" John asked.

"Exactly," the fire marshal said.

"Why not burn the place like in the movies? Dump a gallon of gasoline down the hallway and toss a match?" Paula said.

"This is much more controlled and gives someone time to get out before it goes up. It will light, given time and fuel. We caught this one early. These old homes go up quick once the fire gets established."

"Aren't sofas, fabrics, and stuffing materials supposed to be fire-proof?" John asked.

"Fire resistant. But when that pile of paper on the sofa ignited—boom."

"Paper? What paper?" Paula said.

The marshal shrugged. "Looked like files, paper work, office stuff."

"I didn't have any files in the living room."

"Don't know what to tell you."

"Let me take a look," she said.

The fire marshal looked over his shoulder. The mop-up was done inside, so he led the detectives to the doorway, now shattered from being forced open by the first responders. The smoke smell was overpowering and came with a humid stench of burnt woodwork and lacquer.

A scorched outline on the wooden floor marked where the sofa was before it burnt. Next to the blackened wood wainscoting, a nest of charred papers, held together by memory more than structure, lay on the floor.

Paula touched a page, and it crumbled under her finger. Some of the pages weren't completely consumed. Words, fragments of sentences and bold headings remained behind. She bent to get a closer look at the remains.

"These are the internal affairs files on the SSPNET case," she said.

"What are they doing here? Those were on your desk back at the office. You didn't take them out, did you?"

"Hell no. I know better than that. These damn things are confidential."

"Who could have gotten them here without anyone noticing?" John said.

"Sherman has someone on the inside."

Nothing like a collection of emergency vehicles parked along a residential street to bring out the curious and morbid, some getting a head start on the neighborhood gossip and others trying to leverage something for themselves. Among the crowd were ambulance chasers of the new economy: contractors with business cards.

Paula spotted her neighbor Mrs. Conner in the throng of bystanders. Paula went back outside and joined her in watching the firemen dump another load of smoldering material on the lawn.

"I'm sorry I was short with you on the phone," Paula said.

"Not to worry, dear. I thought you should know."

"Thanks for calling the fire department. It sounds like if they hadn't arrived when they did, it would have been much worse."

Mrs. Conner scrunched up her mouth, lips pulled tight over ill-fitting dentures. "Did they find him?"

"Who?"

"It's none of my business. I should leave you alone; you have enough to worry about."

Paula placed her hand on the woman's arm, not restraining her, but with a touch that urged her to keep talking.

"Your man friend," she responded in a hushed tone, one that implied disapproval of Paula's lifestyle.

"Who are you talking about? Him?" Paula pointed at John, who was still talking with the fire marshal.

"No, it wasn't him. I haven't seen this particular caller before, but he must be a special friend to have his own key to your front door."

Paula got a chill up her spine. "You saw someone with a key?"

Mrs. Conner nodded.

"This man you saw, have you seen him before?" Paula asked.

Mrs. Conner looked hurt. "Paula, I don't judge you on who you choose to be with, nor can I keep track of your social life."

In truth, the widow probably could recite all the dates and times that Paula had brought someone home. Paula saw her parked in a rocker in the front room of her home watching the goings-on around the neighborhood all day long.

"This is important, Mrs. Conner. I didn't expect any company today. What can you tell me about this man?"

The description fit Charles Sherman, right down to the bruises still lingering on his neck.

THIRTY-FOUR

"It was Sherman. He was in my house," Paula said. This was a new level of violation. It was personal and intimate, and John knew the pain this intrusion would inflict.

"And he locked up when he left. How thoughtful. That'd be the last thing on my mind if I were setting out to torch a place," John said.

"He wanted to burn my place, just like the note we found in his prison cell said."

"I thought he meant burn you, like make the DA think you're a bad witness," John added.

"He's doing a good job at that too. Lucky for me, I have a nosey neighbor. Still, the water and smoke damage are going to kick my ass."

They walked through her home after the fire. All the work and sweat she poured into the place   stolen.

John squatted over the burned pile of internal affairs files. "Why do this? What was the point? The DA wasn't going to go for a retrial, so what is this all about?"

"It could be a message. 'You burn me—I burn you.'"

John's cell phone rang and he took the call, listening and responding, "I'll be right there."

"What's up?" Paula asked. She began sorting things beyond salvage into a pile.

"Dr. Kelly wants to go over something on Burger. I can run over; you have your hands full here."

"I'm coming with you. This can wait. Smoke-damaged drapes are the least of my worries right now."

Paula closed the front door and went to lock it until she saw the splintered doorframe from the fire department's entry. She closed the door as best as she could and saw Mrs. Conner peering through the blinds next door. Better than any dead bolt on the market.

They rode to the coroner's office and found Dr. Kelly in the homicide suite, an enclosed room set aside for the autopsies of those who'd died at the hands of another. Larry Burger was partially covered by a single sheet, leaving his head, neck, and chest exposed.

Dr. Kelly was jotting notes while an assistant was suturing Burger's chest closed.

"Any surprises for us, Doc?" John said.

Dr. Kelly sniffed the air. "What's that smell?"

"That'd be us. House fire. I'm surprised you can pick up anything working around this all day."

"You get used to certain odors: decomp, formalin, stomach contents. But you reek. Meth lab?"

"My house," Paula said.

Dr. Kelly stopped writing and looked up. "Oh, damn, Paula. I'm sorry. What happened?"

"An asshole happened." She shook her head, changing channels. "How about Burger here?"

"It is what it looks like. Blunt-force trauma. The X-rays show multiple cranial depression fractures. Multiple brain hemorrhages."

"So the plastic bag down his throat wasn't what killed him?" Paula said.

"The head trauma was fatal, but the petechia in his eyes indicate a lack of oxygen too. The hemorrhage would have killed him eventually, but asphyxiation is the COD. His stomach contained a handful of the pills from the bag that hadn't completely dissolved."

"Oxy?" John prompted.

"That's the chemical analysis. Interesting thing is, the pills were older—pre-2010. They were manufactured before the FDA required antitamper chemicals and binders to reduce abuse of the drug. The pills found in your victim didn't contain the additive."

"He happened to have them sitting around?" John asked.

"Not likely. These are worth their weight in gold. Addicts can crush them and snort the powder, chew them, or shoot up." Dr. Kelly said.

"Are you saying that's what Burger was trying to do?" Paula asked.

"From the abrasions around his jaw and mouth, your killer forced the pills down his throat," Dr. Kelly said.

"But he was already dead before the pills kicked in," John said.

"Quite," Dr. Kelly said.

"The pills were an afterthought. How about the weapon used to inflict this damage?" Paula asked. She stepped closer to the body and pointed at the lacerations around the impact points. There were six separate depression fractures on Burger's face and the back of his head.

"Blunt with roundish edges. I made an impression of the wound." Dr. Kelly took a chunk of resin off the counter and handed it to Paula. The hunk of resin was circular, about the size of a quarter with a jagged striation that ran across the surface. There were five other similar-looking chunks of resin on a counter behind Dr. Kelly.

Paula turned the resin in her hand. She didn't need to compare it with the hammer John found at the Wing killing. The irregular ridge came from chipping out the old tile in her kitchen. The murder weapon—her hammer—had claimed two lives.

"All of the impressions the same?" Paula asked.

"Yes, a single weapon," Dr. Kelly said.

"Can we take this with us?" John asked.

"I can't do anything more with it here," the doctor said.

"Don't bother, it's the same hammer used on Bobby Wing. Someone took it from my garage. Totally different wound patterns, though," Paula said.

"Not completely," Dr. Kelly corrected. "Both victims suffered massive head trauma, multiple depression fractures. The victims had no defensive wounds whatsoever, and neither died immediately. A few more blows with your hammer—the hammer—and your killer could've put them down."

Paula flinched from the attribution. "Why didn't he?" she said aloud.

"There's no question he wanted to kill them. I mean, this extent of injury is a death sentence," John said.

"Inflicting pain?" Paula asked.

"After a point, there's only so much pain the mind can register," Dr. Kelly said.

"There's a punishment vibe here, for sure," Paula said.

"Vibes and feeling and motives aren't something I can measure in the lab," Dr. Kelly replied.

"Torture? Would you say the wounds are consistent with torture?" John asked.

"It's within the realm of possibility."

"When the killer got what he needed from Burger, he stuffed the bag down his throat," John said.

"The timeline works. I can't say if this man was interrogated or not. But your theory holds up against the physical evidence."

"Sherman didn't want anything from these two other than to stop them from testifying," Paula said.

John paced the small exam space. "Are we looking at this all backward? I mean, sure, Sherman wanted a new trial, and the only way he was going to win that case was if these witnesses didn't or couldn't testify."

"Yeah—and?" Paula said.

"All he needed was for Burger to recant or not testify. Why Bobby Wing and George McDaniel? There's something more here. I mean, I know Sherman is up to his ass in this. But what if it wasn't him?"

Paula's arms went stiff, hands clenched at her sides. "It had to be Sherman. We have his DNA at the murder scenes, the fraudulent court dates that line up with the dates of the killings, the badge numbers in his personal property."

"And yet here we are, trying to tie him to a murder with nothing but circumstantial bits and pieces," John said.

"Well excuse me, Mr. Defense Attorney. In case you've forgotten, this is my ass on the line out here."

"We'll nail down the Sherman angle. He's definitely mixed up in this somehow, but it might not be with the murders of Burger and Wing."

Paula shook her head, her frustration with her partner evident. "Then explain to me what Sherman was up to on his field trips from prison if he wasn't killing the very people who could put him back there."

"Think about what McDaniel said. He claimed Sherman has a stash of confiscated drugs, enough to flood the city. The old Oxy that Burger had backs up the claim of confiscated drugs out there. What if this is all about a drug stockpile and not testifying in the next Sherman trial?"

"And who gets control over that stockpile."

Karen Baylor appeared from the hallway. "Detectives." Then she registered the tension on their faces. "Um—sorry. Did I interrupt something? I have something I need to show you."

John registered the worry in Karen's tight expression. "What's up?"

"I'm sorry, Dr. Kelly. I'll wait outside." Karen backed out of the room.

"No worries, Karen. We're done here," Dr. Kelly replied. She tucked the sheets back over Larry Burger's remains and jotted a note on her tablet.

John and Paula followed Karen into the hallway.

"You didn't have to come out here. You could have called us," John said.

Karen shook her head. "I—I couldn't let anyone else hear."

"What is it?" Paula asked.

"I found a second set of DNA markers on Burger's body."

"We know there was someone else there with him," John said.

"The same DNA was on Bobby Wing's body as well."

"Great work, Karen," John said. "That will nail whoever is helping Sherman."

Karen paused.

"What?" Paula asked.

"The DNA is yours, Paula."

THIRTY-FIVE

In the parking lot behind the building where human remains were kept in cold storage, Paula's face looked as gray as one of the dearly departed locked away inside.

"How? How is that even possible?" Paula said.

John, Paula, and Karen gathered in a tight knot near a white coroner's van, still warm from soul collecting.

"Where did the sample come from? Blood, saliva?" John asked.

"Hair. Strands of Paula's hair were on both bodies," Karen said.

"Cross-contamination. That has to be it. Paula was at the Burger crime scene," John said.

"I wasn't at the Wing crime scene at Southside Park." Paula leaned against the van and let out a sigh. "So much for the lieutenant and chief backing my play. Every time I turn around, it's quicksand, and I get pulled in deeper."

"Don't be so quick to throw in the towel. There is plenty of reasonable doubt."

"Great! I have to rely on the refuge of the guilty—reasonable doubt."

"We'll get you an attorney—"

Paula cut him off. "Wait. Karen, how do you know the hair was mine?"

"It was a DNA match. I said—"

"What did you compare it with? I don't have DNA on file in the system," Paula said.

"They didn't need a warrant when they took the coffee cups off of your desk and clothes you kept behind your chair. They will be getting a warrant asking for a swab, though."

"Kamakawa?" John asked.

Karen nodded.

"Who else knows the results?" Paula said.

"No one yet. Not even Kamakawa. That's why I wanted to find you first. Guys, what am I supposed to do?"

"We'll have an attorney arrange for—" John started.

"I'm not getting an attorney. I didn't do anything."

"Paula, think this through," John said.

"I have. Karen, file your report. Exactly the way you always do. The last thing I want to see is you get your ass in a sling because of me."

"But Paula—"

"No buts, Karen. Follow procedure on this. Got it?"

"Yeah, I understand. I'm sorry, Paula. We'll get this sorted out. I promise."

Karen left them and ambled through the parking aisle, her head down, scolded.

"You could have asked her to sit on it for a bit. Give us some time to find out Sherman's angle in this," John said.

"That crazy bastard's angle is clear enough. He wants me to burn. My house was only the beginning of what he has planned for me."

"And he walks as the righteous man."

"To continue his little drug empire, if you can believe McDaniel. That was one of the first places Sherman went after he got out."

John looked away. His eyes tracked a dark-blue Crown Vic as it turned off of the main road and pealed toward the front entrance. The detective wouldn't have given much thought to an undercover car coming to the morgue, but two things set him on edge: no one hurried to this place—the persons of interest here weren't going anywhere—and it was Kamakawa in the driver's seat with the internal affairs captain. They didn't normally burrow around in the morgue.

"You see that?" John said.

"Sammy and his boss, yeah I did. The captain doesn't venture out unless it's something splashy."

"Come on, I have an idea," John said.

The pair got in their car and pulled from the rear parking lot. John parallel parked on the street a half block away. They had a view of the front entrances of the coroner's offices.

"What are we doing here, John?"

"Waiting for someone to drop the next piece of this puzzle." He pointed at another car coming in. "And here it is."

The incoming car pulled to a stop, and the backseat passenger had the door open before the car stopped. District Attorney Linda Clarke stepped from the rear seat and strode inside the coroner's office.

"This can't be good. The DA and Kamakawa together," John said.

A few minutes passed before Paula said, "Look," and pointed to the door.

The mirrored-glass entrance slid open, and the DA led the charge outside, followed by an anxious, pleading captain of internal affairs. He was getting an emasculating lecture from the prosecuting attorney, based on his slumped posture and her finger jabbing him in the chest.

"Sammy can't get far enough away. Check it out," John said.

The junior IA man pressed back against the mirrored door panel and kept it from closing. The door bumped his leg and retracted only to close on him again. He kept his distance from the DA and let the captain take the full force of the verbal barrage.

"You don't like being on the other side of it, do you, Sammy?" Paula said.

"Whatdaya think she's telling them?"

"They don't know about my DNA yet, so it's not that. I think they were here for me. It wasn't a secret that we were heading out here."

John pulled his cell and tapped a number. He waited while the connection went through.

"Who you calling?" Paula said.

John put a finger up. Paula put up a finger in response, a gesture that meant something else entirely.

"Hi, Doc. It's John Penley. Did you have a visit from two guys from the department?"

He listened and nodded. "What were they after? You mind telling me?"

Another pause. "I see. I'm sorry you got put in the middle, Doc. Did you happen to see the DA, Miss Clarke?"

A pause.

"I couldn't agree more. Thanks, Doc. We owe you one. I know—put it on my tab." He disconnected the call.

"Well?" Paula said.

"Dr. Kelly said Kamakawa is focused on the hammer kills and wanted to know if you'd contacted her to cover for your part in the crimes."

"Oh, I bet that went well. My money's on the good doctor there."

"You've seen her rip up defense attorneys on cross-examination. She's brutal. She told Sammy and the captain that her examination didn't provide any evidence linking you to the killings. She told them in *her* examination, she found nothing. And that's true. She didn't. Karen did."

"That's some fine hairsplitting."

"What about DA Clarke?" Paula asked.

John pulled the car from the curb. He glanced in the side-view mirror and saw Clarke was returning to her car. The IA captain was anchored to the spot where the DA had left him.

"Clarke was after you, Paula. She wasn't happy that Dr. Kelly wouldn't conclusively tie you to the murders."

"Once that DNA evidence comes out, I'm toast." She slouched in the passenger seat. "When that happens, I'm going down for the two killings, and it'll look like I framed Sherman all along." Paula nibbled on a thumbnail.

"My gut tells me there's more to it than that. Clarke keeps getting lucky with all this evidence."

"Yeah, evidence that buries me a little deeper hour by hour."

"It's clear Sherman's obsessed and put you in the leading role in his little revenge play," John said. "That drawing of you on his cell wall reinforces that point."

"He blames me for everything."

"At least that's what he wants you to think."

"What do you mean? He's doing pretty damn good job of it."

John gripped the steering wheel and waited at a stop sign. "The bogus court dates align with the Burger and Wing killings, the allegations of a stolen drug stash—he's working at something else, something bigger."

"He seems to have found the time to fuck my life up, frame me for the ex-cop killings, and burn my home."

"He wants everyone distracted—looking at you."

"That's because he blames me—we've come back to this again." Paula smacked a fist on the dash.

"If Sherman wants you so bad, why weren't you his first stop when he got out?"

Paula considered it for a moment. The increased pressure of paranoia didn't dull her reactions; they were sharpened. Slowed down, like she was at the gun range. The range master at the academy would drill by the mantra, "Slow is smooth, smooth is fast." By consciously slowing the mind down, you could avoid reckless mistakes. She was doing the same now. Avoiding mistakes and reactions that would trap her in Sherman's noose.

"If Burger was going to recant his testimony and free Sherman, then killing Burger first would make it look like I killed him to hide the payoff for false testimony. Damn, Sherman thought this through."

"But the Wing and McDaniel hits too? There's nothing that says that they were going to roll on him."

"What would a jury think? That's a whole lot of smoke for me to try and prove there was no fire," Paula said.

"You nailed him before. What was the one thing that broke that case?"

She paused for a moment. "He got too bold, you know? Sherman believed that he was untouchable and started making mistakes."

"He'll do the same thing again. That whole leopard-can't-change-his-spots deal."

Paula nodded. "The biker house. Why did Sherman go there first? Of all the places in the city to go, he went there, the spot where McDaniel was gunned down."

John stayed silent while Paula thought it through.

"Let me make a call," she said.

Within minutes, Paula had the connection between Sherman and the bikers. Specifically, the big man they'd seen in the driveway, an Aryan Brotherhood wanna-be named Hal "Junior" Burton. Junior and Sherman shared a cell at Folsom.

"I want to hear what Junior has to say about their time together," Paula said. "How long has Sherman been planning my undoing? I have less than a day and a half to find out, or Sherman wins."

THIRTY-SIX

John pulled the car to the curb at the meth house. Junior was in the garage, parked on a lawn chair that bowed under the man's weight. The half-drained bottle of whiskey on the floor next to him didn't bode well for civil conversation.

"Why isn't this house boarded up? Didn't they take down a lab in the bathroom?" Paula asked.

"There wasn't enough of a lab operation to get anyone's attention. We should check out the property records and see who pays the taxes on this place."

Paula pointed at the front door. Another biker leaned in the open doorway, one arm hidden behind the threshold. "We got one over there. No telling what kind of weapon he's got behind door number one."

The door guard watched with red-rimmed eyes as John and Paula got out of the car.

"Hi there, Junior," John said.

They walked to the corner of the garage, where they could talk to the fat man without yelling and keep an eye on the watcher at the front door.

"Do I know you?" Junior took a pull from the whiskey bottle and wiped his beard with the back of his hand.

"You should. You and your fellow motorcycle enthusiasts almost ran me down after you had your place shot up the other night."

"Yeah, the neighborhood ain't like it used to be, what with all the immigrants and shit."

"That must be it," John said.

"You're cops. Unless you got a warrant or some such, get outta here."

"See this, this right here is the reason the neighborhood isn't what it used to be. People aren't friendly anymore. You used to be able to go up to someone and just have a friendly conversation with them."

"Fuck friendly conversation, and fuck you," Junior spat. He was starting to slur his words.

"We aren't here to bother you. We're just interested in a friend of yours, Charles Sherman."

The big man drained the last inch of the whiskey and tossed the bottle out onto the driveway. It shattered near Paula's feet. The guard at the front door coughed up a rough laugh.

"We did some checking, and you and Sherman were cellies at Folsom. I bet you were catching and he was pitching," Paula said.

"You got a mouth on you," Junior said.

"I bet that's what Sherman said about you too."

Junior's arms braced on the lawn chair, and he lifted his bulk a few inches, then slipped back into the chair. Too drunk to make good on his attempt at bravado.

"Bitch, get outta here."

"Bitch? Oh, it's 'bitch' now? You haven't seen me release the bitch on you, you fat worthless piece of white trash."

Junior's eyes widened slightly, then he began to laugh. A whiskey cough made his face turn red, and when he recovered, he said, "I like you."

"Yeah, yeah, we're all friends here. What can you tell me about Sherman?" John asked. He wanted to defuse Paula before she went off like an IED at an Iraqi crossroad.

"No harm in me telling you. Sherman was supposed to come through on a promise, and he's late. He's got some powerful dudes looking for him now."

"This have anything to do with the black bag he picked up from you," John said.

"Hypothetically?" Junior slurred.

"Sure, hypothetically," John responded.

"Well then, if some friends of mine, say, gave me some money to give to Sherman to buy something and he didn't come through—then he's in a world of shit."

"And you too," Paula finished.

"Hypothetically, fuckin' A," Junior said.

John pointed at the heavy lug-soled boots Junior wore. They bore metal toecaps with dark river mud and what looked like bloodstains.

Junior tracked John's line of sight.

"What?"

"You have those fancy metal things on the toe of your boots."

"So?"

"What's that about?"

"Keeps your boots from wearing when you shift your ride."

"And for kicking ass?" Paula added.

"There's that," Junior said.

"That mud come from the river? You been hanging out down there?" John said.

"Ain't no crime if I was. It's a free country."

"We're gonna need to take a look at those," John said.

"The fuck you are."

"You're gonna hand them over with a smile, or we're gonna pull 'em off you," Paula said.

"You think the Aryan Brotherhood would like one of our patrol units camped out here day and night? That might put a crimp in business, don't you think?" John asked.

Paula nodded. "But it might help with that whole neighborhood decay problem Junior is so concerned about."

"I bet it would cut down on traffic and all the unsavory elements driving by."

"If the Brotherhood doesn't get their profit out of this place, I don't think they'd care—would you, Junior?" Paula asked.

"Whatever."

"When they find out that their business went under because a lowlife wouldn't give up a pair of worn-out boots, well, I'm sure they'll understand."

"They wouldn't care," Junior said. Flop sweat began to form on his creased brow.

"But they'd probably—hypothetically—care that you ratted out the details of the drug operation to the cops?"

Junior looked confused. "What? What are you talking about?"

Paula glanced over at the door guard and said louder than she needed to, "I can't promise you protective custody, but for what you've given us, the federal prosecutors will have no trouble handing down a RICO indictment."

Junior's face pruned up as he tried to follow along.

"Thank you, Junior. It takes a strong man to go up against the Aryan Brotherhood like that."

The door guard stiffened.

Junior finally got it. "I ain't done no such thing." He looked to his man at the door. "I didn't do nothing."

"Word will get around that you did. And your friend over there doesn't look too happy about the prospect of crossing the Brand," John said.

"Give us the boots," Paula continued.

Junior struggled to reach his feet and tugged the laces loose. "Man, you ain't right."

Paula pulled on a pair of latex gloves, took the first boot, and held it at arm's length. "God, these stink."

"Where'd you get these boots?"

"We get them at a cycle shop in Southside. Perry's."

"We?" Paula asked. She looked at the doorman's identical boots. She took the second boot from Junior. "We'll get these back to you."

A broken yellow toenail poked through the hole in a dingy sock and Junior sat back in the lawn chair again. "Now nobody needs to tell nobody about any bullshit informant bullshit."

"Not if it's bullshit," Paula said.

John and Paula returned to their car, and by the time they'd pulled away from the house, the doorman was in the garage having a heated exchange with Junior.

"You're still gonna have a patrol unit parked outside, aren't you?" Paula asked.

"Absolutely. Think of it as our contribution to urban renewal."

THIRTY-SEVEN

"I swear I can smell those boots from here," Paula said. Junior's stained leather boots were sealed in an evidence bag and locked in the trunk, but the threat remained.

John pulled the sedan into an empty spot as far from the main entrance to the police headquarters as possible. He kept it running as he popped the trunk release.

"Stay here while I run these boots in for Karen Baylor to take a look."

"I'm not a dog you can tell to stay in the car. I'm coming with you."

John took her elbow. "IA probably has the DNA results—your DNA on the bodies—now. We don't have time to try to explain that to Sammy Kamakawa."

Paula didn't jerk her arm away. Instead, she took his hand and held it briefly. "I haven't done anything, no matter how it looks. You don't need to cover for me. I don't want you to get caught sideways because of me."

"That's what partners do," John said.

"Sherman wants me to react, and so far, that's all I've done. He's been calling the shots and I let him. No more. I'm doing this by the book."

Paula got out of the car and grabbed the evidence bag with Junior's boots from the open trunk. She held them out and said, "Junior fits the general description of the man Bullet said he ran into out on the river road, right?"

John stood by his car door and locked up the sedan. "He does. You want to pull Bullet in, have him look at some photos and see if he can ID Junior?"

"If Karen can pull Burger's blood off these, it puts us that much closer. And we know that Junior and Sherman shared a cell in Folsom."

"Junior is taking care of the potential witnesses for Sherman? DA Clarke will have to listen to that," John said.

"We can make the case—that's all we can do."

Inside, the detectives found Karen processing evidence from what looked like a very nasty crime. A once gray sweat shirt, now black from the blood that soaked the fabric, was spread out on a table before her.

"Detectives," Karen said, "make a note that alcohol and tree trimming do not go together."

"Ouch. Chainsaw?" John asked.

"Yep. His wife handed him the chainsaw and she 'may have' pulled the trigger as it plunged into his stomach—three times."

"Damn, did he make it?"

"Yeah, he did, but I have my doubts about their marriage."

Paula placed the evidence bag on a nearby table. "Could you check these out? They may have blood from our vic."

Karen pulled off her latex gloves and put on a fresh set to avoid cross contamination. She selected a small vial that held a clear liquid and a swab built into the cap.

"I had the phenolphthalein out for chainsaw boy." Karen uncapped the vial and scraped the swab across the stain on Junior's boot. She replaced the swab and shook the vial, raising it to the light.

"No catalytic reaction. The Kastle-Meyer test would have pulled the hemoglobin from the blood, if it were present. That stain is not human blood."

"Dammit," Paula said.

"Junior wasn't there."

Paula stared at the boots. "Can you analyze the mud in the soles and tell if it came from the Garden Highway crime scene?"

Karen thought for a second. "I can narrow it down to the general area. Will that help?"

"Definitely."

"What are you thinking?" John asked.

"If we can identify Junior as one of the guys Bullet overheard, we can pressure him to give up what he knows. He'll roll on Sherman."

John nodded. "Yeah—yeah, that fits."

"I might have to cut a section out of the leather and sole for testing. Will that be a problem?" Karen asked.

"None whatsoever," Paula said. A slight smile creased her face before disappearing. "How did the IA Captain take the DNA news?"

"Actually, I haven't had time to get around to that." She pointed at the bloodstained sweat shirt. "Seems that something keeps getting in the way."

"I appreciate what you're trying to do, but please don't jeopardize your job and your med school admission over this."

"It's not fair," Karen started.

"That's not what this is about. Do me one favor? When you do get those results out, give them to Lieutenant Barnes first, okay?"

Karen nodded.

John and Paula left the lab area, and John made a path for the back door. Paula stopped. John saw her bite the corner of her lip, the way she did when she was sorting something out.

"We should get back out there," John said.

"I need to do something first." She went in the opposite direction.

John lost sight of her as she shut the door after she went in Lieutenant Barnes's office. He went to his desk, grabbed a file, and pretended to read while watching the lieutenant and his partner talk.

He glanced at the file—the prison documents on Sherman's correspondence and movement since he was sentenced. How could one man generate so much paper? John knew how—convicts were quick to appeal, complain, and litigate anything. The paper was a defense against the constant stream of—

John sat straight. "That's it." He spread the documents on his desk and separated them into piles. One for classification, one for correspondence, and one for movement. That last pile was thicker than the others by double.

The stack of body receipts for Sherman's out to court appearances was an inch thick by itself. All the out to court demands were accompanied by a minute order from department 140 of the superior court. But Paula had verified before that his case was never called.

John looked at two of the body receipts side by side and noticed another identical factor. "Son of a bitch."

He took the body receipts and threw open the lieutenant's door.

"Wallace. Sergeant Wallace was the transport officer for every one of Sherman's court appearances."

THIRTY-EIGHT

It took less than five minutes to confirm that Sergeant Wallace was on duty and was finishing up booking in a prisoner at the main jail. His shift was scheduled to end in an hour.

John and Paula circled the area around the jail and located the silver Ford pickup registered to Wallace two blocks away. John parked on a side street where they could watch the truck.

"So what'd you and the lieutenant have to talk about?" John said, breaking the silence.

"I needed to know that the lieutenant still believed in me, trusted me even in the light of all this crap. I'm not sure I trust me. I needed to hear it from him. I told him everything I know and told him to expect something pretty damning from Karen."

"He hasn't pulled you off on admin leave. That has to mean something. Besides, isn't it enough that your own partner trusts you?"

"You don't have a choice," she said. A gathering of people waited at the crosswalk, three blocks down. Paula squinted. "You didn't think to grab the camera, did you?"

"Backpack, in the back seat."

She leaned over the seat and grabbed the camera. The telephoto lens focused in on the pedestrians. One of them wore a black Sacramento sheriff's uniform. "There's our man."

They waited until he was a few yards away from his truck before they approached.

"Sergeant Wallace. We need to talk," Paula said, holding her badge up.

"That so?"

"And I'd rather not do it out here on the street."

"What's this about, anyway?" Wallace asked.

"We need your help on an old case," John said.

Wallace cocked his head. "Really? Which one?"

"Let's take a drive and we'll talk it over," John said. He gestured to their car.

"I'll follow you," Wallace said.

Wallace gave the appearance of cooperation when he agreed to go with John and Paula. That appearance was short-lived. When they arrived at the detective bureau, Wallace told them to get his union representative or he wasn't going to say another word.

It took more than an hour for Parker, the union rep, to sober up and creep out from some watering hole. A telltale odor of booze swept in the door with Parker when he arrived. A terminally pissed-off ex-cop, John got the sense Michael Parker popped from the womb an angry man. A perpetual scowl, tight jaw, and sarcastic demeanor were a package of unpleasant times for everyone.

"Parker, I didn't know you repped for the sheriff's department," John said.

"What you don't know could be measured in metric tons. What are we doing here? And why are you interviewing Sergeant Wallace and not the sheriff's internal affairs unit?"

"We're not conducting an internal affairs investigation. We were going to talk to the sergeant when he said he wanted you here first."

"I want it noted that Sergeant Wallace came here on his own free will."

"Noted."

Paula led them to a small break room, deliberately not one of the rooms used for interrogation, to keep Wallace as compliant as possible. A table near the back kept them out of the traffic hitting the microwave and vending machines. Paula pulled out a chair and set a file and notebook on the table.

Parker dropped into another chair. He unbuckled his belt and let his gut breathe. "So let's get on with it."

After everyone had settled, Paula ran a hand across the file. Everyone's attention went to the internal affairs stamp on the front. It was Parker who bit first.

"I thought this wasn't an IA witch hunt against the sergeant?" Parker said.

Wallace eyed the file under Paula's hand. Something in his expression darkened. He'd seen his share of IA files.

"Do you smoke?" Paula asked.

Wallace tilted his head. "What?"

"What the hell does his need for a smoke got to do with anything?" Parker asked.

"Just making sure the sergeant's need for a *smoke* break is attended to." The word *smoke* was loud and clear. "Sergeant, how long have you known Charles Sherman?" Paula continued.

"I dunno, why?" Wallace asked.

"Sherman, the ex-cop?" Parker said.

"Or former prison inmate," John added.

"You can't say how long you've known Sherman? I mean, you guys go back to Solano County, and you both worked the SSPNET task force."

"Yeah, so?" Wallace said.

"I'm just saying you know him, is all," Paula said.

"So?"

"When's the last time you saw Sherman?" Paula asked.

"Last time I worked with him was about two, maybe three years ago."

Paula leaned forward. "That's not what I asked. I don't care when you worked with him. I asked when you last saw him."

Wallace shrugged. "Couldn't say."

"And why's that?" John asked.

"Listen, I have nothing to do with him. He's why I got out of the task force. I saw what he was doing, and I didn't want to get caught up in all the bullshit."

John pulled the prison body receipts from a file and pushed them, one at a time, across the table. He let Wallace stew for a minute before he spoke. "These prison records say something else. You definitely had something going on with Sherman."

Wallace picked up one of the receipts, glanced at it, and pushed it back to John.

"I picked up a prisoner, so what?"

"You knew who you were picking up at the prison?"

"I go where they tell me to go and pick up who they tell me to. Simple as that."

"And you picked up Sherman six times over the last year?"

"If you say so."

"According to the prison records, you were the only transport officer to pick up Sherman for his court appearances. Is that unusual?"

Wallace shrugged.

"So what? Prison inmates go out to court all the time," Parker said.

"How's that work exactly?" Paula asked.

"The court issues an order for removal, and the sheriff's department picks them up," Parker responded.

"That's right. Except, in this case, all the removal orders from the court were fakes. There were no court appearances, and Sherman was never booked into the jail for holding. So how's that work?" Paula glanced from Parker to Sergeant Wallace.

"I just transport who they tell me to. It ain't my job to call the court and see if they still need them or not," Wallace said.

"So where did you and Sherman go? You didn't book him into jail. So was it a nice romantic moonlight drive?" Paula said.

"I pick 'em up and drop 'em off. If someone's telling you they don't have any booking record, then that's on them, not me."

"Where is Sherman?"

"How the hell would I know?"

"Because you picked him up from the hospital and took him to your place," Paula said.

"As a favor."

"I thought you didn't have anything to do with him," John said.

Paula lifted the lip of the internal affairs file and peeked inside. "You left the SSPNET task force just before the shit hit the fan, didn't you?"

"If you mean before you and the rest of the rat squad railroaded those guys, then yeah, like I said, I got out just in time."

"How long had all the skimming of drug seizures gone on?"

"Don't know nothing about that."

Paula patted the file again. "Really? Because what I have tells me you were the senior man on the task force when you left. You'd have to know something was going on. Everything you'd set up, Sherman managed to screw up. Was he too greedy?"

"I didn't have anything to do with that. You've got nothing to say I do, or I'd have gone down with the rest of them. What Sherman did, what those guys did, skimming evidence, I guess they were greedy."

"Where were you when Larry Burger and Bobby Wing were killed?" John asked.

"Working."

"Don't you need to know the dates of the murders before you know if you were working or not?" John said.

"I'm always working," Wallace said.

"You don't have any idea where Sherman is?" John said.

"Nope. You want me to tell him anything for you if I see him?"

"Sure, tell him I can't wait to see him in prison again," Paula said.

Wallace nodded. "If he's done what you say he has, killing righteous cops and such, that's where he belongs. You want me to go find him? He might trust me."

"No, we have that all locked down," Paula said. She kicked her partner's foot under the table.

Wallace nodded again. His expression went from pissed to depressed in ten seconds.

"So if you see him, let him know we're onto him," Paula said.

"I don't think I'll be seeing him."

"Why's that?" Paula said.

"He's got no reason to see me, and I got no reason to see him neither."

"We about done here?" Parker asked. "I got another appointment."

"Yeah," John answered. The only appointment Parker had was a two-for-one happy hour special at a local cop bar, John figured.

Paula stood and grabbed the file from the table. "Thanks for your time, Sergeant."

Parker and Wallace strode out of the break room.

"You notice Wallace almost swallow his tongue when he saw your IA file? I thought all these were burned at your place," John said.

"Yep. They were." She opened the file and dumped the take-out menus on the table.

"He thought he missed one."

John's cell rang. "Penley." He smiled and said thanks. "Karen got the GPS tracker on Wallace's truck."

"Now we can let Wallace lead us to Sherman. Did Karen have any issue putting that tracker on his truck without a warrant?"

"She knows we need this to get you out from under the Sherman case. We've got your back, Paula."

"Wallace was a little eager to help find Sherman, don't you think?"

"Maybe he figured with Sherman gone, he'd take over Sherman's stolen drug stash. He had to know about it from the task force work."

John grabbed one of the food delivery menus. "You hungry?"

"I'm too pissed off to eat."

"How would you feel about delivering to a poor shut-in?"

THIRTY-NINE

"This is the poor shut-in you were talking about?" Paula said. They sat across from the meth house. Junior was getting his drunk on in the garage, and two other bikers were getting out of a blue panel van. There were only three motorcycles in the driveway, so they were likely looking at the sum total of the current biker population.

"Run that plate, would you?" John said. He pointed at the blue van. "That's the van I saw at the biker house when McDaniel was shot."

"And it's back here?" she said.

Paula started running the plate, then a motorcycle rumble sounded from down the block. A single biker parked behind the van, got off his ride, and approached Junior. He wore sunglasses, but as soon as he took off his Nazi-style bike helmet, Paula recognized him. "Wallace."

"Didn't take him too long to finish up with his union rep. He damn near beat us here," John said.

Wallace spoke with Junior, who held out a bottle of beer to the newcomer. The conversation started off slow, then grew animated with Wallace gesturing toward the van. Junior raised his bulk from the lawn chair and tossed the full beer bottle.

"You see that?" Paula said.

"Something's got Junior a bit pissy."

"He doesn't look like he's taking it out on Wallace, based on the body language. That and the two other bikers are staying out of the way."

Wallace put his hand out to his side and shrugged his shoulders, a gesture that said, "I don't know."

Junior took a step forward and pointed a fat finger in Wallace's face.

"Okay, it just got personal," John said.

Paula finished entering the vehicle information into the computer. A flash hit the screen that stated the van was reported stolen six months ago.

"Oh, this is rich, the registered owner who reported the van stolen is Mr. Wallace there."

A biker behind Junior tossed a set of keys to Wallace, who walked to the back of the van. He opened a rear door and pulled out an aluminum ramp, and he pushed his bike into the van's rear cargo space.

"He's repossessing his own van?" John said.

"Look there, on the floor next to Junior," Paula said. The black nylon bag delivered by the bikers the last time they watched the house had reappeared.

Wallace went back up the drive and spoke to Junior once more. Wallace pointed at the bag, and Junior kicked it behind him, keeping it away from Wallace. Junior spoke, and it didn't take a lip reader to make out the demand: "Get out of here."

Wallace made a step toward the bag, and the two other bikers moved between him and the bag. One had a hand behind him, like he was reaching for a gun tucked in his waistband.

Wallace got the message and put his hands up and backed off He went to his van, and as he got in, he yelled back at the bikers, "I want my money!"

"Not my problem," Junior replied. "Now get the fuck outta here."

Wallace closed the van door and patted a heavy shoulder holster back into place under a leather vest.

"You catch that?" John said.

"Yeah. Wanna take him down now?"

"We don't have enough to make it stick. The bag might have some forensic value, but we didn't see him in possession of the damn thing. And we can't say for certain what's in it—drugs, money, or a

Mary Kay delivery. I'd have a hell of a time getting a judge to get that warrant based on what we have now. Besides, one of them is going to lead us to Sherman."

Wallace started the van and sped away from the biker lair. John and Paula waited another ten minutes until Junior stopped pacing and returned to his lawn chair throne.

"You got 'em?" John asked.

"Yep." Paula turned and grabbed a paper evidence bag.

They walked up the drive under Junior's glare. "What the hell you doing back here? Want my boxers now?"

"I thought you'd be more of a tighty-whities guy," John added.

Paula tossed the paper bag in front of Junior. "As promised."

Junior opened the bag and dumped his boots onto the garage floor. A missing strip of leather on the toe had been thoughtfully covered with duct tape.

"You and Wallace have a falling out?" John asked.

"You been doing your neighborhood watch thing again?" Junior asked.

"Just happened to see him drive off in a huff, is all," John said.

"Well, just happens that I don't need cops around here, his kind or yours."

"I'm glad you have standards to uphold. Say, mind if I take a peek in that bag?"

One of the boys picked it up and brought it inside the house.

"Matter of fact, I do. Now, as I told Wallace, get the fuck outta here."

"And here we came all this way to give you your stuff back," Paula said.

"Gee, thanks." Junior pulled back the taped section on the boot.

"Turns out that wasn't blood on the boot."

"I coulda just told you that."

"Whatever you and Sherman have going is over," Paula said.

"That right?" Junior didn't seem amused. His eyes flicked in the direction that Wallace had fled.

"Yeah. I hope you didn't expect anything outta him."

Junior hoisted himself up from the lawn chair, grabbed his boots, and started for the house. "When they say one door closes, another opens—well, sometimes it don't." Junior smacked a button on the garage door panel by the back door and sent the garage door down. John and Paula were left outside on the driveway.

"He wasn't concerned about Sherman," Paula said.

"Like he already got what he needed from the black bag."

They walked back to their car, and Paula glanced at her watch. She turned when she reached the passenger door. "How long did it take us to get here?"

"I don't know, twenty minutes maybe."

She bit her lower lip.

"What?"

"Wallace went home, changed clothes, got his bike, and still got here almost the same time we did."

"Yeah, he was in a hurry. So?" John said.

"He thought Sherman was gonna be here to make the deal."

"That means Wallace doesn't know where Sherman is."

John made a call to the officer watching the front of Wallace's home. "Go do a knock and talk. See if Sherman's home."

"What are you thinking?" Paula asked.

John waited to respond until he heard back from the officer. He disconnected the call.

"If Wallace doesn't know where Sherman is, then neither do we. The place is empty. Sherman's in the wind."

FORTY

Paula suggested they go back to Wallace's place and check it out. When they got there, Wallace's Ford truck was gone, but there was no ping from the GPS unit to indicate it had moved. According to the technology, the pickup truck was here. They circled the block, using the alleyway behind the home, and found the blue panel van tucked next to the back fence of Wallace's yard.

Paula hopped out of the passenger seat and pressed her face against the dust-covered window of the garage that made up a third of the back property line.

"The motorcycle is here," she said.

She got back in the car with John. "He unloaded the bike and put it in the garage. Why not park the van in there too?"

The vehicle was big and boxy, but it would have fit easily in the old garage. "There is a space all cleared out for another car. We figured Sherman had an out when we came here the last time, right? Maybe it was the van, set to go in the alley."

"And then it turns up in Junior's driveway, packing only God knows what was in that bag he didn't want us to see."

"A drop vehicle. Park it somewhere and Junior's boys know where to pick it up."

Paula activated the GPS program on a tablet computer and the red dot on the screen showed the device at this location. "He must have found it and tossed it in the yard somewhere."

"Maybe," John said. He pushed open his door. "Hang on a second." He got out and went up to the van, went on one knee and fished a hand up in the fender well of the rear wheels. Inside the passenger wheel well, he found the GPS unit, power light still strobing.

He came to Paula's window, dusted off his pant leg, and hooked a thumb at the van. "He found it all right. He put it on that hunk of rust."

"He wanted us to think he was still here," she said, tapping the tablet.

"Or maybe he put it there so *he* could track the van."

"He could get access to the program to track that unit. It's not like it's rocket science or anything."

"Wallace wants to find out where Sherman went."

Paula's brow creased. "Or he's trying to get Sherman to lead him to the stolen drugs. The stash McDaniel talked about."

"Wallace doesn't know where it is."

"Want to pull it and shut it down?" Paula asked.

John took a step toward the van and stopped. "If he can track it, so can we. Let's let Wallace lead us to Sherman's stash." John placed the GPS unit back under the blue van's fender well.

John got back in the car and pulled through the alley. While they drove back to the detective bureau, Paula scanned the side streets and parking lots for Wallace's chrome-tailed truck.

"If we ask for a BOLO for the truck, Wallace will find out and go to ground, don't you think?" John asked.

Paula was lost in her own thoughts.

"Hello?"

She jarred back to the present. "Sorry, what?"

"What took you away there?"

"Sherman. I mean, why risk everything to make some deal with Junior? I get the whole bit about them sharing a cell for a while, but Sherman literally got a get-out-of-jail-free card from the DA. Why mess with a lowlife like Junior at all?

"His play has to rest in the Burger and Wing killings. They represented a threat to his potential freedom. I can see the hit on Burger to stop him from testifying, but Wing and McDaniel? They weren't gonna roll on him." She looked at her partner. "What if it was never about the testimony against Sherman? Burger, Wing, and McDaniel all knew what happened to the drugs siphoned off from the task force arrests."

"Burger, Wing, and McDaniel in the drug business? I don't know. How could Sherman have run a drug operation from inside a prison cell?"

"He'd have to have someone on the outside, someone like Junior or Wallace to make the connections," Paula said.

"What if Burger and the others were connections too and someone started getting greedy? Those pills we found in Burger's throat—could they have come from the stolen drugs? They were older, according to Dr. Kelly."

Paula shook her head. "Maybe Burger had a role in it, but if you were running a high-risk operation, would you trust a pillhead like him?"

John parked in the lot, and they made their way into the office, where a brown paper-wrapped package sat in the center of his desk along with six phone message slips. Four of the six messages were for Paula.

The two remaining messages were from the principal at Kari's school. *Great.*

John called the number, and it rang three times before it picked up. At first, John thought it was a recording, from the sickly sweet voice on the other end.

"Mrs. Thompkins." The insincere voice sounded like it belonged on one of those late-night infomercials hawking kitchen knives or nonstick cookware.

"John Penley, returning your call."

"Mr. Penley, thank you so much for calling. I need to speak with you about your daughter." There was paper rustling in the background. "Kara."

"Kari."

"Pardon?" she said.

"Kari. My daughter's name is Kari."

"Yes—yes. Well, Kari's behavior is causing some concern here at the school. I'm afraid that she's become a distraction to our learning environment."

John squeezed the bridge of his nose. "What are you saying?"

"We take threats of violence very seriously."

"Violence? You mean the spat she and her friend Lanette had?"

"I cannot downplay the seriousness of this unkind behavior and the hostile environment it creates for all the children."

The language—unkind, hostile, children—set his teeth on edge. "It was a disagreement between two teenaged girls."

"You don't seem to understand the seriousness of today's infraction—"

"Today? What about today? She's on suspension."

"Your daughter disregarded her suspension and threatened the safety of another student. We have a zero-tolerance policy, and with her history of violence—"

"Wait. History? She had one single altercation with another girl. Don't blow this out of proportion."

"One cannot condone threats of violence against another student. Moreover, she came to the school campus after being suspended." More papers rustling in the background. "Kara told the other student, and I quote, 'I will kick your skanky ass if you get in my face again.'"

"That's it? Kick your skanky ass? That's the threat of violence? And my daughter's name is Kari."

"This is serious, Mr. Penley. I need a parent to come and remove her from school grounds. Kari has been suspended until the board reviews this for expulsion."

"Are you fucking kidding me?"

"Mr. Penley, I never."

"I wouldn't doubt it." He slammed the phone onto the cradle.

He dialed Melissa, and the phone went directly to voice mail. "Well, shit."

John grabbed the message from the medical examiner and dialed the extension for Dr. Kelly.

After connecting with her, she put him on hold while she got to her office.

"John, you still there?"

"Yep. Did I pull you out of anything?"

"*Anyone* would be more accurate. But it's always that way around here lately. I wanted to give you an update on the ballistics on your victim."

John paused. "Which victim are you talking about?"

"McDaniel, George. White male, midthirties."

"He was alive this morning. What the hell happened?" John said.

"I'm sorting that out, but I wanted to give you the ballistics information and let you run with it."

"Yeah, yeah. Two high-caliber rifle slugs, I'm guessing .223," he said.

"Are we talking about the same case here? McDaniel had two gunshot wounds all right. Two .380-caliber bullets from a handgun."

"Are you certain?"

"It's kinda what I do."

"I didn't mean it that way, Doc. It's just not what I expected."

"I will get back to you with a determinate cause of death. It may, or may not, be resultant from the gunshot wounds."

They hung up, and the unsettled feeling in John's gut threatened to eat through his stomach lining.

He dialed Melissa again and got sent to voice mail immediately. Was she screening his calls? "Dammit."

Paula looked across the desk. "What's up?"

"I need a minute of your time. Can you put on your best I'm-sorry face?"

FORTY-ONE

Three more attempts to reach Melissa on her phone, and all went directly to voice mail. John was about to try again when he pulled into the J. C. Marshall High School parking lot. Buses started to line up for the afternoon exodus from school. Adult-looking thick-necked boys—men, really—jostled one another in displays of peacock-like horseplay. Was one of these chin-stubbled animals Cameron, the one responsible for Kari's change of attitude?

John pulled the sedan to the curb near the office and went in while Paula sat on the trunk watching the adolescent display of dominance.

The principal's office was easy to find, a corner room festooned with those motivational posters with their pabulum of teamwork, communication, and respect. Kari sat on a chair in the outer office, looking bored out of her mind. She rolled her eyes when she saw him enter.

"Kari, let's go," he said.

A woman with long gray hair, blue jeans, and a macrame vest over a paisley blouse came from an inner office. "Mr. Penley."

He recognized the voice from the phone. "Mrs. Taskins, I'm here for my daughter—Kari."

"Thompkins," she corrected. "And we need to talk about your daughter."

"What's to talk about? It sounded like you already made up your mind."

"I'm concerned about her willful disobedience by violating the terms of her suspension and her need to express violence."

"Violence? Telling someone to get out of her face isn't an expression of violence."

"We cannot tolerate such harmful behavior."

"Oh, for shit sake. If the 'children' aren't learning boundary issues and respecting another kid's space, then I have to question what's happening in this institution."

Kari's eyes widened.

Mrs. Thompkins placed a hand over her heart. "We have no tolerance for threats. We draw the line at the safety of all the children. If you are having trouble supervising your child's activities—"

"Seriously? Who's watching the drug deals going on in the parking lot right now while you're all twisted up about Kari warning another girl that she'll kick her butt if she doesn't leave her alone?"

"We can't have her—"

"It sounds like you're condoning the bullying behavior by this other girl."

"No, we don't tolerate—"

"I think the school board will be interested to see the environment fostered here, where a girl like Kari isn't safe."

"Now, Mr. Penley, there's no need to bring the board—"

"Come on, Kari, I'll take you home, where it's safe."

"Mr. Penley?"

"Let me know when my daughter will be safe back here."

John and Kari left the office and headed out of the administration building.

"Dad, that was awesome."

"Don't get too excited, young lady. I'm still not sure if I need to be pissed at you. What the hell were you thinking going back to school today?"

"Paula, you should have seen Dad with Mrs. Thompkins. It was so cool."

"Ramona Thompkins? Is that crazy old bat still working here?"

"You know her?"

"I went here more than a few years ago, and nutty old Mrs. Thompkins was the guidance counselor."

"What did you do?" John asked his daughter.

"It was Lanette again. She was getting all up in my face about Cameron and how I wasn't good enough for him—"

"Which one's Lanette?" Paula jutted her chin at a knot of girls that seemed overly interested in what was going on with Kari.

"She's the tall one with the dark hair," Kari said.

"You called her a skank and said you'd kick her ass?" Paula said.

"Yeah."

Paula hopped off the back of the car and approached the girls. Two of their number left as soon as she started in their direction.

Lanette had her hands on her hips when Paula started, and within seconds, the girl was hugging herself and looked to be on the verge of tears. Paula pointed a finger at her, and Lanette jumped like she'd been stabbed.

Paula turned and came back to John and Kari. Lanette and her posse had vanished.

"What did you do? Am I gonna get another call from the school? You could get expelled too, you know," John said.

"I reminded Lanette that Cameron gets to make up his own mind, and he'd rather spend his time with someone like Kari than a skanky skinny bitch like her."

"You didn't."

"Not in so many words. But I don't think she's gonna be a problem anymore."

Kari hugged Paula. "You're the best."

John pointed at a gathering of awkward teenaged boys huddling around a bank of lockers. "Which one of these misfits is Cameron?"

Paula followed Kari's gaze to where one of the guys making furtive doe-eyed glances at Kari. He was gangly—not man and not child, but something in between.

"I think I know which one," Paula said. "Maybe I'll go have a chat with him too."

Kari's face turned white. "Paula, please no." She grabbed Paula's elbow.

John gave his best stay-away-from-my-daughter look, but the kid was too focused on Kari.

"Get in, both of you," he said.

On the drive home, John asked, "You try to get ahold of Mom?"

"Yeah, I got voice mail."

"Me too. Was she going anywhere that I forgot about?"

Kari shrugged.

John glanced at his partner. "Did Dr. Kelly get to you about our latest vic?"

"Nuh-uh."

John saw Kari in the rear view. She seemed lost in thought. Probably about Cameron.

"George McDaniel died."

"Really?" Paula said. "He didn't look that bad when we saw him at the hospital. What did Dr. Kelly say about COD?"

"That means cause of death, right?" Kari chimed in.

"Do we need to get you earmuffs?" John asked.

"Whatever." She slouched back in the seat.

"Dr. Kelly didn't have that yet. She called me because the ballistics were off from what I saw happen. The drive-by shooter sprayed automatic rifle fire from the car," John said.

"Yeah, I remember seeing the bullet holes in the meth house and Wallace pointing them out with Junior."

"Well, the slugs in McDaniel were from a .380."

"A little handgun?" Paula said.

"Probably. But the driveway shooter had a rifle, I'm certain of it."

"Then you have a second shooter," Kari called from the back seat.

John looked at his partner and then in the rearview mirror. Kari was looking out the window, trying her best to look bored.

"The rifle fire was a distraction. Everyone, including me, was concerned with the rifle fire coming from the street. I wasn't even looking for another shooter," he said.

"If it wasn't Sherman in the drive-by, who'd want to take McDaniel off the board?"

"I saw someone with a shotgun. The handgun had to be Junior or someone from his crew."

"We need to check out .380 gun registrations. It's a long shot, but we have to cover it. One of those rejects might've a registered weapon."

"I don't think there were any tears shed over McDaniel getting shot. Junior and his crew didn't even come and try to see if he was okay. They took off on the trail of the shooter—or that's what it looked like at the time."

"McDaniel knew about Sherman's stash, and he wasn't gonna give it up without immunity," Paula continued.

"So McDaniel was just one more, like Burger and Wing, who knew too much about the business. Who's next?"

FORTY-TWO

John gave Paula the keys and had her drop him and Kari at home. Melissa's car wasn't in the driveway, and the house was locked up. Tommy should've been home from school by now. The old fear for Tommy's health returned with a white-hot vision of kidney rejection, immune system compromise, and renal shut-down. The boy had lived through all these hells before, and the transplant was supposed to make sure he never went down that declining path again.

Kari went to her room and closed the door as soon as they got inside. Some things remained constant. He checked the answering machine and the big red zero blinked back at him. Melissa hadn't called, and there was no handwritten note pinned under a magnet on the refrigerator saying she needed to dash off somewhere.

Paranoia swelled against the banks of reason. Under the best of circumstances, a cop swallowed a healthy dose of paranoia to explain human behavior and prepare for what's behind the next door. This felt different. Lately, Melissa's emotions had whipsawed from distant and cold to a guarded truce.

He dialed Melissa's cell again and it went to voice mail as he heard the front door open. His blood pressure started to throttle back when he heard Tommy's voice.

"Hi, Dad."

"Hi, you doing okay?"

Tommy looked at him with a quizzical expression. "Yeah, I'm okay. Are you?"

"Yeah, sure, fine. Everything's fine. Where's your mom?"

"She's in the car. Said she needed to do something first."

John went outside and Melissa was still in the driver's seat and puffing away on a cigarette, eyes closed and head tilted back. She'd been the one who pressured him to quit smoking, especially when Tommy was waiting for a transplant.

He rapped a knuckle on the window. Melissa turned and took another drag and looked at him with red puffy eyes. When she didn't roll the window down, John tugged on the door handle and found it locked.

"Open up, Mel. What's going on?"

She put the window down a few inches, and stale cigarette smoke wafted from the crack. "I can't do this right now."

"Do what?"

She gestured to the house and him with the lit end of her cigarette. "This—all of it."

"What are you talking about?"

"I'm tired of Kari's abuse. I don't know what to do about it."

John caught a whiff of booze when she spoke.

"Where have you been, Mel? I've been calling you."

"You've been calling, the school's been calling, Lanette's parents have been calling, everybody's been calling. I don't know what to say."

"Come on, Mel. Come inside."

Her eyes flicked over at him, and something darker lurked behind the usually soft blue.

"I'm a shitty mother. I can't control my daughter, I nearly killed my own son last year."

There it was, that same guilt. Her black-market deal had nearly killed their boy, but it wasn't her fault. But it seemed the guilt she kept repressed had eaten away at the woman she was, leaving behind an insecure shell of the person he loved.

"You're a good mom; come on out."

She chuckled. "They teach you that in hostage negotiation training?"

"The kids need you. I need you. Come in and I'll put on some coffee, and we'll talk."

"I'm such a mess. I didn't want Tommy to see me like this."
She rolled the window closed. A barrier, physical every bit as it was
emotional.

"Mel, come on. You shouldn't be driving." He tapped on the
window with a knuckle.

She popped the car in gear and backed out of the driveway.

John trotted after the car until she shoved it into drive and sped
away from the house—from him and the kids. He watched Mel's
car turn a corner and disappear.

"Dad? Is Mom coming back?" Tommy stood in the doorway.
The boy looked small and frightened.

"Yeah, Tommy. Mom needed to go and take of something."
John hoped the boy didn't ask what that was, because he sure as hell
didn't have an answer.

John went inside and told Tommy to get started on his homework. Kari's door was closed. She'd already walled herself off.

Alone in the kitchen, John leaned against the counter and tipped
his head back. He let out a ragged breath. "When did life get so
complicated?"

A slight rap sounded on the front door. John went, expecting
another solar panel sales call—frickin' predators hawking sunshine.
Instead, Connie Newhouse, in her Sacramento County Sheriff's
uniform, stood in the doorway.

"Hey, Connie, come in," John said. "What brings you over?
Can I get you a drink?"

"No, thanks. I need to get home and get Lynne to soccer
practice. But I wanted to make sure you got this, personally. I
didn't want it going through channels and getting lost in the PD's
human resources black hole." She handed him a thick file marked
"Confidential."

"What's this?"

"Sergeant Wallace's personnel file."

John took the file and thumbed through the volume.

"With the unsubstantiated court appearances you discovered,
the department suspended him pending further investigation. He's
officially on the beach until this gets sorted out." Wallace was effec-
tively stranded, so to speak, on administrative leave, but with pay.

"Glad you did that. Why bring the file to me? Isn't your internal affairs gonna need this?"

"I asked them to let you work your case first, and they'll take our administrative action based on your findings."

"In other words, if I can't nail him down on more than the phonied court orders, they won't have much to work with?"

"Something like that. But there're some things in there you need to see. A half dozen complaints of excessive force, reprimands . . . and that's just since we got him from Solano County. When you're done looking it over tomorrow, give me a call and I'll pick it up, or you can drop it by my office."

"Thanks, Connie, I appreciate the heads-up."

They said their good-byes, and John promised to return the file tomorrow. Connie left, and John closed the door behind her, turning back to his broken family.

FORTY-THREE

John's bedside phone jarred him awake. It took a couple of rings before his mind figured out where the shrill, earsplitting sound was coming from. He grabbed it, looked over, and saw that Melissa hadn't come home.

"Penley," he whispered as he walked down the hallway and into the kitchen.

"Detective, this is Lieutenant Mendez, watch commander. You have been requested on scene."

"Hi, Felipe. Congrats on the promotion. Long overdue. So what'd ya have?"

"Thank you." The lieutenant's voice softened a bit and carried a less formal tone. "The victim called in—"

"The victim? This isn't a homicide callout?"

"No. I guess I should have led with that. But the victim called in and asked for you and Newberry, specifically."

"Who is it?"

"Responding unit reported Gerald Balderson."

"Doesn't ring a bell."

"Goes by the name of Bullet."

"Okay, now we're getting somewhere. We get any story as to what happened yet?"

"Sketchy. Something regarding what you guys were asking him about. That's all he'd tell our guys."

"Tell you what. Have a unit sit on him until I can get there. Call Newberry and tell her I'm on the way. Wait—do you know what contact number she left? She had to move out of her place."

"I have her cell number."

"Okay. Where do we have Bullet?"

"He met the responding unit behind a convenience store in Natomas."

"I know the place. Call Newberry and let the officers know my ETA is about twenty minutes."

He hung up and dialed Melissa's cell. It went to voice mail. He called her sister Andrea and a groggy voice responded. "Hello," she said.

"Andi, it's John. Is—"

"Mel's here, John."

"She okay?"

"She will be."

"I need a favor. Can you come and watch over the kids? I got a call out. I don't know if Mel—"

"Yeah, no problem. Give me fifteen minutes, 'kay?"

"Thanks, Andi."

While John was dressing in the dark, Paula called. She'd been at the detective bureau running gun registrations for .380-caliber handguns in the county. He popped by and picked her up. She was bleary-eyed and jittery from an energy drink. The one in her hand wasn't the first one of the night.

"Those things aren't good for you."

Paula made a show of taking a big gulp of the caffeine-and-stimulant-laced drink. "Says who, the coffee growers lobby? Everything's gonna kill us."

"I'm just saying, that stuff right there will raise your blood pressure, and I'm guessing yours is high enough as it is."

Changing the course of the conversation, Paula asked, "Why did Bullet want to talk to us in the middle of the night?"

"Something got him spooked."

"That little tweaker was probably hallucinating that he saw crocodiles in the Sacramento River."

"Any luck on running gun registrations?"

She shook her head. "Hundreds. Nothing that ties to Junior and his white boys so far."

"You should have come back to our place and gotten some rest, Paula. You look like you haven't slept in days."

"Gee, thanks, that's exactly what a girl wants to hear. And I can't sleep. Between Sherman finding a way out of prison to murder guys tied to his task force and the DA's hunt for a scapegoat because she's gonna lose some political clout, I'm way past counting sheep."

John pulled into the same convenience store parking lot where Bullet was found scavenging in a dumpster. This time, they found him hiding behind it. The uniformed officers said he wouldn't come out until the detectives arrived.

The patrol unit took off once John and Paula checked in with them.

"Come out, come out, wherever you are," Paula said. She was not in the mood to play a rousing game of homeless hide and seek.

Bullet peeked around the side of the metal dumpster.

"Get your ass out here," Paula snapped.

Bullet looked unsure, like he wanted to bolt back into the brush behind the store.

"Don't you dare. You got me out of bed, so you owe me an explanation," John said.

Bullet skulked from behind the waste container and came to the paved part of the lot where John and Paula waited.

"I'm sorry. I didn't know what to do." Bullet's voice was raspy and weak.

"What's wrong with your voice?" John asked.

A mottled purple bruise was visible in the light from the storefront. A dark stain spread under Bullet's jaw.

"I got hit in the neck. A sucker punch."

"That why you called us out here? To snitch out one of your homeless pals?" Paula asked.

Bullet shook. "No, it ain't like that. The guy who done this. I think he was on the road when that guy got himself killed."

"Burger? The man who was murdered on Garden Highway? You saw the man who did it today?" John said.

"He was there. I knew he looked familiar. I was too slow putting it together."

"You're sure? You saw the guy?"

"It was his voice. It was so dark before that it was hard to see him, but I'd never forget that voice."

Paula pulled her cell phone and thumbed through a collection of photos. "Is this him?"

She held out a prison mug shot of Sherman. Not exactly an unbiased photo identification. A defense attorney could argue she should have assembled a "six-pack" of similar looking photos from the DMV database.

Bullet shook his head. "No, that ain't him. I'm talking about a big, beefy dude. His name's Junior."

Paula put the phone away. "Junior killed Burger for Sherman."

"Wait, what?" Bullet said.

"How long ago did you last see him?" Paula asked.

"Must be close to an hour, maybe less."

"We gotta get a perimeter set up. He's on foot," John said.

"He didn't kill nobody," Bullet said. John and Paula stopped. Bullet looked from one to the other. "He didn't kill nobody. Did you hear what I said?"

"You just told us that you saw him up on the road when that man was killed," Paula said.

"No, I didn't."

"Goddammit, Bullet, I don't have time for games," Paula took a step closer to the man, and he cowered, waiting for a blow, like a man used to taking a beating.

"I said I saw him and heard his voice. But he wasn't the one who done the killing."

"There were two men?" John said.

Bullet nodded and looked for approval, hoping he'd said the right thing.

"If this man didn't kill Burger, then who did?" Paula said. She held Sherman's photo again. "You sure?"

"No."

"No he didn't, or no you're not sure?"

Bullet closed his eyes and shook. "Please, I'm trying to tell you."

"Okay, okay, take a breath and tell us what you remember," John said.

Bullet gulped for air like he was surfacing from the deep end of the pool. "I followed a man, not that man, out to the highway. I listened to them talk, and he's the one who stomped the living shit outta that guy after he mentioned your name, Detective," he looked at Paula.

"Go ahead. Where does this other guy come in?" John said.

"The dude who done the killing came back to the fire road. Junior was in the blue van, and him and the killer dude talked some, and that's when one of 'em saw me and they split."

"Are you certain the guy in that picture isn't the one you saw kill the man on the highway?" John said.

A quick nod. "I'm certain."

"That doesn't mean that Sherman didn't set the whole thing up," Paula interjected.

"Would you be able to recognize the killer again if you saw him?" John asked.

"Yeah, but I don't wanna get involved. I done enough. You guys don't need me for anything else."

"You're involved up to your ass, cupcake," Paula said. "What did he look like? What was he wearing?"

Bullet's eyes shut tight, and it hurt to watch him think that hard. John felt sorry for him. All the drug use had turned the man's mind into a Swiss cheese–like mess.

"He was big. It was dark."

"Think. What did you see?"

He shook his head so hard that John feared Bullet would give himself a concussion. "I can't say."

"Can't or won't?" Paula asked.

"I don't know. There was something familiar about the guy. But I can't say where I've seen him before."

"It was Sherman," Paula said. "It has to be."

FORTY-FOUR

Bullet was afraid to return to the homeless camp because he thought someone would come back and finish him. John found a housing voucher and dropped Bullet at one of the single room–occupancy hotels downtown that catered to the down and almost out. As much as Sacramento tried to eradicate the places that attracted people like Bullet, the number of people needing those lifelines grew. The city couldn't solve the homelessness epidemic in the capitol, but they could keep them out of sight. It was easier to pretend the lost ghost souls didn't exist.

The face that John and Paula saw in the hours before daybreak was the side that the tourist guides didn't publicize. The parks teemed with homeless. They weren't camping, because that was against the city ordinances, but they were on the grass and sprawled out on benches until they were rousted to move on. The light-rail stations attracted a different element after dark. The late-night trains ran more drugs than people.

"What's in it for Wallace? Why would he risk so much picking up Sherman on those bullshit court appearances? And why would Junior be there if he wasn't doing the killing? What am I missing?" Paula said.

"The second man at the scene has to be Sherman. We have his DNA at each of the crime scenes—he was there. Wasn't he?"

"My DNA was at the scene too. Bullet made noise about someone else as the killer and not Sherman. He seemed sure about that—as much as a meth head can be. Shit, I need more time."

"We're closing in, partner," John said.

"That's not good enough. According to the lieutenant, I'm on my last twenty-four hours. The Green Mile, and I didn't even get a last meal."

"There's one other guy who matches Bullet's description." John reached over the back seat and passed Wallace's personnel file to his partner.

"What are you doing with this?"

"A friend dropped it off last night. Take a look through there and see if anything pops for you. I took a peek last night, but I didn't know what we know now. It might change things."

Paula opened the stiff-backed file in her lap. "He's got a few disciplinary actions here."

"Supposedly use-of-force issues," John prompted.

"At least two of them took place in the jail. He was assigned there after his transfer from Solano County. An inmate filed a complaint that Wallace and others beat him down after he grabbed a food tray from a female deputy."

"Don't mess with room service."

"Another complaint about excessive force. Apparently, he broke a prisoner's arm when he resisted getting fingerprinted," Paula read.

"Yeah, booking isn't a fun place to work."

"Here's another where the inmate claimed that he got rat packed after he refused to come out of his cell."

"Sounds like a cell extraction. What else?"

"Here's one, more recent. While on transportation duty, Wallace took a prisoner down and stomped on his ribs. The man went to the hospital and was treated for injuries. Wallace reported the prisoner tried to grab his weapon."

"Guy has a way of being in the wrong place at the wrong time, doesn't he?"

"The complaints weren't sustained, with the exception of the one where he broke the guy's arm in booking. The report said Wallace escalated the situation and failed to use proper procedure to defuse the prisoner's behavior. He was reassigned to transportation soon after."

"Maybe he was the guy they all called on when shit went bad. But there's a pattern here, like the guy liked to mix it up. I get the feeling there's more to it than that," John said.

"Wallace's training records are spotty for all the required stuff, but he was a trainer for weaponless defense, a marksman for Solano County's tactical team, and assigned to the SSPNET task force."

"A marksman wouldn't have missed McDaniel," John said.

"Unless he wanted to. You think he was the driver who put down the rifle fire at Junior's place?"

"It fits," John said.

"You know how Wallace said he barely knew Sherman but admitted he worked with him on the task force?"

"Yeah?" John said.

"He and Wallace were partnered up back in Solano County. They've been working together for years."

Paula shut the file when her phone chirped. The phone screen displayed an alert. "Wallace's van is on the move."

She put down the file on the floor and slid the tablet computer from the console.

"Heading west on J Street."

John whipped the car into an abrupt U turn, a move that daytime traffic would have made unthinkable. There were few vehicles on the road at this time of night. The old, faded van was easy to spot, and their tail would be easily spotted too.

John hung a quick right turn and went two blocks south to the next one-way that paralleled J Street. "Let me know when he turns, so I can keep out of sight."

"We can't be sure who's driving. Remember, Wallace can track the van too," Paula said.

The red dot held its course for ten minutes until it turned on Sixty-Fifth Street to the south. John turned south on another less crowded street a few blocks away.

"He's stopping," Paula advised.

John turned toward the mark on the map, and when they pulled within a quarter mile, John switched off the headlights and crept through the dark commercial district streets.

Paula pointed to a storage facility. "The GPS puts him there."

They got out of the car and approached the yard on foot. The streets were dead quiet, and they heard the clatter of a roll-up door inside the facility. They followed the fence line to a back corner where a space between units gave a line of sight into an aisle of the storage facility. Rows of orange metal doors kept silent vigil. The blue van wasn't there.

"Give me a boost," Paula said.

John laced his fingers together, and Paula stepped in his hands with one foot and jammed a toe in a fence link. She scrambled up and dropped down on the other side.

"You be careful. Got your radio on?"

She nodded and slipped out of his sight.

A light crackle of radio static and Paula's voice whispered through John's radio, "The van's moving. I didn't see which unit he stopped at. Hold on—moving for a better look."

John pressed his microphone button once to signal he understood.

A few silent seconds passed, and John thought about scaling the fence after her. It was a bad idea to let her go in alone. As if Paula could've been stopped.

"It's Sherman. I saw him as he passed me."

The rumble of an engine drew John's attention from the fence. The blue van tripped the motion sensor on the gate-opening device. Sherman pulled through the gate and turned on the main road, heading back into the city.

"Paula, we gotta get moving," John said through the radio.

"I can't tell which unit he was in. There must be a hundred back here. I'm on my way to you."

Paula jogged through the front gate before it closed, just as the van's taillights disappeared.

A nagging thought flashed in John's mind. Had Paula let Sherman escape?

FORTY-FIVE

Sherman loved the game, but it was never going to be everlasting. The plan was to destroy Newberry, then cash in the stolen drugs and disappear. He could live like a king in some nonextradition country. The problem was that Junior and his cadre of knuckle-dragging mighty whiteys couldn't move the product fast enough. He needed someone with a thicker wallet.

He'd gotten into this situation with Junior and his Aryan Brotherhood backers out of necessity. The social opportunities available to a disgraced cop in prison were somewhat limited. In prison, everyone had wanted a piece of him, and only the Aryan Brotherhood had stood between him and a shank in the kidney. The gang's interest wasn't from love or even the fact that Sherman was a white boy. Predators acted based on the what's-in-it-for-me factor, and their protection came with a price.

Sherman had proven himself fending off a handful of half hearted attempts to put him in the infirmary. The gang saw something they could exploit, and Sherman became an enforcer, collecting rent and sending physical messages to those who disrespected the Brotherhood. The work put Sherman in good standing with the shot-callers, and he enjoyed the reputation. But he'd never bought into all their racial-superiority bullshit.

The gang demanded a test of loyalty. Gang members who worked in the yard office manipulated cell moves and housing arrangements to serve their needs. One of those needs was the discipline of an informant who gave up information about an Aryan

Brotherhood operation on the street. It was a minor drug lab in Stockton, and the police acted on the tip. The snitch was marked, and the green light was given for a hit.

The man was moved into Sherman's cell, and the rat didn't last the night. He was stabbed in his sleep, and when officers came by for count, they found the informant dead on his mattress and Sherman covered in his blood, sitting by the cell door drawing designs on the cell floor. Within a day, he was in administrative segregation at CSP-SAC and headed for the cage in the PSU.

Sherman knew it was time to call in the favor for his loyalty. If Junior couldn't move the volume he had, the AB could. Sherman would go around the middleman and deal directly with the gang.

Sherman pulled the blue van into a garage of a low, squat bungalow that looked like it last saw fresh paint in the 1950s. The place had the markings of a house teetering on foreclosure: dry lawn, a handful of windows boarded up, and neighborhood trash strewn on the sidewalk. The house didn't stand out from the rest of the block. Sherman owned the place and had for the better part of four years.

He parked the van and tucked the keys under the sun visor. He walked to the garage door and surveyed the houses nearby. No curious faces appeared in the windows. Everyone here knew better than to take an interest in someone else's goings-on. Sherman closed the garage door and placed a new combination lock on the hasp. He gave the dial a spin and walked away.

The pocket of his blue hoodie sagged from the prepaid cell phone he'd gotten at the 7-Eleven when he put five dollars of cheap gas in the van's tank. Enough to get the Aryan bastards the goods, but Sherman didn't feel like funding their entire road trip.

He kept to the shadows along the commercial roadway, skirting the yellow pools of light that spilled from the few unbroken lamps. He found the dark doorway of an auto-dismantling business identified by the greasepaint-lettered signs on the front. A thick layer of dust and nicotine glazed the window, but the outline of a greasy counter and a pair of plastic patio chairs marked this as the office of the dismantling operation.

Sherman knew this particular yard from the task force operation. Stolen cars used by high-end traffickers would end up here after a one-time drug drop. The cars disappeared or, more often than not, got what the shop owner called "an extreme makeover," where all parts with a vehicle identification number were removed and swapped out with another scrapped car. Combine that with a cheap layer of paint, and you had the automotive equivalent of an untraceable gun.

The benefit of "shopping" at this time of night was the complete absence of salesmen, or in the case of this yard, crackheads moonlighting as chop shop welders. The four cars parked out in front of the shop's office were lower-end Hondas and budget imports. Business had slacked off since the state began issuing driver's licenses to undocumented immigrants, who could now buy a car on the legitimate market rather than relying on predatory lending in places like this. There weren't for sale signs on the cars, but those who needed a ghost car knew where to find one.

A gray Honda Civic caught Sherman's eye. There were hundreds like it that flowed in and out of the city during the twice-daily commute crush. An empty hole where the door lock should be meant he didn't have to smash the window to get in. He pulled the door open on uneven hinges and sat on a cushion that held the impression of a butt much larger than his.

A bright new chrome ring around the ignition meant it had been recently replaced. He glanced through the filthy storefront window and saw the cabinet on the wall behind the counter where the keys were stored. The owners hadn't bothered to change it since the last time Sherman was there. Granted, that last time, he'd carried a badge.

The front door had been forced open so many times that Sherman almost fell through when he put a shoulder into the metal frame. With keys in hand, he returned to the Honda and started the engine. He pulled out of the parking lot with his untraceable car. The best part was that the salvage owner couldn't even report it stolen.

Sherman grabbed the cell phone in his sweat shirt pocket and dialed a number from memory. Someone picked up after the fourth ring, harsh music screaming in the background.

"Yeah?" a voice said beneath the wail of death metal.

"Lemme talk to Simmons."

"Who's askin'?"

"Sherman."

"Who the hell's Sherman?" the voice called out to someone.

There was a rustle of the phone as it was passed around and the ear-splitting death metal mercifully backed down a dozen decibels.

"Hey, little pig, how's it hanging?" Simmons said.

"I'm selling a house," Sherman said.

"That right? The whole thing?"

"All of it."

"Why don't you use our regular broker?"

"Junior can't handle a house this big."

"How big we talking here?" The metal music disappeared as a door closed in the background.

"It's all yours for one-point-five."

"That seems a bit high for the neighborhood."

"The appraisal is worth twice that. You're getting a bargain."

"I could see one."

"How about seven-fifty plus a side job?"

"Must be a personal side deal if you're willing to spend that much for it."

"Something that needs doing, and I need to be seen somewhere else when it goes down."

"So seven-fifty plus the side job? You understand if the home inspection doesn't pan out, we're gonna have a big problem, right?" Simmons asked.

"No issues on my end. Can you keep yours?"

"It's gonna take me a little bit to pull together the funds, but yeah, it's doable. And as a gesture of good faith, I'll handle your side project up front."

"Good."

Sherman shoved the phone into the passenger seat and drove toward downtown. Almost done.

FORTY-SIX

Paula couldn't sit still. It wasn't from the caffeine she'd downed in the last twelve hours; she was one of those people who could drink a double espresso an hour before bedtime and still sleep soundly. The agitation came from feeling the noose tighten around her neck, and it felt like every move she made tugged on the rope.

Sherman's release from prison was being cast as a perversion of the justice system. Or, even more damning, the result of corrupt cops. The only thing the two views agreed upon was that Paula Newberry was at the center. She either engineered his conviction with tainted paid-for testimony or had a hand in making sure the case against him evaporated before a retrial happened.

The district attorney was clear about her opinions. Others were starting to line up and turn their backs on Paula—literally. She'd walked down one of the hallways and officers would turn away. A sign that she'd betrayed the faith.

"Newberry, my office," Lieutenant Barnes said, pulling her out of a dark cloud.

She got to the office door and Barnes motioned her in.

"I'm not sure where John went off to," she said.

"Close the door."

"That's never good," she muttered.

"The city council meets tomorrow. What do you have?"

"We have a witness to the Burger killing. Not the most credible of sources, but he puts Junior at the scene, along with a second man as the killer. That has to be Sherman. His DNA was on the victim."

"You figure he was taking out the witnesses who could have gone against him in a retrial?" Barnes said.

"Sherman knew these guys were the only thing that stood between freedom and more time behind the walls. Could be that he lured these guys in and took them out. They used to work with the guy—hell, they might have still trusted him."

"Sherman and Wallace—their relationship goes back to Solano County before their SSPNET assignments. Could Sherman have played that loyalty to get Wallace to fake the court removal orders?"

"That makes sense," Paula said.

Barnes looked up and signaled Penley into the office.

"What's up? I was getting some info on the gun used on McDaniel," John said.

"The drive-by that wasn't," Barnes said.

"Yeah. Karen Baylor echoed what Dr. Kelly said. McDaniel was shot with a .380-caliber handgun. She identified the gun through NIBIN." The National Integrated Ballistic Information Network maintained a database of almost three million visual images of bullets and cartridges collected at crimes scenes.

"It's been used in a crime before?" Paula asked.

John nodded. "Yep, a drug-lab takedown. Any guesses?"

"SSPNET," Barnes said.

"That's why you're the lieutenant. Specifically, Deputy Wallace confiscated the firearm and reported it destroyed."

"The gun used on McDaniel isn't supposed to exist," Paula said.

"No trace, no paper work, no nothing. But it turned up in this shooting, and it's my bet that Wallace gave it to Junior. Wallace had to be the gunman in the truck distracting everyone from the real shooter. Even the rust bucket blue van looks like the one I saw when the shooting went down."

"Where's the gun now?" Paula said.

"If they have any brains, Junior and his misfits tore it down and spread the pieces from here to Reno."

The lieutenant picked up his desk phone on the first ring. "Lieutenant Barnes. Yeah, they're right here. I'll let 'em know."

"That was a call from the officer on Ronland's protective detail. Ronland got attacked this morning, and our guy didn't see a thing.

He went knocking on the door when Ronland was late for work and found him."

"Shit. How is he?" Paula asked.

"In surgery at the trauma center. Doesn't look good—stabbed in the chest. Why don't you guys head on over and see what's happening. If he comes out, we're gonna need to know what he can tell us."

"That's the last of them, isn't it?" John said.

"Last of what?" Barnes asked.

"The SSPNET crew. Anyone who could have been in a position to challenge Sherman is gone," John said.

"Except Wallace. Wallace knows he's looking at criminal charges due to his role in Sherman's little excursions from prison. He'll be lying low if he hasn't already split. He doesn't know we have the NIBIN hit on the gun."

"And Sherman?" Barnes asked.

"I lost him at the storage yard. The van went north and—I just lost him," Paula said.

"The GPS unit ran out of juice or something. Its last reported location was at the storage facility. I asked for a warrant to get in there, and I'm waiting for the night judge to give us the go-ahead," John said. Then to Paula, "*You* didn't lose anyone. Sherman slipped us both."

Barnes nodded. "Paula, if there's anything you need to tell me, now's the time. I can't help you if—"

"I didn't let Sherman get away. Jesus, Lieutenant, you too?"

"I have to ask, Paula. If Sherman has something on you—something he's using to—"

"Dammit. I have nothing to do with that asshole."

"Don't make it personal," Barnes said.

"Listen to what you're saying. It *is* personal. Sherman made it that way. I'm so busy covering my ass that I can't think ahead."

"Remember when you came here from IA?" Barnes said. "You were so caught up in making sure you did the right thing or followed the exact letter of department policy that you lost sight of the big picture. Brice Winnow exploited that blindness when he kidnapped Tommy Penley. Don't let Sherman do that to you."

Paula went silent. Her jaw was tight, and it looked like she was about to respond.

"But you learned to work through that," Barnes went on. "Every case is personal if you let it get to you. You're a better investigator when you focus on what matters. Taking down Sherman isn't what this is about."

The room went cold.

"It's about solving cases. Burger, Wing, McDaniel—all of them. They are what this is about."

John needed to break the tension in the room. "We gotta get to the trauma center and get us a dying declaration from Ronland," John said. "No sense in letting Wallace run free. Can you get us a BOLO for him—his blue van and that shiny Ford truck of his?"

"Will do," Barnes said.

John and Paula grabbed their gear from their desks and started for the car. Officer Stark was coming on shift and glared at Paula. She'd had about enough of him.

"You got a problem, Stark?"

"With you? Yeah, I do."

"You worthless waste of space. You and Sherman are just alike," she said and jabbed a finger into his chest.

"Get your hands off me." He turned to John. "I'm telling you, Penley, she's gonna drag you down just like she done all the others."

"You and Sherman were pretty buddy-buddy back then, weren't you?"

"We had some times together. Sherman was good people," Stark said with a glare toward Paula.

"You guys have any place special you'd hang when you were having your 'times'?" John asked.

"Why would I tell you?"

"Because something ain't right about Sherman and Wallace, and I think Sherman may be getting the raw end of the deal," John said.

"Him. Yeah, Wallace is a piece of work. Only met him twice when Sherman brought him around. That dude is one messed-up critter. On my boat one time, he started talking about how much easier it would be to drop drug dealers in the river instead of booking 'em."

"Does Wallace want anything from Sherman?"

"Like what?"

"You tell me."

"I dunno. Wallace was the jealous type. Sherman had a new car, Wallace went and got one. A bigger house, better flat screen—it was always one up with that guy. The overtime checks must have been something on that task force," Stark said.

"Yeah, I'm sure it was the overtime," Paula said.

"I heard the rumors too, Newberry, but Sherman never showed off like he was on the take. You were wrong about him." He headed away to the preshift briefing.

"How much of that do you believe?" Paula asked.

"There was a time when Stark was a decent cop. I'd say he knew something was off about Wallace; he just couldn't see it for what it was."

They headed to their car, and the morning sunlight glared in their eyes. There was someone leaning on their car, but it wasn't until they were ten feet away that they were able to see him clearly.

Charles Sherman rested on the front hood, arms crossed and casual.

"Hi, Newberry. Looking for me?"

FORTY-SEVEN

Paula's hand went for her weapon.

Sherman put his hands out in mock surrender. "You'd like nothing better, wouldn't you?"

"I'm gonna be the one to put you down, one way or another," Paula said.

"What are you doing here, Sherman?" John asked.

"I have a meeting with the DA and the chief of police about my suit against the city—and you."

A news van rumbled up to the front of the police department building.

"Ah, here they are," Sherman said.

"What do you have for these scavengers?" John asked.

"Seems that I'm gonna be the story of the hour."

"When we take you down again?" Paula asked. Her hand backed away from her weapon.

"I'm an innocent victim here. The city's agreed to make this go away."

"Really? I didn't know the city invested in bullshit," she said.

"I wish we could have ended this differently, I really do. But you didn't give me any other choice."

"Yeah? How's that?"

"Stick around and find out."

An officer in uniform came from behind Paula and John. "Excuse me, detectives, the chief needs this guy." The public information officer looked like he was hating life about now. "Mr. Sherman, this way."

"That's my cue." Sherman rose from the car's hood and strode past Paula and John.

The PIO shook his head and said, "Sorry, guys."

"You want to stay back and watch the show? I can go sit on Ronland and wait for him to come out of surgery."

Paula sighed. "No, if I stick around, they might catch me on camera with my hands around Sherman's neck."

They got in the car and pulled out of the lot as Clarke and her entourage from the DA's office arrived. She was dressed in red and ready for prime time.

"They are gonna exonerate him. The only one who stands to lose in that scenario is me," Paula said.

"Focus on what you can control, give up the rest," John said as he found a parking spot in the trauma center lot.

"You sound like a walking twelve-step meeting."

"I am your higher power."

She smacked him on the arm.

They badged their way into the trauma center and got an update on Ronland. He was in surgery, and as soon as he was out, they'd send someone to let them know.

The trauma waiting room was a sociological experiment. The worried faces of domestic abusers tensed when anyone entered. Rival gang factions claimed opposing corners of the room. A fragile detente allowed the gangs some time to patch themselves up before the next conflict over turf brought them back here. In the middle were mothers with sick children, a piece rate craftsman who'd hacked off a finger, and parents of an accident victim waiting their turns for assembly-line medical care.

A lone woman sat, stiff-backed, on the edge of one of the plastic sofas in the waiting room. In her midforties, the woman clutched a wadded handkerchief in her hands. Her face bore a striking resemblance to George Ronland. John nudged Paula, and they went to her.

"Excuse me, are you here for George Ronland?" John asked.

The woman froze; her eyes widened.

"What's happened? Is he all right?"

"We're with the police department, ma'am."

A wave of relief swept through her. "You startled me. I'm trying to hold it together." She dabbed the handkerchief under her eyes. "I'm George's sister, Patricia."

"George mentioned he was living with you. Is that right?" John asked.

"Yes, he is."

"Were you home when he was attacked?"

She shook her head. "I left early. I had a seven fifteen flight. I was at the airport, about to board, when the hospital called. I'm George's emergency contact."

"I'm very sorry. Do you have any idea who might have wanted to hurt your brother?"

A crease formed in her forehead when she looked at John. Her eyes now bore anger, not worry or grief. "I have a good idea who's behind it."

"Care to share?" Paula said.

"Since George left his job in law enforcement, he's been harassed by white supremacists and other cops. Rather than blame a white cop for testifying against them, they try and lynch the black man."

"You ever witness any harassment?" John said.

She narrowed her eyes. "I didn't have to witness it. I saw the result. George would come home, and you could see it on him. The weight, the guilt they put on him was awful."

"You said white supremacists; what makes you think that?"

"I saw them leave the house once as I came home. Their motorcycles blocked my garage door. Those men with their Nazi tattoos and white-power patches on their leather vests didn't like a black woman telling them to move their shit."

"When was this?"

"About a month ago."

"Anyone stand out that you can recall?"

"The leader—I think he was, anyway, because he was the loudest and was in my brother's face—I remember him. A huge man, long stringy hair and a scar on his left cheek."

"Sounds like Junior," Paula said.

"Can you remember anything they were saying?" John said.

Patricia paused for a moment. "No, it didn't make any sense."

"What didn't?" John pressed.

"The big guy, the one you called Junior, said something about one of theirs getting out of prison and George had to take care of it."

"It?"

"I don't know what they wanted him to do, but from the look on my brother's face, he wasn't happy about it. He wouldn't talk about it after they left, saying some people are too greedy for their own good."

"Family for George Ronland?" a woman at the check-in counter called from behind a thick glass barrier.

Patricia stood, and the woman behind the barrier said, "Dr. Pierson will be out in a moment."

"Do you and George have any other family I can call for you?" John asked.

"No. All we have is each other, which is why I know he didn't do anything to deserve this."

A set of automatic doors opened, and a slight woman in light-blue scrubs entered. "Ronland?"

Patricia gathered her belongings and went toward her. John and Paula followed at a respectful distance but held close enough to listen.

"Ms. Ronland?"

"Yes. Is he?"

"He's been badly injured. But he's a strong man. He has a tough next twenty-four hours ahead of him, but barring any infections or unforeseen complications, he should pull through."

Her shoulders relaxed. "When can I see him?"

"He's in recovery now. Let us get him out from under the anesthetic and settled in a room. It's going to be a while, at least a half hour."

John held his badge for the doctor. "We need to collect his clothes and process them as evidence."

The doctor nodded. "Already done. Along with the knife. If the assailant had pulled it out, the blood loss would have been unrecoverable. Leaving it in place may have saved Mr. Ronland's life. I gave the weapon and the clothes to the officer who rode in with him. I really need to get going." She didn't wait around for a response. Another busy night in the trauma center.

John spoke to the woman at the counter while Paula took Ron-land's sister back to the waiting area couch. The televisions were muted, but the scrolling closed caption text captured the dialogue.

Local news coverage interrupted the network morning talk show, and the image went to the parking lot outside of the police department. The department's emblem loomed behind a podium with the chief of police in midstatement.

". . . Cannot tolerate the disregard for legal process. Justice matters for everyone." The scene scrolled the message.

Linda Clarke stepped to the podium. "Thank you, Chief. We must be transparent, even in times of difficulty and in times of shame. My office was less than diligent in vetting the evidence against Charles Sherman. As a result, he was not afforded a fair and unbiased legal process. The city council and the county board of supervisors have agreed to a settlement with Mr. Sherman to help atone for our missteps in this matter. In addition to a financial settlement, we are taking steps to rectify the problem and hold those who were responsible accountable for this travesty."

Paula's soul turned to ice, and it shattered into crystals when Sherman took the podium. He played the victim to a tee. Chin down, eyes searching up for the camera. What a crock.

"I appreciate the district attorney's sentiments. But that can't change what was taken from me. My life, my career, and my future are gone. Because of one person. While the terms of my settlement prohibit me from disclosing anything further, she will get what's coming." A steely glint formed for a moment, then he returned to character. "As for the money. I'll be donating it. All of it will go to homeless services here in the city."

"Huh, didn't see that one coming," John said from over Paula's shoulder.

"What's he planning? He's always got something going," she said.

"I don't have to be a fortune-teller to see how this one ends—he's untouchable."

"I guess my time is running out. That had to be part of his deal."

The interior hospital doors opened once more. Instead of another doctor looking for a patient's next of kin, a uniformed Sacramento police officer entered, carrying a large brown paper bag.

"That must be Ronland's guy."

John waved him over.

"You need a ride back to your car? I understand you rode in with Ronland."

"That'd be great. I don't want to call my sergeant for a lift. He's already giving me a load for letting Ronland get hit under my watch."

"You didn't *let* anyone get hit. From what my lieutenant said, if you hadn't found Ronland, he would've been toast."

The officer set the bag on the floor next to the sofa. The top was open, exposing the plastic evidence containers with bloody clothes and the hilt of a butcher knife.

Paula pulled the rim of the bag open an inch more, taking a look at the contents. She bit her lip and let go.

"Where did you get that knife?" she asked.

"That was stuck in Ronland's chest when I found him. I thought he was gone, man."

Paula got up and took a quick step away. John sensed her agitation and took her by the elbow.

"Hey, what's up?" he murmured.

"That knife. John, it's mine."

FORTY-EIGHT

A shattered television screen gave up the ghost with a final crackle and spark after Wallace threw a beer bottle through it. In his mind, Wallace nailed Sherman in his holier-than-thou face.

Good for you, asshole. Now what about the rest of us?

"Hey, you gotta pay for that!" The bartender whacked the bar with a yellowed baseball bat.

A pair of pool players stopped and got behind Wallace. One held a cue stick and laid it alongside the bar to make his presence known.

"What the hell is wrong with you, dude?" the stick-wielding man asked.

"Call the cops on this dick," someone said from behind Wallace.

"Nah, take his ass out back and beat some sense into him."

"I get paid first," the bartender said. The baseball bat tapped in front of Wallace.

"How much you want?" Wallace said.

"How much you got?"

Wallace got up from his barstool, and the men behind him pressed closer.

"Easy, boys."

Wallace peeled two hundred dollars and tossed it on the bar, and while the cash distracted everyone, he pulled a pistol from his waistband and pushed it against the head of the man with the cue stick.

"Drop it or die," Wallace hissed.

The pool cue bounced off the wood planked floor.

The bartender gathered up the loose cash. "Hey, this don't cover it."

"Close enough. Or do we have to talk about it?" Wallace pushed the muzzle of the gun hard into the pool player's forehead. A red ring formed on the skin under the business end of the pistol. Wallace took the man by the shoulder and walked backward to the front door, keeping his eyes on the malignant crew in the bar.

When he felt the door at his back, he kicked it open with his foot, pulling the pool player with him. Daylight made the pool player squint, and Wallace glanced back to make certain there was no one between him and his motorcycle.

The man was about to say something before Wallace pulled back his gun hand and coldcocked him in the forehead with the bottom of the pistol grip. The man's face bled from the split skin, and Wallace gave him a boot to the stomach, pushing him back inside the doors.

He kick-started his bike, and the tire tossed gravel as he tore out of the parking lot. Wallace sped away from the biker bar and let up on the throttle when his rear view lost sight of the place.

Wallace cruised past his home and slowed when he noticed a black-and-white patrol car blocking his driveway. An officer stood behind his Ford truck and looked to be running his license plates. He kept moving and turned right onto the next street. Another car blocked the alley entrance. The house was off-limits.

But he finally knew where to head next. There was no way he was going to let Sherman win. He'd worked too long to make sure his secret stayed buried with the dead.

Wallace cut a path toward the police station, where the news broadcast showed that pious son of a bitch basking in the media's adoration. With all the attention, it wouldn't take long before a zealous journalist started digging into Sherman and his time with the SSPNET task force. Hell, they'd probably already signed a movie deal for the inside story. That could not happen.

A block from the station, a news van passed Wallace in the other direction. Wallace drove his bike into the parking lot, and the engine rumble vibrated, causing a few heads to turn.

Most turned away. An expensive street bike was pretty common in cop circles. But one man kept staring at the approaching rider—Sherman.

Wallace saw Sherman's eyes widen in recognition, and he tried to back into the knot of people gathered at the podium.

The bike slowed, and Wallace drew his pistol.

Sherman yelled and pointed at the gun.

Wallace let loose three shots at Sherman. He rocked back on the throttle and saw Sherman collapse. A gunshot from one of the nearby officers flicked off the side of his bike's frame. Another caught the bike's seat an inch below his butt. He'd felt the heat from that one.

He braced for another shot, and it didn't come. He sped out the downtown corridor and hit the freeway before every patrol car in the division was on him. He gripped the handlebars as the relief bled between his fingers. He'd put down the only threat left that could expose his role in the SSPNET.

FORTY-NINE

Paula held the plastic evidence bag with the blood-smeared butcher knife and turned it over in her hands.

"There are hundreds, if not thousands of knives like that, Paula," John said.

"Not like this." She rotated the bag so the hilt was against the plastic and an elaborately embossed monogram showed through. In the center of the scrollwork, the initials *P. N.* stood proudly. "My mother got these for me when I bought my house. They were a housewarming gift."

John caught the monogram in spite of her trembling hand. "There has to be an explanation for this. The break-in you had, your garage—this could have been taken at the same time."

"This was in a butcher block on my kitchen counter. Sherman had to have taken it when he was in my house."

John took the evidence bag and rolled the top closed. He gave it back to the officer. "Get these to Karen Baylor in the forensics investigation unit, got it?" John tossed him the keys to his sedan.

"Yeah, got it."

The hospital employee behind the counter waved them over. "Mr. Ronland is out of recovery." She gave them the room number and directions to the fourth-floor ward that served surgical patients.

After two elevators and a serpentine path through pale-colored hallways, they finally found Ronland in a room with another recovering patient.

A sheet covered Ronland from the waist down, exposing a heavy gauze pad on his chest, three inches to the right of center and about a fist's width from his collarbone. Patricia sat at her brother's side, and she didn't look happy to see the detectives.

"Has he woken up yet?" John asked.

"No. The doctor wasn't sure how long he'd be out."

"How'd he do in surgery?" Paula said.

"Punctured lung and an embolism. Lost a lot of blood." She flipped a hand to the IV pole, which held four different bags: blood, pain meds, anticoagulants, and antibiotics.

The sight conjured bad memories for John of when his son was tethered to a similar hospital bed by wires, tubes, and monitors.

"I'm glad he'll be okay," Paula said.

"You call this okay? He almost died. And for what? Because of you people. You don't give a damn about him or his life. You guys just bleed him for what you can—literally—and leave him for dead."

"I'm sorry. I didn't mean it that way."

"Sorry doesn't cut it." Patricia got louder as the exchange continued.

"What did you mean about us bleeding him for what we could? Other than—" John started.

"My brother made mistakes. He faced them and took his medicine like a man. He paid his debt and was doing his probation like he was supposed to, and you guys wouldn't leave him alone."

"I only talked to him for a few minutes at the car wash."

"You guys picked him up and took him downtown, threatening him to cooperate in another case against one of the people he worked with."

"Charles Sherman?" Paula asked.

"That sounds right," Patricia said. "My brother claimed that man was the one responsible for bringing everybody down back then. George tried to put it all behind him, and you wouldn't let him."

"Who took him 'downtown'?" John asked.

"How the hell should I know? All I know is we were having dinner, and they showed up at my house and dragged him off."

"Who?"

"Who, who, who. You sound like a goddamned owl. The police took him. The officer with that black uniform, all Nazi-acting—"

"Black uniform? Sheriff's department?"

"It doesn't matter who took him. Police is police. He cooperated with a roomful of white cops and look where that got him."

A moan came from Ronland.

Patricia turned to her brother. His eyes were open, small slits peering back at her.

"Patti, what's a guy gotta do to get some sleep around here?"

She hugged him, and he groaned.

Ronland noticed John and Paula in the room.

"No, I don't know who did it. So you don't have to waste time with me. Didn't see him. He came from behind. White guy—that's all I know."

"Your sister said something about you getting picked up and brought downtown. What was that about?" John asked.

Ronland's eyes shifted to his sister and then, with some difficulty, back to John. "She did, huh? She should mind her own business."

"It was Wallace, wasn't it? The guy who picked you up in his sheriff's uniform?"

He nodded. "Yeah, it was. He had Sherman in the car with him to prove that he knew what he was talking about."

"What's that?"

"He wanted to get the band back together. Wallace still had an inside track on contraband and drugs seizures—not as big as before, but he wanted to continue where we left off."

"What was Sherman's role in this new operation?"

"Sherman didn't say much; it's like he was preoccupied or didn't want to be there. I don't know. It was weird."

"What did Wallace want from you?"

"He didn't say until after he dropped Sherman off. Then all he wanted me to do was follow Sherman and find out where he was hiding his stash back from when we were skimming off the task force. I said I wasn't interested."

"Follow him? Wallace wasn't with him?"

"No. Wallace had to drop Sherman off and leave. That was the only way Sherman would agree to work. No one but him could know where he hid his stash."

"What's up with that? He didn't trust Wallace?" Paula asked.

"Sherman didn't trust anyone. The deal was that Wallace would get Sherman out of prison on these little field trips, and he'd hand over some drugs to sell to the white boys. Then Wallace would take him back to his cage."

"How many trips did Sherman make?"

"I don't know. It looked like Sherman had done it a lot, because they had their act down tight."

"He happen to mention anything else?"

"This was after Bobby Wing got killed and Wallace made some comment about no one having the heart to take a risk anymore. Rich coming from the only one of us who didn't go to jail or prison for that bullshit."

A spark lit in the back of John's mind.

"Paula, how did the case against the SSPNET begin?" John asked.

"An informant."

FIFTY

The trauma center waiting room had thinned out as the morning bled into midday. The mothers with sick little ones were gone, and amputated fingers were glued and stitched as much as possible, but the crews of opposing gang members remained.

When John and Paula pressed through the double doors, the gang colors were brighter than they were in the dark morning light. Or there were more of them. The red bandanas and Cincinnati Reds ball caps of a local Bloods gang set outnumbered the Crips in their blue T-shirts and Dodgers paraphernalia, and it wasn't a friendly baseball rivalry.

Paula pointed to the knot of Crip members with hands that snaked into their pockets as the provocation continued.

"Is that Deshawn Cooper?" Paula asked.

John found the youngest Crip in the group, Deshawn, who had turned eighteen a month ago.

"Let's see if we can't de-escalate the situation here," John said.

Paula nodded, and they walked between the two opposing sides.

"Deshawn? What's going on?" John asked.

The teenage gang member didn't like the attention, and the other members looked at the interaction with the police with suspicion. "'Sup, Detective?"

"How's your mom? She still selling her art? I might drop by her place and pick up another one."

"She paints?" Paula asked.

"You know that cityscape we have in the living room? Deshawn's mom did that."

"I thought that was some computer Photoshop thing from a photograph. There's so much detail."

"Moms doesn't use software to do that. It's all by hand," Deshawn said.

"Damn." Paula was impressed.

The boy looked proud for a moment and then remembered where he was. A false front shut the emotion down.

"I'm glad she's still painting. After your brother died, painting is what kept her going," John said.

"I guess."

John sat on one of the waiting area seats, careful not to sit in anything left behind by bleeding, vomiting, or contagious patients.

"Deshawn, what's going on here?" John asked.

"Just waiting on someone."

"Got anything to do with those guys?" John asked. He tipped his head toward the red-clad group.

Deshawn shrugged.

"Damn right it does," the Crip next to Deshawn said. "We was minding our own business, and they come and disrespected us."

"How's that?" John asked.

"They was in our hood flying their colors where they don't belong."

"That's it? Their fashion choice?" John deliberately minimized the gang color. "Hell, kids can't wear anything but damn near green plaid because of all this."

"That's enough for us."

Lives lost and broken in defense of imaginary lines and perceived slights of disrespect. Generations sucked up into the gang life because nothing else existed in the community for them. Deshawn followed in his brother's footsteps, and how much longer before a trigger pull would put him in an early grave?

"You still haven't told us why everyone is having a street criminal convention here," Paula interjected.

"Jo-Jo went out in the street," Deshawn answered. "They run him down with their broke-ass ride."

"They ran him over?" Paula asked.

"Yeah, busted him up pretty good too. At least one leg was all twisted up and shit. Bleeding from his head from where he hit the pavement."

"And they was laughing about it. Who gonna be laughing now, punk?" the other Crip said, loud enough to get a reaction from the other group.

"Who you calling a punk?" a Blood responded.

Paula turned to the closest Blood and pointed her finger in his face. "Knock that shit off! Now!" With the mad dog neutered, she turned to the other Bloods.

"What are you doing here?"

"Those bitches shot Lil Bobby."

"Bobby Steves from Third Avenue?" Paula said.

"Yeah, that's right."

"Bobby is supposed to be lying low on his association with you guys because he just got out of jail. It's a condition of probation."

"Man, who else is he gonna associate with? He lives, sleeps, and breathes red."

"How bad is he?" Paula asked.

"Can't keep Lil Bobby down. He'll be back."

"The cops get who shot him?"

"Yeah. But—"

"No 'but.' It's done. You're even. One-for-one. You can leave one man here to take Lil Bobby home if they release him, but the rest of you gotta go."

"We can't leave with them here."

"I'll take care of them too. They will be on their way. You guys split now, or I swear I'll call the gang task force and get them to search all of your houses and impound your cars."

"Man, you're not right," the Blood said.

"So I've been told."

Paula pointed to the door, and a few of them started out.

The Blood said, "This ain't over."

Paula stepped to him and jabbed a finger in his chest. "It's over if I say it is."

When the last one left, Paula went to the Crip contingent. "Same goes for you. Leave someone here who can let his family know what's going on, and the rest of you hit it."

"Damn, Penley, you got you a bulldog here," Deshawn said.

"I think I need to make sure she's up to date on her shots."

Paula shot him a scowl.

"Deshawn, you get your butt home and take care of your mom," Paula said.

"Yes, ma'am."

When the last of them had departed the waiting room, the hospital employee at the counter gave Paula a thumbs-up.

"The department could cut back on their crowd-control budget if they'd turn it over to you," John said.

"Most of these kids didn't have a chance for anything positive in their lives. They just need to be told what to do and have a way out."

"Who are you and what have you done with my partner?"

"You know I'm right. There is nothing for these kids, and the ones who get out are the ones who survive. Drugs, gangs, no jobs, no positive role models, some bounced around in the foster care system; I'm surprised it isn't worse."

They walked out the double glass hospital doors into the sun. The glare off the car windshields reflected back at them. John put on his sunglasses and Paula raised a hand to cut the bright reflected light.

A gunshot rang out and echoed under the hospital portico. John dropped to a knee and pulled his weapon.

The screech of tires under a high-powered engine from a car speeding away pulled John's attention to the left.

"One of your gang converts wasn't happy about leaving."

John stood, holstered his weapon, and turned. Paula was splayed on her back on the pavement with a bullet hole in the center of her gray jacket.

FIFTY-ONE

Wallace pulled a dust-coated blind aside when the rumble from a pair of motorcycle engines vibrated the beer cans on the window-sill. A pair of bikers dismounted their rides in Junior's driveway and unstrapped their helmets as they walked toward the garage. Wallace couldn't hear what was being said, but the voices carried an urgent tone.

Wallace opened the door to the garage, and the two bikers looked at Junior, who gave them a nod.

"What's going on?" Wallace asked.

"Seems like that lady cop friend of yours bought it," Junior said.

"Newberry? No kidding? What happened?"

One of the newly arrived bikers, who sported dark sunglasses, stroked a long red beard. He hooked a thumb at the other biker and said, "Me and Spider was making a run, and we was near the hospital when a sweet GTO went screaming outta the parking lot."

"Dudes were runnin' outta there, red rags and blue rags. We figured they was up to the usual, killing each other, so no big deal," Spider said.

"Then the GTO pulled past us, and it was Simmons's people. They must of dusted it up with some of the locals. We pull in, and there's people going everywhere. That lady cop was down, and that Penley asshole was standing over her."

"You sure it was her?" Wallace said.

"No doubt. It was her."

"How'd it happen?"

"Couldn't tell at first. It coulda come from any of them red-and-blue-wearing gangster wannabees. We split before the cops showed up and got us swept up in the show. Caught up with Simmons's crew at their place."

"The bar on Sixty-Fifth?" Junior said.

"Yeah, we go in and they was whooping it up like after a big score. They started talking and joking about the shooting. It was them. They put the cop down," Red Beard said.

"Simmons sanctioned a hit on the cops?" Junior asked.

"I didn't see him there, but they was acting all chesty like they just made their bones by killing a cop."

"Why would they make a move on Newberry?" Wallace asked.

Junior climbed out of his lawn chair. "The cops see you guys at the hospital?"

"No."

"You sure?"

"The only other cop there was too busy looking at his partner on the ground. He didn't see us."

"The Brotherhood would only make a move like this if it was necessary. That kind of action brings too much heat. I remember when one of them went after a prison guard out on the street. The shit that came down after that was unbelievable. Every AB member behind bars got their asses kicked," Junior said.

"What was Newberry to them?" Spider asked.

"To them—I don't know. She should have been just another cop to Simmons. They're more concerned about the feds moving on an organized crime indictment," Wallace said.

"If she was working with the feds, that might explain their taking that kinda risk," Junior said.

Wallace went to the beer fridge, snagged a cold bottle, and leaned against the door. The vibration of the door couldn't counter the sense of uneasiness that grew in his belly. The beer only made it sour.

"There was only one person with a hard-on for Newberry, and you know who I mean," Wallace said.

"Sherman," Junior said.

"Bull's-eye," Wallace responded, tipping his beer at the big man. Then to the two bikers, he said, "Sherman ain't gonna be a problem no more."

They looked at each other before Spider said, "No?"

Wallace ignored the question, stared at the beer bottle, and peeled a section of the label with a thumbnail. "If Sherman and Simmons were in business, that's not good for you. You know that, right?"

Junior didn't say anything in response, but his ruddy complexion went a few shades darker.

"What you saying?" Red Beard asked.

"You said Sherman owed you a delivery today," Wallace checked his watch, "in about an hour. He's not coming. If someone from Simmons's crew does, you'll have your answer."

"No way. We're tight with Simmons," Red Beard said.

Junior remained silent when his two men needed reassurance.

Spider stepped forward. "Tell him, Junior. Tell him the Brand's got our back."

"Hey, I got no beef with you, Spider. But you gotta get real. Look around. You see the Aryan Brotherhood around here except for when they want something?" Wallace asked.

"You're talking outta your ass," Red Beard said. The biker's hand slid around to the bone handle of a knife strapped to his belt.

"Step off, bitch," Wallace said in a low voice.

"Who's this guy think he is? He got no right to come in here and talk shit."

Wallace looked out at the driveway and saw a GTO pull to the curb.

"Looks like we're gonna see who's talking shit now."

Red Beard strutted out to meet the visitors. He greeted them with a slick handshake and bro-hug. He was trying too hard.

"Man, he looks like his daddy just showed up," Junior said.

The driver was a man with a slick-shaved head. He wasn't tall, but his arms were thick and sleeved with spider webs and brick tattoos, a graphic illustration of a man who'd done lots of prison time. Life on the installment plan.

"Who's the bald dude?" Wallace asked.

"That's Simmons's number two. Goes by Stubbs."

Wallace figured out the genesis of the name when the man ran a hand over his bald head, the ring and little finger were missing.

Stubbs nodded to Junior, who waved back.

"I take it you weren't expecting Simmons's second in command today?"

"Nope."

Stubbs sauntered to the garage with Red Beard in tow like a dutiful puppy.

"How you doin', Junior?"

"You tell me, Stubbs. Wanna beer?"

Stubbs had already opened the door and rummaged around for the coldest bottle.

Wallace wandered back to the workbench, away from the middle of the garage where Junior and Stubbs stood.

"What brings you out here today?" Junior started.

"We got us a little problem with our distribution network," Stubbs said.

"How's that? I get you guys what you want. Nothing's changed about that," Junior said.

"Let's say there's competition out there now, and Simmons decided to go with the new guy." Stubbs never looked away from Junior as he laid out the news.

"Yeah, who's this new guy?" Junior asked.

Stubbs shrugged. "Ain't my deal."

"You're a little early for the pickup today. I won't get it for another hour."

"That's kinda why I'm here. There ain't gonna be a pickup. And we need our money back."

"That's not how this works, Stubbs. You know better. That money was fronted for the shipment."

"The deal's off, and Simmons wants his money."

"He can't get what I don't have."

"I'd hate to tell him you don't have his money."

"Sounds like he got what he paid for after hijacking my connection."

"He don't see it that way. You're on the hook for what he gave you."

"How am I supposed to make good on that when Simmons took my connection for himself?"

"That's your problem," Stubbs said.

"I'd say that's your problem," Wallace said from the sidelines.

Stubbs turned. "Who the hell are you?"

"Just a guy who knows Sherman won't be giving you anything."

"I think he knows better than to cross Simmons."

"I'd suggest you keep your business with Junior," Wallace said.

"You leave Brand business to us."

Stubbs tossed his beer bottle against the back door, sending shattered glass fragments around the garage.

"Thanks for the beer. Best have the money back to Simmons tonight."

"You tell him if he wants something from me, he best come and tell me face-to-face and not send his errand boy," Junior said.

Stubbs stiffened. "Boy, you better watch your mouth."

A metallic click stopped Stubbs from his advance toward Junior. Wallace had thumbed off the safety of the .380 pistol, the barrel less than three feet from the man's head.

"You go home and tell Daddy that he got his answer," Wallace said.

"You're a dead man," Stubbs said.

"Yeah, yeah, I'm quaking in my boots. Now leave."

Stubbs turned and went to his car. He stopped briefly and gave Wallace a glare from a distance, a look Wallace had seen a few thousand times from cell-front warriors, those jail inmates who'd threaten officers from the safety of being behind bars.

Stubbs sped away, and the car's tires chirped when he shifted into second.

"I appreciate the backup, but that probably wasn't the smartest thing you ever done," Junior said.

Wallace put the .380 down on the workbench. "Maybe not, but you got your answer. Simmons and the AB just took sides, and they picked Sherman over you. My question is, what're you gonna do about that?"

"What I shoulda done from the gate. Take over Sherman's supply."

"That ain't gonna be so easy if he made a deal with Simmons," Red Beard said.

"Nah, that makes it easier. If Sherman gave them the stash, we know where they're hiding it—with Stubbs and his boys at the bar."

"You talking about taking out their place? Man, that's suicide," Red Beard said.

"They'll never see it coming," Junior said.

"With Sherman out and us holding the supply, they have no choice but to deal with you," Wallace said.

Junior grabbed a beer from the refrigerator and drained it. "You were right, Wallace. Let's figure out when we do this."

FIFTY-TWO

From a fleabag motel room, Sherman drained a beer, popped open another, and gave thanks to the stopping power of an inch-thick oak podium. Three pistol slugs had dug into the dense wood before the police reacted, tackling Sherman to the ground.

The squalid room was the kind of place where hourly customers came and went without raising concern from the front desk attendant. When Sherman checked in, he didn't need to show any identification and simply scribbled a fake name on a yellowed ledger below five John Smiths and three Jerry Browns. It seemed there were a few unidentified men and septuagenarian California governors at this spot.

The desk attendant didn't bother to look at the ledger and tossed the key across the counter in exchange for a one-hundred-dollar bill, which went into the man's pocket.

The motel was one of those horseshoe-shaped affairs with a total of twenty-four rooms, twelve on the second floor and twelve on the lower. Number nine was in the far right corner on the ground floor. If sleep were the object, the rattle of the ice machine two doors down would have made it impossible. But he was happy the mechanical grinding almost muffled the grinding of another sort in a room nearby.

Sherman flipped on the light to reveal hues of 1970s brown, mustard, and avocado. The colors dated by the construction of the place, but the dust and spider webs in the corners of the room testified to its neglect. He flipped the light off, and dust motes rode a slip of light that fell through a torn curtain.

He placed his cell phone on top of the dresser and pulled a chair to the window where he could watch the parking lot. Why had Wallace turned on him? The press conference? Getting Newberry's image shredded was always the plan, and blaming her for the killing was the piece Sherman loved the most. He'd seen what it was like for a cop behind bars, and it was a pity that Newberry wouldn't get her turn.

Sherman parted the curtain and settled. He smiled when he realized that was the first chair he'd sat in that hadn't been bolted to the floor in three years. A small thing, insignificant to most, but being able to sit where you wanted was liberating.

Less than twenty minutes after he checked in, a black-and-white police car prowled through the parking lot. Sherman closed the curtain until the police car finished its sweep of the lot. They made note of the license plates in the no-tell motel. But they had no reason to look for him—yet. The disposable prepaid cell phone rang and startled Sherman. He pushed his chair back from the window and grabbed the cell. Caller ID showed the number he'd used to call Simmons before.

"You have something for me?" Sherman said.

"That side job you wanted us to handle is done." The voice on the other end was Simmons. "How's about we get on with the real business?"

"I'm gonna need proof that Newberry is out of the picture; then we can get on with it."

"Turn on the television, little pig, and you'll have all the proof you need."

Sherman found the remote and the black plastic was sticky to the touch. He hit the power button, waiting a few seconds for the old screen to warm up. A local news broadcast was in progress. Sherman turned up the volume.

"Hang on a second," Sherman said into the cell phone.

The news anchor read from a script. "A broad daylight shooting leaves a decorated police officer dead. Details are scarce following the attack at the UC Medical Center. The identity of the officer is not being released pending notification of the next-of-kin, but sources inside the hospital tell us that the officer, a woman, was an eleven-year veteran and a detective with the Sacramento Police Department. The gunman fled the scene, and there is an active search under way in the area."

Sherman flipped through the channels, and two other local networks posted similar stories. He turned the volume down.

"Looks like you came through for me. I was gonna say thanks, but you probably got as much out of doing that as I would have."

"Like I said, you must've had your reasons. That was some expensive takeout," Simmons said.

"Now how about we get on with business. Still in the market for a house?"

"Still need to take a look. That gonna be a problem?"

"Whatever happened to trust? When you pay the asking price, you can look at it to your heart's content," Sherman said.

Simmons laughed—more of a course cough deepened by a night of whiskey drinking. "I'm talking to a man who stole drugs and went out of his way to screw his partners. Trust is something earned."

"Point taken. Okay then, one hundred thousand, nonrefundable, credited against the final payment. One man, you choose."

"We can do that. When and where?" Simmons asked.

Sherman glanced at the television screen and a banner scrolled at the bottom of the frame. It read, *Vigil planned for fallen officer.*

"Seven PM in front of police headquarters on Freeport."

"You have a strange sense of humor," Simmons responded.

"Make sure your man has the hundred K with him or no deal."

"Yeah, yeah. He'll be there."

"He comes alone or it's off. I'll find him. Have him wear a kid's backpack, let's say pink."

"What?"

"I'll find him."

Sherman disconnected the call and turned off the phone. He pulled the battery out of the phone and laid both parts on the dresser. He smiled at the thought of a muscle-bound Aryan warrior with a pink backpack in a sea of cops. That should be enough to put the man off balance and leave Sherman in control.

Sherman shut off the television. They weren't showing any images of Newberry, or even releasing her name. That would come, but for now, he closed his eyes and the image of her he'd drawn on his cell wall came to the front of his mind. He'd spent so many hours with her in that concrete box that he'd memorized every curve and contour of her face.

When the news began flashing that photo, he'd be ready to tell them his story. How she lied and railroaded him. She'd paid off a witness for testimony. Then who'd be holding vigils? He made sure that legacy went with her to her grave.

FIFTY-THREE

"This is messed up," the police department's public information officer said.

"We had to get the news out," John said.

"The media depends on us to be a trustworthy voice, and this kind of move is only going to kill that image."

The pair stood behind the smoked-glass doors of the department's public safety center on Freeport, watching a makeshift memorial built with candles and flowers from people who'd come to pay their respects. Handwritten messages to the fallen officer fluttered from their places in a chain-link fence.

The PIO rubbed a hand through his close-cropped hair. "This is giving me a migraine."

"Anything yet?" a voice called out from over his shoulder.

The PIO turned. "You shouldn't be here."

Paula wore a bulky blue sweat shirt and had her hair tucked under a River Cats ball cap. She ignored him and looked through the smoked glass at the procession of well-wishers. She rubbed the spot on her chest where the slug hit. The lightweight ballistic vest prevented a fatal wound, but she was still sporting a deep bruise from the impact.

"Nothing. But Sherman won't be able to keep away," John said.

"Weird watching your own memorial," she said.

John glanced at her. "When did you start wearing that vest? It's not exactly department-issued body armor."

She darted her eyes away. "When I heard Sherman might get out—I had this gut feeling."

"I'm glad you did."

"It made me feel like an old woman seeing ghosts in the shadows."

"Nah, I just thought you'd put on a couple pounds," John said as he stepped out of the range of a backhand.

"Ass."

"You get ahold of your mom? Let her know what's going on?"

"Yeah, she knows."

"The lieutenant sent a unit over there, right?"

"He did. She's probably feeding him right now. He's supposed to keep everyone away from her. Hard to do if he's in a food coma."

"She understood how important it is not to talk to anyone?" John said.

"It's killing her, but she gets it. The upside of being dead is that I get to skip one of her matchmaking attempts."

"You actually faked your death to avoid a date. That has to be a new low."

Paula's expression turned dour. "You got the slug to Karen for a ballistic run on NIBIN?"

"Hoping we can get a hit in the system."

"I want it back when she's done. I might try my hand at making a necklace out of it so I can wear it to Sherman's next trial."

"He was across town at the chief's press conference when you got shot."

They watched a few people place candles and condolence messages at the base of the fence.

"While you were getting checked out in the ER, I talked to that kid Deshawn again."

"The one with the artist mom?" she said.

"That's him. He told me he didn't see the shooter, but the car they drove away in belonged to guy named Stubbs—apparently a heavy with the Aryan Brotherhood."

"What's their end for taking a shot at me?"

John shrugged. "Deshawn mentioned the AB controls the drug trade in North Sacramento and sells 'pills by the truckload.'"

"That lines up with what Ronland told us. You think Sherman used them as a distributor for his stolen drugs?"

"I bet Burger bought those pills from the Brand—the same pills he helped steal."

"Who's that by the fence?" Paula said.

She pointed to the left side of the fence, in front of a cluster of candles. Linda Clarke, the district attorney, posed before a news camera giving an interview. The news van hadn't been there before the DA made her appearance.

The PIO checked his cell phone and messaged the station filming the spectacle.

"This isn't going live. They're recording it for the late evening news segment. So we have some time to unwind this."

"Unwind what? One minute she wants to string me up by my thumbs and the next she shows up for a photo op mourning my untimely death. Let her look stupid," Paula said.

"Who organized this vigil tonight, anyway?" John asked.

The PIO shrugged. "It's all over social media."

A crowd had gathered on the sidewalk and overflowed into the street. One traffic lane was blocked, and uniformed officers worked crowd control to keep the mourners out of the path of traffic. The usual assortment of community activists made use of the gathering to protest city hall and abuse at the hands of the police. A few signs popped up about who mattered and who didn't. A small number of professional protesters shouted and paraded for the camera, but when they didn't get the reaction from the media that they'd hoped for, they faded into the background.

The activity caused a traffic bottleneck when the crowd blocked another lane.

"There!" John pointed.

"Sherman?" Paula said.

"The car. That's the GTO Deshawn saw leaving the hospital when you were shot."

Paula put her hand on the door, and John grabbed her wrist. "Stay put. We got this."

John raised a radio and thumbed the key. "Green GTO coming your way. Is it Sherman?"

"Negative. White male, midthirties, bald, heavy tats. Want me to stop him?"

"Not yet. Keep an eye on him."

"10-4."

"Who was on the radio?" Paula asked.

"Tucker. He's one of the ones we can trust with your little secret. Besides, when he heard it was you, he couldn't stay away. I think he's still sweet on you. Though God only knows why."

"You're such an ass." Paula pressed to the window and picked out Tucker in uniform directing traffic around the swelling crowd. A wistful smile crossed her lips.

"Looks like the festivities are about to start," John said.

A local minister from one of the God-in-a-box, nondenominational Christian churches sprouting all over the region stepped in front of the crowd. From where John and Paula stood, they couldn't hear the words being spoken, but heads bowed in unison and a stillness spread.

A crackle from John's radio sputtered.

"The GTO is making another pass. The driver is definitely checking out the scene," Tucker said.

"I see it," John said.

"He's parking about a block up. Getting out of the car. He's alone. He's getting something from the car. A backpack—a pink backpack," Tucker said, laughter in his tone.

"Say again?"

"A pink kid's backpack. I swear this skinhead is sporting a Hello Kitty backpack."

"Any sign of Sherman?" John asked.

"Negative."

John thumbed the radio key again. "Team one on the GTO. Team two on the skinhead with the pink backpack. Approach, but do not engage."

The two teams signaled back, and eight of the "mourners" split off from the crowd and set up in positions to watch the car and their target.

"A third of the people paying respects are plants. Damn, that stings," Paula said.

"Live a better life next time if you want a better turnout."

"I can see the guy with the backpack," Paula said, pointing at the back of the crowd. "Doesn't look familiar. Definitely not one of the SSPNET guys, but with those prison tats, he's got to be hooked up with Sherman somehow."

The man scanned the crowd and didn't seem to be interested in the prayers being offered for the fallen officer. The more time that passed, the angrier he looked.

A passing Honda slowed as it reached the skinhead. John couldn't see the driver and asked Tucker if he had a line of sight on the man behind the wheel.

The driver tossed something at the feet of the man with the backpack, flipped him off, and drove away.

"I missed him," Tucker said.

The man bent over to pick up the object at his feet—a paper bag from a fast-food place.

John watched as he opened the bag and rustled around inside. He sorted out something and nodded to himself. The backpack came off his shoulder, and the fast-food bag was held tight in his left hand.

"What is he waiting for?" John said.

The man's attention keyed on the line of traffic like he was going to try to run between cars. He waited until the Honda reappeared and timed his jump into traffic. Instead of dashing between the cars, he ran to the open rear window and tossed the pink backpack in the back seat.

"You see that?"

"Tucker, stop that car," John said. "Team two, take him down."

A hand came out of the car as it accelerated.

A loud pop sounded, and half of the mourners bolted from the sidewalk into the street.

One of the protestors dropped his sign and yelled, "The cops are shooting at us!"

Vehicle traffic snarled in seconds as drivers slammed on their brakes to avoid the fleeing bystanders. An old woman froze in midstride and Tucker moved her out of the path of an oncoming city bus.

Tucker keyed his radio, "Lost him. It was a firecracker as a diversion. No shots fired."

"Team two. Eyes on target?"

"Affirmative. Target in custody."

The PIO pressed a thumb into a throbbing temple. "Jesus, this is a total cluster."

The undercover officers dragged skinhead to the closest door, where John and Paula had watched the events unfold. John opened the door for them, and the officers led their captive inside.

"Take him to interrogation," John said.

Paula watched as the man went by, but she still couldn't recognize his face. She shrugged to her partner, indicating she didn't know who this thug was, or if he was the one who'd shot her. She'd hoped for Sherman, not this stand-in.

She continued to eyeball him as the officers pulled him down the hall, hands cuffed behind his back. Missing fingers on his left hand.

FIFTY-FOUR

Sherman changed direction and drove downtown, parking the Honda in an underground parking garage off of Fifth Street, far enough away to make certain he hadn't been followed and close enough to take a light-rail train to a stop within ten blocks of his squalid little hidey-hole of a motel.

A fistful of the cash in his backpack could get him a room at the Sheraton across from the capitol, and he could live off of room service and pay-per-view for a week. But the long game meant watching Newberry's legacy go up in flames.

The light-rail stop on K Street near the corner of Fifth was a busy connection, one of the reasons Sherman chose the line. He'd be able to mix with the crowd and blend in. He stepped into the middle car seconds before the train lurched forward. The passenger mix was benign in the afternoon. Half-day government workers and students heading for classes at Sac State made up most of the ridership. A homeless man staked out a rear corner seat and slept.

Sherman hadn't felt claustrophobia in his prison cell, but the walls of the light-rail car began to press down. Sherman felt everyone's gaze—heavy on him, judging him. When he'd whip around and look, he couldn't catch them watching. They knew who he was. He felt it.

He had trouble breathing. There wasn't enough air in the rail car. He tried opening a window, but it was sealed.

"Dude, you okay?" a young man with an open backpack full of books asked.

The train conductor announced the next station, and Sherman pushed his way to the door, squeezing out as it opened. His pink backpack stole a few glances. He took off his shirt and wrapped the backpack in the sweaty fabric and walked off the platform.

He walked straight to his motel and made certain the room was as he had left it and that no one else was hiding under the bed, in the shower, or in the closet. With the drapes drawn, he tossed the Hello Kitty backpack on the bed and ripped the zipper in his haste to open it. He held the bag by the straps and shook it over the bed.

Simmons had lived up to his end. In wrapped bundles, one hundred thousand dollars fell from the backpack. Each one hit the surface and kicked up a swirl of dust. All Sherman smelled was freedom.

He went to the dresser and reassembled the cell phone, snapping the battery in place. He redialed the last number and waited.

Simmons answered on the first ring, without the chorus of heavy metal music this time. It sounded like he was in a vehicle on the move. "You got some balls on you."

"Thanks for noticing," Sherman said.

"I'm gonna rip your throat out."

"I kept my end of the deal, and you did yours. As far as I'm concerned, we're good to go."

"How do you figure? My guy didn't show up after the exchange."

"Not my problem."

"It's your problem now."

"He wasn't smart enough to get away. I did, so I don't know what his problem was. Unless he wanted to keep what he saw for himself."

"I want my money," Simmons said.

"I can do that, or do you want to finish this deal and we both walk away happy?"

Simmons didn't reply right away and the traffic noise heightened in the background. Downtown sounds—horns, chirping crosswalks, and construction activity. The AB boss was retracing Stubbs's route.

Someone in the car with him said, "There, that's his car. Shit, there's cops all over it."

"What happened to Stubbs?" Simmons asked.

"I didn't see him after we made the exchange. He had time to split."

"If you crossed me—"

"Just stop with the threats." Sherman parted the drapes to see if anyone had approached. "You want the shipment? Here's how it's gonna go down."

FIFTY-FIVE

The interrogation room pulsed with anger, and Stubbs pulled at the eyebolt in the table that held his handcuffed wrists secure. Left to stew in "the box" for forty minutes, the white supremacist had worked up rivulets of sweat on his bald head. An observation camera in a corner delivered a feed to a screen outside.

"He must have taken a hit before the drop. His body temp looks like it's up, and look at the tremor," John said.

"Meth will do that to ya. A little artificial courage before he wore his pink fashion accessory out in public," Paula said.

John hefted an evidence bag in his hand. The wrinkled fast-food bag inside weighed about a pound. "Let's see what was so important to bring him out here."

"Other than my memorial? I've heard it was the social event of the season."

John unrolled the greasy, stained white paper bag and tipped the contents onto a white blotter in the center of the table.

Individual plastic baggies, some bearing an SSPNET evidence sticker, poured out. Twenty-four in total.

"Oxy, Vicodin, methadone, Ecstasy, and a little heroin and meth thrown in for good measure," John said, sorting the bags.

"A menu of what's available?"

"The SSPNET evidence bags corroborate what McDaniel told us about skimming off the confiscated drugs."

"I'd bet it was Sherman on the other end of that exchange," Paula said.

"Makes sense, but why would he make this kind of drop in the middle of a bunch of cops? It was like he was daring us to catch him."

John pulled a set of three photos from the fast-food bag and laid them on the table. They showed the blue panel van, back doors ajar, packed with bags and boxes. One of the photos featured a close-up of the open boxes, filled with bottles of OxyContin, and evidence bags, each with a handful of pills.

"Jesus, that's a shit-ton of drugs," Paula said.

"The stash Sherman loaded up that night at the storage facility."

"No doubt. And I was a minute late, or we could've taken him down with this haul."

"Let's ask our friend in there why Sherman hung him out to dry. It looks like a going-out-of-business sale," John said.

John scooped up the drugs and put them back into the bag.

Paula hit the room first, threw open the door, and took the chair directly opposite Stubbs.

The Aryan Brotherhood member turned a lighter shade of white. He hadn't expected to see Newberry alive and in the flesh. He recovered quickly, hiding behind a veneer of prison thug.

"Nice to meet you, Erica." Paula looked at a printout with Stubbs driver's license. "Seriously, Erica? Were your parents high or something?"

"It's Eric. The extra letter was a mistake on the birth certificate."

"I guess I know why you go by Stubbs, then," she said.

"I bet you've been paying for that mistake all your life. Might make someone overcompensate to prove they're a real man and all," John said.

"Ain't nobody questions that. I'll show you if you want."

John stood behind his partner and dangled the fast-food bag. "How about we start with this gem?"

"Ain't never seen it before. Is that your lunch?"

"You were on live television in possession of this bag full o' goodies. There's enough here to make a case for possession for sale."

Stubbs tightened his jaw and turned away.

"We can make that all go away," Paula said.

"You oughta know by now, I ain't a snitch. So you can stick that bag up your ass."

"Now why you gotta be like that? If you don't play nice, you're the one who's gonna be taking things up the ass when you go back to prison, Erica," she said.

Stubbs pulled against the restraints. Paula was getting under his skin.

John sat down and poured the contents on the table. "Why would Charles Sherman set you up for a takedown?"

"Because he's a weak-ass punk."

"What was in the backpack you tossed in his car?"

"Don't know what you're talking about."

"Your pink girlie backpack, Erica. What was in it?" Paula pushed.

Stubbs's face reddened. "No wonder Sherman wanted you dead. I get it now."

"She has that effect on people," John said.

Paula leaned forward. "So Sherman arranged for you to take me out? You missed, asshole."

"I don't know what you're talking about."

"Why didn't Sherman take care of business himself?" she pressed.

He shrugged, and the restraints jangled. "Maybe 'cause he don't have the stones for it."

John fanned out the photos in front of Stubbs. "I don't care about your little bag of takeout. I want this. Is Sherman trying to move it?"

Stubbs tipped his head up at John. "What's in it for me?"

"You walk on this possession charge."

"Wait a second," Paula said.

"You walk on the possession," John said in a louder voice.

Stubbs grinned. "I see who wears the pants in this family. Yeah, okay, I walk on the possession, not that you coulda proved they were mine."

"So tell me about Sherman," John said.

"Sherman's a pussy. Always has been. Even inside, he was a scared rabbit."

"You knew him from prison?" John said.

"Yeah, he came to us for protection from everyone. White, black, brown—everybody wanted a piece of that cop."

"Who's 'us'?" Paula asked.

Stubbs cracked his neck. "Let's call them concerned citizens."

"With a penchant for cross-burning," she responded.

"A pen-what?"

"Never mind. Back to Sherman. What was he trying to set up?" John asked.

"He's been nickel-and-dime dealing through a guy named Junior for the past year or so."

Paula shot a kick under the table at John when Stubbs mentioned Junior's name.

"Yeah, so?" John said, urging him on.

"Now that he's out, Sherman wanted to get out of the business and liquidate his inventory. It's no surprise where that came from. Everyone knew it. You all knew it and turned a blind eye." Stubbs pointed a shackled hand at the photo of the drug-laden van.

"Okay, so why screw you in the process?" John said.

"It's gonna cost you."

"We already told you. You get to walk on the possession beef," Paula said.

"This is worth more than a nickel's worth of time. I need more." Stubbs regained some smugness and leaned back in his chair.

"I think Erica's full of shit," Paula said.

"Could be," John responded.

"He doesn't have anything else, or he would have put it on the table already."

"Well, if he doesn't want to play ball on the possession for sale changes, we can book him and let the public defender's office try to punch holes in the case."

Stubbs looked from one detective to the other. "Hey, I'm right here."

They ignored him, which made the gangster uneasy, and he began to rock in the chair.

"With all the video, that's not likely. Is he a second striker?" Paula said.

"Are you a second striker? 'Cause you're looking at a ton of time if that's the case—more than a nickel's worth."

Stubbs looked like he was having trouble keeping up with the conversation, and the tremor in his hands became more noticeable.

"I want an immunity deal," Stubbs said.

"Immunity from what?" John said.

He paused.

"Tell us where this is." John tapped the photo of the drug van.

"I—I don't know."

"That's not helpful," Paula said.

"He was supposed to take me to it."

"Now why would Sherman take you there?" she asked.

"On account of the hundred grand that was in the backpack."

John whistled. "Now we're talking. You bought the whole damned thing?"

Stubbs shook his head hard enough to send sweat droplets onto the table. "Now, do I look like I got a hundred grand to toss away? And you know that's worth way more than a hundred K. It was more pay-to-play, and I was just the bag man."

"Who was the money?" John said.

"Not going there. It don't matter. Sherman crossed some very powerful Brotherhood players, and he has no idea that he's already dead."

"The backpack was a down payment?"

He nodded.

"And the hit on my partner?" John asked.

"Part of the deal, so I hear."

"How much money's in play here?"

"A half million, maybe more. And that still leaves a lot of meat on the bone for profit."

"What do you have on Sherman? Come on, you gotta give us a taste," John said.

"The name Leo Simpkins mean anything to you?"

"Sounds familiar; help me pin it down."

"Simple Simpkins was the guy Sherman killed in prison."

"Oh, yeah. The DA didn't prosecute that one. Lack of evidence and diminished capacity, they claimed."

"What if I can get you a witness?" Stubbs said.

"Sure, who's that?"

"Me," Stubbs said.

FIFTY-SIX

Junior rode shotgun with a cut-down 12-gauge on the seat between him and Wallace. He pointed to someone leaning on a motorcycle ahead in the shade of a tall but diseased elm in William Land Park. As they pulled closer, Wallace couldn't tell which one was more diseased, the tree or the man with his yellow-cast skin.

"What you got, Dutch?" Junior said.

Dutch leaned on the driver's window, and Wallace smelled stale beer and rotting teeth. "Stubbs got hisself into some shit."

"What'd you see?"

"He tossed a backpack or something into a passing car."

"You see who was driving?"

"Yeah, it was Sherman," Dutch said.

"Son of a bitch!" Junior punched the dash with a fist. "I thought you said you put him down."

"Fucker's like a cat—he's got nine lives," Wallace said.

"I seen the cops take Stubbs down like they was waiting for him. They ain't booked him yet. Our eyes on the jail say he ain't showed there."

"That means they're sitting on him and pressuring him to roll," Wallace said.

"Stubbs ain't like that. He's solid wood," Dutch said.

"Hey, I know he drank the Kool-Aid and he's down with the cause and all that, but does he know enough to bring it all down?" Wallace asked.

"Stubbs is righteous," Junior said.

"Righteous doesn't give me warm fuzzy feelings," Wallace said.

"He won't open his mouth. We have people everywhere and he knows it."

"Then he's on your property card, not mine," Wallace said.

"He's ours to deal with—if there's a problem. You feel me?" Junior said.

"Yeah, yeah, he's your problem." Wallace turned in his seat and faced Junior. "Sherman's got you by the short curlies. You got no verification of the stuff he's holding, and you're no closer to finding it before he sells it to Simmons and his crew. How stupid are—"

Dutch moved fast, pressing a switchblade under Wallace's jaw. "You need to show some respect," Dutch growled. Wallace felt a warm trickle down the front of his neck.

"I'm starting to think I don't have much use for you," Junior said.

Wallace glared back at the huge man, stone-faced. Junior picked up the 12-gauge cut-down and placed the barrel under Wallace's chin. "Dutch, you might want to step out of the splatter zone."

Dutch removed the knife from Wallace's throat and took a long pace back.

"What can you do for me now?" Junior asked.

"I got you here, didn't I?" Wallace answered.

"Can you get me to Sherman?"

"Maybe."

The barrel pressed harder into the soft spot under his chin. "Can you or not?"

"Dutch, you have eyes on Simmons?" Wallace asked.

From a safe space near the back window, Dutch didn't step forward but answered, "What's it to you?"

"Of course we do," Junior said. "Since he cut me out, I've had Red on him."

"You follow Simmons, and he'll take you to Sherman," Wallace said.

Junior's eyes narrowed with a slow burn of recognition. "Dutch, call Red and get an update."

"On it, boss." He pulled a cell from an inside pocket of his leather vest, next to the bone handle of the knife that had been at Wallace's throat moments earlier.

While Dutch was calling, Wallace lifted his chin away from the gun barrel and Junior didn't press back.

"You need me to get to Sherman. Even if you can find him, he's not gonna deal with you or Simmons face-to-face. I can get him to agree to a meet," Wallace said.

"You'd be surprised how persuasive we can be. He might need a friend in his issues with Simmons and the Brand," Junior said.

"You gonna take on the whole lot of them? Not likely."

"But Sherman don't know that."

Dutch came to the window, ducking first to make certain the 12-gauge wasn't pointed in his direction.

"Simmons is out. Red says he's been circling downtown for twenty minutes," Dutch said.

"He alone?" Junior asked.

"Nope. Two of his guys with him. They're just riding around."

"They're looking for Sherman," Wallace said. "Follow them, and we'll find him."

Junior pulled the shotgun away and put it by his leg against the door. "Let's go see what we can find out. Dutch, meet up with Red." Junior told Wallace to pull away from the curb and take Freeport into downtown.

As they passed the police department headquarters, Stubbs's GTO was being winched onto a flatbed tow truck. Wallace slowed down and scanned the few people left on the sidewalk. A man stood over the candles and flower offerings trampled during the disruption.

"That's Penley," Wallace said when they drew close.

"Looks like he's waiting for someone."

"Gimme that shotgun," Wallace said.

"What you got in mind?"

"We'll never have a better chance to take him out. The cops will be so busy dealing with that, they'll forget about Sherman, and he's all ours."

"You forgetting the part where they'll come after us for shooting a cop?" Junior asked.

"Risk and reward, Junior. Hand it over."

Junior slid the gun over, keeping it low and out of sight. Wallace grabbed the cut-down shotgun and cradled it in his right hand, resting the barrel on his left forearm. He slowed the vehicle and leveled the barrel out the window. His finger caressed the trigger, waiting for the opening when he was directly behind the detective.

Less than ten feet between Penley and the barrel. Wallace pulled the trigger, and nothing but a loud click sounded. He squeezed the trigger again, and another click as the firing pin fell on an empty chamber.

Junior held the 12-gauge shells in his palm and rattled them. "You think I'm gonna give you a loaded gun and let you screw this up?"

Wallace tossed the gun in the back seat.

"We're after that drug shipment and Sherman—nothing else."

Junior's cell phone rang. He listened and hung up after a short conversation.

"Turn left on Twenty-Ninth. Simmons is circling around Capitol Park."

"That's it. That's where Sherman will make the deal. Security, public spaces, lots of cops. That's him. That's where we take him down."

FIFTY-SEVEN

John's cell phone vibrated in his pocket and a quick glance showed his home number. "Paula, can you finish up with our boy Eric here? I need to take this."

"No problem, I think we've come to an understanding. Haven't we?"

"Whatever," Stubbs replied.

John stepped out of the interview room and accepted the call. "Mel? Are you okay?"

"Dad, it's me," Tommy's voice sounded on the other end.

"Tommy, is everything all right?"

"Mom's here. Just thought you should know she came back."

"Okay, Tommy. Give me a couple minutes and I'll be right there." John hung up and immediately dialed Mel's cell. It went straight to voice mail. So she was back but still avoiding his calls.

John ducked into the interview room and pulled Paula aside while Stubbs scribbled out his statement on a legal tablet.

"I need to run home for a bit. You got this?"

"Yeah. Everything all right?"

"I'll find out when I get there. It's Mel—"

"Just go and do what you need to do."

"You stay out of sight. You hear?"

"Yeah, yeah."

John left his partner in the middle of an interrogation, something he'd never done before. The pang of guilt at leaving Paula had built into a full-blown storm of self-doubt by the time he arrived home.

He turned the doorknob slowly—he'd felt less nervous going into crack houses. Melissa wasn't waiting at the door to confront him. John heard her laugh in the kitchen.

He eased his way to the edge of the counter and saw Melissa and Kari talking.

"What'd I miss?" John said.

"Kari was telling me about you and Paula at school."

"Mom, you should have seen Aunt Paula. She was so awesome. I thought she was gonna make Lanette pee herself."

"Oh, God, I can picture Paula doing that," Melissa said.

Kari hopped off the seat at the counter and started to her room. "I've got to get some homework done. I'll help you with dinner after."

There was a slight tremble of an earthquake, or the universe shifted on its axis. John and Melissa looked at one another.

When Kari had closed her door, Melissa looked at John and whispered, "What just happened?"

"I don't know, but I'll take it."

"I'm sorry, John."

"Me too." He hugged her and said, "It's gonna be okay. We'll get through it." He felt her shudder in his arms.

She held him tight. "I don't know how you can say that. That principal at Kari's school as much as said I was a bad parent for allowing my daughter to become a schoolyard thug."

"I wouldn't worry about Mrs. Thompkins and what she said to you. I may have dropped an f bomb on her."

Melissa pulled back and looked up at her husband. "You didn't."

"Yeah, I may have."

"Another reason I love you. I'm sorry I'm such a mess."

"Nothing to be sorry about. And I think Paula may have nipped the Lanette problem in the bud. My guess is we'll get a call from Mrs. Thompkins reconsidering the whole situation."

"She is a piece of work," Melissa said, drying her eyes with her sleeve.

"Mrs. Thompkins or Kari?"

Melissa laughed, and her brightness came back.

"Come on. I'll make the kids and us some dinner," John said.

"You cook?"

"I can microwave with the best of them."

"Not really."

FIFTY-EIGHT

Paula was pecking away at a report on the information that Stubbs had offered when her cell phone chirped. The screen showed a blocked number. She held the phone to her ear, listening. The faint whoosh of city street noise carried through.

"Hello?" she said.

"It's so nice to hear your voice, Detective," Sherman said on the other end. To Paula's ear, he sounded surprised to hear her.

"I'm not that easy to kill. Next time, have the balls to face me like a man."

"I'm calling to help you, Detective."

"Who says I need your help?"

"You're looking for Wallace. I can tell you where he's gonna be. I need him out of the picture as much as you do. You understand that, don't you, Detective?"

"I know why I'm looking for him, but I don't much care what he did to hurt your feelings."

Sherman sighed. "Fine. Don't believe me. You getting him will clear you and me from the killings. I had nothing to do with them. You have to help me to help yourself."

"You gonna come in and show us where Wallace is hiding?"

Sherman laughed. "You'd like that, wouldn't you? Wallace isn't hiding. In fact, he's palling around with some Aryan Brotherhood types."

"And they want your stash," she said.

"Of course they do. But they aren't gonna get it."

"That's kinda risky, don't you think?"

"I've got my reasons. I'll turn the stuff—all of it—over to you."

"Not that I'm not the trusting sort, but why would you do that?" Paula asked.

"Like I said. I've got my reasons."

"All right, tell me."

"Wallace and his racist pals will be at the state capitol in about an hour."

"The capitol? What do they have going on there?"

"It's not because they've had a sudden crisis of civic consciousness. That's where the deal will go down."

"I need you there," Paula said.

"Why, Detective, I'm touched. See you in an hour." Sherman disconnected the call.

Paula sat back in her chair and questioned Sherman's motives. Nothing was straightforward with this creep.

She dialed John and gave him a rundown on Sherman's demand for a meet up. "He's trying to sell us Wallace," she said.

"What's his angle? I mean, he's not gonna just hand over his stash without something in it for him."

"I don't have much of a choice but to go with it. Unless I get Wallace, I'll never get the DA off my back."

"You can't trust him," John said. "You think he'd actually turn over his stash? This is a big risk."

"I can live with that." Paula rose from her chair and grabbed her jacket. "Sherman said the deal is going down in an hour at the state capitol. That's a whole lot of space to cover."

"I'll make a call to the highway patrol. They run security at the capitol. I'll meet you there. We can get set up in their offices and watch the surveillance feeds of the place," John said before he hung up.

Lieutenant Barnes approached Paula's desk. His expression was tight, his emotions buried deep.

"You need to find someplace to be," Barnes said. "Don't tell me where. The DA and her investigators are on the way over here to see the chief. Clarke is pissed off that we hid the fact you were alive and let her run with her television interview, and she wants to nail down this case. If I don't know where you're off to, I can't tell them where to find you. Get it?"

"They don't have anything. It's all circumstantial."

"They pulled hair and fiber from the bodies and DNA off the hammer used on Wing and the knife from the Ronland stabbing."

"I know. They should have my DNA on them. They're mine. Someone—Sherman—took them from my place. My DNA is on the murder victims."

"This was the bombshell you warned me that Karen had? Never mind. Not now. It doesn't look good, Paula. Find someplace to be and we can work out your surrender."

"Or, we could nail the killer," she said.

"Time's run out."

"So I have one shot to make sure it isn't me."

FIFTY-NINE

Sherman glanced at the dash-mounted clock. He was going to miss his flight if he dicked around with Simmons. But he needed the money to start his new life near the equator. He checked for a text message confirming an electronic deposit from Simmons—no unread messages.

Simmons's number was in the recent calls list, and he tapped the name harder than he needed to connect the phone call.

"That you, little pig?" Simmons asked.

"I think we may have had a miscommunication. You were supposed to have sent me the agreed upon amount."

"You won't have any need for the money when they send you back to prison."

"Who said anything about going back to prison?"

"You did a stupid thing, setting up Stubbs like that. I'm not gonna risk you setting me up by taking my money and running."

"Like I said, Stubbs isn't my problem," Sherman said.

"It's your problem if you want to see another dime of my money. I want a face-to-face meeting. You get what you want when I get what I want. Simple as that."

Sherman had set up the electronic transfer to avoid an ambush by Simmons and his knuckle draggers. This wasn't how he wanted it to go at all.

"You hear me, little pig?"

"Once that deposit is made, I will meet you."

"I wanna meet first."

"When I get the message that the money has hit my account, I will text you a partial address of the house. I'll meet you in the capitol rotunda and hand you the keys."

"The ro-what?" Simmons said.

"The dome? Under the dome. That's the big round part on top," Sherman said.

"Don't push me. You screw me on this, and I swear you won't walk out of there alive."

"You have twenty minutes to get that money in my account." Sherman ended the call.

Sherman pocketed his phone and got out of the car. He darted across three lanes of midday traffic, and a taxi had to slam on the brakes. When he got to the sidewalk surrounding the park, Sherman confirmed that no one had followed him across the busy street.

He pulled the collar of his jacket up. It was far too hot, but with his head down, he didn't stand out among the state workers out for a stroll around the park. Halfway through his first circle, his cell phone vibrated in his pocket. He continued walking and looked at the phone. Simmons made the deposit.

Sherman tapped out a response on the keypad and sent off a text to Simmons. It read: 4587.

He pocketed the phone again and tossed a rolled-up paper bag, another fast-food container, in the bushes at the base of the south steps of the capitol. He took the stairs at a casual pace. The eyes of the security team at the metal detector were already assessing him. He didn't look bad for a few days out of the prison psych ward, but he didn't fit the bill as a corporate lobbyist either.

Sherman dumped his pockets into a plastic container, including his cell phone, which buzzed when he placed it into the bucket.

One of the security officers asked him if he needed to get the call, and he said he'd wait. A few steps through the metal detector and he was passed through after a pat down. One of the security screeners shrugged at his partner like he had expected to hear the metal detector hit on the scruffy-looking visitor.

Sherman peered out the south windows and caught a glimpse of Junior, Wallace, and two other thugs. They'd arrived together, and it looked like they had come to a temporary truce so they could hunt Sherman down. They split up in pairs, with Junior and Wallace heading toward the same entrance he'd used.

Junior and Wallace working together. How long had they been planning this out behind his back?

SIXTY

A five-minute drive from the police headquarters put John on Fifteenth Street at Capitol Park. He nosed the Crown Vic into an open space near the Vietnam Veterans Memorial. Paula met him on the curb while he tossed an *Official Police Business* placard on the dash to ward off the parking enforcement officers who saturated the downtown corridor.

The east steps of the capitol loomed beyond the bronze-and-granite memorial to the Vietnam Veterans, and every time John walked through the walls listing the 5,657 names of the Californians who died in the conflict, a strange sense of loss came over him. He recognized only one name on the memorial, a distant family friend he'd never met, yet his sacrifice along with the others felt deeply personal.

"Sherman tell you where the meet was supposed to go down?"

Paula scanned the rose garden and surrounding treelined paths for any sign of Sherman or that they had been baited into an ambush. "No. He wasn't specific. God, there must be a hundred places someone could hide out here."

They walked in the direction of the east steps, and John called the highway patrol security offices. While he was on the phone, he pointed up a light pole to a black camera dome, one of several he could make out, arranged throughout the park.

John finished and pocketed his cell.

"They agreed to let us set up in the security offices. We can monitor these cameras from there and pinpoint Sherman and whoever he's meeting with without a chance of him stumbling upon us out here in the park."

They climbed the granite steps, white in the midday sun, to the east door of the capitol. A highway patrol sergeant opened the door for them. "Hi, John, I thought I'd keep you out of the main security screening points in case the guy you're looking for passes through one of those two areas."

"North and south entrances, right?" John asked. "Oh, Brian, this is my partner, Paula Newberry."

Paula shook the CHP man's hand and noticed his brass name-plate. "Brian Wilson? Like from the Beach Boys?"

"What can I say? My parents were surf bums back in their day."

Paula got a vision of Brian in a skintight wetsuit with a stubble of dirty-blond beard. She held his grip a bit longer than she meant to and pulled away when she realized it.

"Nice to meet you, Sergeant," she said.

"Come on, I'll give you the ten-cent tour," Brian said.

The entry on the east side of the building led to a few small committee hearing rooms that ringed the building. The path ahead opened to a wide marble hall lined with glass cases on both sides. Each case contained a display for one of the fifty-eight California counties. Everything from Hollywood to grapes to Silicon Valley tech. No mention of human trafficking, the half-decade-long drought, or California's other cash crop—marijuana.

Brian tapped out a code on a silver push-button keypad mounted next to an unmarked door. He held it open for John and Paula, and once inside, it looked like any security command center, except the cameras were focused on committee hearings instead of the liquor aisle at Walmart.

"John tells me you're looking for Charles Sherman," Brian said.

"Yeah, you know him?"

"Only secondhand. He's written the governor a dozen times, each letter more bizarre than the last. Not outright threats; it was that rambling, 'I've been framed,' crap." Brian's face changed as if he'd just thought of something. "That's where I know your name from," he said, looking at Paula.

"I was the investigator on the case that took him down. Let's just say that I don't think I'll be getting a Christmas card from Sherman."

Brian led them to a series of monitors covering the main halls and both entrance screening areas. "The legislature is in session, so it's busy." He tapped a few keyboard commands and displayed video of crowded waiting areas outside hearing rooms on several floors of the capitol building.

"I locked down the governor's office and added extra coverage on the floor after you called."

A screen showed two uniformed highway patrolmen outside the oversized mahogany door.

"That's it?" Paula asked.

"That's all you can see. We have executive protection team members inside and roaming the hallway. Have to keep the public from panic."

"Can't lose votes. I get it," she said.

Brian chuckled. "Something like that."

Another patrolman came in and handed Brian a folder. "The file you requested, sir."

Brian handed the file directly to Paula. "I had the letters that Sherman sent to the governor pulled. Maybe they'll help."

She opened the file, and the first page was a pencil-scribbled letter addressed to the last governor. The printing was small, precise, and spread edge to edge, taking up all the space on the page. In every line, a single word was underlined and darkened from multiple passes with the pencil. *Innocent, framed,* and *not guilty* were heavy favorites. One word appeared more often—*Newberry.*

She flipped the page over, and the diatribe continued, taking up the top half of the page. At the bottom was a drawing of Paula, identical to the one on his cell wall. She held it up.

"What do you think? Good likeness?" she asked.

"Good God. What a freak," Brian said.

"I don't think he quite captures the moodiness of the subject," John said.

Paula rolled her eyes.

"Can we run back the security feeds—say, for the last twenty minutes?" John pointed at one of the screens.

"Sure. We'll rewind the feeds from both of the main entry points."

A series of keystrokes set two of the monitors in rewind mode, bodies shuffling backward at an awkward pace.

"There. Where's that?" John asked.

"North steps," Brian said.

"That's our boy," Paula said.

In the background, a rally of school employee union workers was in progress. There looked to be more than a hundred people, some with signs asking for more education funding and others seeking a recall of politicians who ignored schools.

"He's already inside. If we had a bit more notice, we could've kept him outside the security envelope," Brian said. The CHP man shot John a worried glance.

"If he passes through the metal detector, then he doesn't have a weapon, right?" she said.

"He won't have a metal object on him—that's all that says."

"If he's meeting someone here for a 'business meeting,'" she said with air quotes, "wouldn't that mean the other party has to clear security too? This is the most secure neutral territory he can get."

"That's a lot to read into this, especially if this is the guy who wrote those letters," Brian said.

"Brian, we need to let this play out. Sherman is going to make an exchange here. You already have extra security in place, and if he makes a break for the horseshoe, we can move in," John said, referring to the semicircular ring of workspaces within the governor's office. "One thing at a time. Let's find out where he is now."

Brian nodded, lifted the radio, and gave the east security team a description of Sherman.

"We have a visual: main corridor, near the governor's office," a voice over the radio sounded.

"I want at least two bodies on him," Brian said.

"He used to be an undercover cop, he'll smell those guys coming," Paula said.

"I need someone on him."

"I'll do it," Paula said.

"Like hell you will," John said.

"Give me one of those earpieces, and you guys can play flight controller from in here."

"He knows you," John said.

"That's the point. He wants me here, remember?"

"Then I'm going with you. Give me an earpiece too."

John tapped on the video screen. "What's he doing?"

Brian zoomed the image with a joystick. "He tucked a piece of paper into the frame of that display case."

"That's it, that's the drop. Let's move," Paula said.

Brian gave them earpieces and placed the microphone wire so it snaked down from their collars to their wrists. They both tossed their jackets back on and tested the connections.

"Where's he headed?" Paula asked.

"West corridor past the elevators," Brian's voice carried over their earpieces.

John and Paula entered the hallway, and Paula grabbed John by the arm. "You watch the drop. I'm on Sherman."

Before he could respond, she joined the back of a tour group heading toward the capitol rotunda.

"I see him," she said.

Then her transmission stopped.

SIXTY-ONE

"Paula?" John said into his microphone.

No response from his partner came to his earpiece.

"Brian, do you have her?"

"I see her. Her comm must have gone down. I can't get a response from her either. She's still heading toward the rotunda, keeping some distance from Sherman."

John took a step away from his observation point over the drop so he could cover Paula when Brian whispered in his ear.

"You have three guys coming your way from the north entrance. All white, big, and not dressed for a senate hearing. Biker leathers, seedy-looking types."

John tucked back along the display cases at the opposite end of the long corridor, more than one hundred feet from the bikers, and watched their approach. As Brian described, the men wandered the hallway, and it didn't look like they were there to lobby against the motorcycle helmet law. He recognized Junior as one of the men. The taller of the threesome held a cell phone low as if reading a text. Sherman had managed to lure them all here, as he'd promised Paula.

They moved up the hallway, interested in the county displays, checking out the names above the individual glass cases. The tall man pointed at El Dorado County, the one where Sherman planted the piece of paper in the frame. They stood in front of the scene of gold discovery in Coloma, looking nervous and apprehensive.

"The tall one is Simmons. He's a big boy with the Aryan Brother-hood. The big one is Junior, and I'm not sure about his sidekick, but the white pride tattoo on his arm tells me all I need to know," John said.

"That's who Sherman was supposed to meet?"

"Looks like it."

Simmons spotted the paper's edge in the fold of the glass frame. He had trouble pulling it out and dug it out with a thumbnail. He unfolded the scrap of paper, and his face flushed. "Fucking games!"

A woman with a ten-year-old boy held her hands over her son's ears and glared at him.

Simmons wadded the paper and tossed it on the marble floor. He tapped a message on his cell phone with an angry finger.

"Is Sherman on his cell phone? Can you tell?"

"Looks like he got a text message," Brian said.

"Still have Paula in sight?"

"Affirmative. She's watching Sherman from the tail end of a tour group by the Columbus statue."

Simmons had the look of a steroid-enraged cage fighter; corded knots of muscle on his neck and veins puffed up on his arms, ready to pop.

"He's one unhappy camper."

Simmons made a phone call, barked orders at someone, and shoved the phone in his pocket when he finished. He paced near the display, and his companions leaned against the glass case with crossed arms and watched the faces parade by. Junior pushed his sunglasses up on his head when an attractive woman in a tight skirt and heels went past.

"Sherman's on his phone again," Brian said.

John saw Simmons fumble for his cell phone. The gang leader looked at it and pointed down the hall, and then he and his side-kicks moved toward the rotunda.

"They're coming toward Paula. Is she out of the way?"

"For the moment. That tour group is gonna move on at any moment, and she'll need to find cover."

John stepped from his vantage point into the main hallway and the crowds of visitors, legislative aides, and lobbyists. The leather-clad bikers stood out, making a tail easy at a distance. John snagged the wadded paper that Simmons had tossed.

"Sherman's on the move," Brian said.

"Where?"

"Staircase, north end. He's going up. Paula's following."

"Dammit. You have anyone up there?"

"I'll get them heading that way."

John followed Simmons and his men to the rotunda. It looked like they expected to find Sherman there. They walked around the huge Columbus statue and peered into the hallways that dumped into the circular open space.

John unfolded the paper and all it bore was a number: "7th." Seventh what?

"Is there a seventh floor?"

"Nope. Why?"

"Room seven, or something significant about the number seven?"

"No, nothing that I can think of," Brian said.

From his spot at the edge of the rotunda, John caught a glimpse of Sherman at the railing on the second floor, overlooking the space below—and his pursuers. Sherman glanced over his shoulder and didn't show alarm when Paula appeared nearby.

John caught Paula's eye, and he tapped his earpiece. She shrugged in response. As deep as Sherman's obsession with Paula ran, she showed little discomfort with the man less than twenty feet from her. She had her weapon out and hidden under the flap of her jacket. The barrel pointed at Sherman. A sour knot flipped in John's gut.

Simmons kept glancing at his phone, and the more time that passed, the more the anger became palpable. Even his biker friends backed a few feet away.

"Brian? Do you have eyes on the three bikers in the rotunda?"

"We do, and the exits are covered. Want us to move in now?"

"Hold for now. I'm moving," John said.

John cut across the wide expanse of the rotunda, keeping the statue of Columbus making an appeal to Queen Isabel between him and Simmons. At the last moment, he cut left to the elevator bank as one of the cars opened.

A holdover from days past, an elevator operator sat on a narrow stool inside the door. "What floor?" she asked.

"Two, please."

The old car moved up and sounded a loud bell when it arrived at the next floor. John stepped out onto the circular walkway that overlooked the rotunda below and looked up to the elaborate dome. The walkway was also a main passage between the old and new parts of the capitol building. An oddity of architecture, the third floor of the new building aligned with the second level of the old structure.

John stepped into the flow of pedestrian traffic and spotted Paula and Sherman at the railing directly ahead. They were on the opposite side of the circular walk, both focused on Simmons below.

John took a position on the rail, to Sherman's left and in Paula's view. She glanced up and gave a slight nod, one that said, "I've got this." John moved a few steps closer to Sherman with each passing group of tourists.

"Nice of you to join us, Detective," Sherman said.

"Paula, what are you doing?" John asked.

"Walk away, John."

"Paula—"

"I'm tired of picking up the pieces of my life because of him." Paula punctuated her statement with a jab of the gun barrel against her jacket. She'd closed within a few feet of Sherman.

"And here I thought you came to apologize to me and take care of our friends down there."

"You mean Beavis, Butt-Head, and friend of the Brotherhood? Not much of a show," Paula said.

Sherman took his cell phone from his pocket.

John tensed. "Easy now." His hand covered his weapon.

Sherman held the phone with two fingers to show it wasn't a threat. He tapped a text message and hit send, then pointed at Simmons below.

Simmons grabbed his cell and glanced at the message. "I'm tired of these God damned games!" His voice echoed under the capitol dome.

"What did you say to him?" John said.

"I told him to hang tight, and he'll get what he wants."

"This is your big plan?" Paula asked.

"You haven't got a clue. You put me in there with them. You and your high-and-mighty act."

"Nobody twisted your arm to steal drugs. You're the one who took everyone down with you. And look at them now: they're all dead."

"Their blood is on your hands, Newberry," Sherman said.

Paula's weapon came out. "How the hell can you say that? Your blood—literally, your blood—was on their hands."

"Paula, he's not worth it. He's trying to get you to—"

Sherman's expression darkened. Paula's comment shook him and he stepped back from the rail. "What did you say?" He looked confused and unfocused.

"I said it wasn't my blood on those guys, even though you tried to make it look like I killed them."

"I—I didn't kill Burger. Who—who else?" Sherman asked.

"Wing, McDaniel, Ronland almost—" she said.

"Wallace—" Sherman hissed.

"What about him?" Paula said.

Sherman pointed over Paula's shoulder. Wallace stood ten feet away, his arms down, but the tip of a ceramic knife peeked out from his right hand. The perfect weapon to carry through a metal detector.

Paula faced Wallace, her back to the railing, and held a hand out.

"Stay where you are. Don't come any closer," Paula said.

John closed up ranks and edged closer to his partner while grabbing Sherman by the shoulder.

From behind Wallace, a ring of CHP security fanned out and began to move tourists from the area.

Wallace took a step closer. "You cut a deal with the DA."

"What deal?" Sherman said.

"You and the others were gonna roll on me."

"What are you talking about?" Paula asked.

Sherman dangled the cell phone over the railing. "Your friends down there would be interested in what I have to say. It's right here in my phone. You want it? Come get it."

Simmons caught the motion above and recognition crossed his face when Sherman and Wallace came into view.

Wallace sidestepped closer to the railing, and Paula blocked his path.

"Drop the knife," she said. She aimed her weapon. "Put it down."

Simmons saw Paula with her weapon pointed at someone but decided he and his sidekicks shouldn't stick around and find out who. He kicked a trash can as he passed but hadn't realized it was concrete, and the only thing that gave was his toe. He limped down the hallway toward the south exit. He sent one final message to Sherman.

"You're a dead man" popped up on Sherman's screen.

With one hand, Sherman tapped in the final piece of the address that Simmons needed and the location of the keys in the rolled-up bag near the capitol steps. He tossed the phone off the balcony. The phone shattered when it hit the marble floor.

Wallace rushed forward and swung his knife hand. Paula lined up a shot and as her finger covered the trigger, a large group of middle school students on a tour crossed behind Wallace. Any misplaced shot or a bullet that went through Wallace could take out a kid. John's line of sight was also compromised.

Sherman laughed. "You were never one of us. First chance you got, you bailed."

"We had a deal," Wallace said.

"You shouldn't make deals with people in prison psych wards. They tend to be unreliable."

"I took those guys out because they knew. You're next," Wallace said. He was quivering as he spoke; the knife pulsed with each word.

Wallace lunged forward, slashing the air as he advanced. One slice flashed in Paula's face and she fell aside, leaving nothing between Wallace's knife and Sherman. All Sherman did was extend his arms, offering himself as a sacrifice.

Wallace raised the blade overhead and thrust the knife down. Paula dove between the men and threw her hip into Wallace. The move pushed the attacker off-balance, and the tip of his knife shot past her shoulder.

Sherman sidestepped the attack and backed away, blending into the frantic crowd.

Paula's forward momentum pulled Wallace off his feet and sent him over the railing to crash on the marble floor below.

"What were you thinking?" John asked.

"I need Sherman to prove my innocence," she said. "Where is he? Do you have him?"

John craned his neck and scanned all the bystanders who'd gathered to watch events unfold. Cell phone videos and selfies were being taken all around, but Sherman had slipped away in the turmoil.

"He's gone."

SIXTY-TWO

"I'm so sorry, Paula; I let him slip away," John said.

"It wasn't your fault. But I'm pretty much screwed now."

"Sherman used the crowd as cover to get past the security. He dropped his dark jacket and the camera missed him. We got Wallace though. The fall from the rotunda wasn't enough to do more than break a few bones. I've got a couple uniforms watching him, so—"

"He's here, right? Is he talking?"

"Wallace is getting bundled up by the paramedics. He's gonna need a good orthopedic doctor after his humpty dumpy act."

"I gotta talk to him."

"That can wait. Besides—"

"No, it can't wait. Sherman is still out there, and Wallace knows more than he's let on." She pushed John aside and cut down the rotunda stairs to the landing zone, where Wallace was being loaded on a gurney.

Wallace lay on the gurney with both legs splinted, a neck brace, and a bruise, already purpling, on his shoulder, suffered during his tumble from the balcony.

He was awake, and his eyes narrowed when Paula came in.

"Where is he?" Paula said.

"If I knew, I wouldn't tell you," Wallace said.

"What do you owe him?" she asked.

"Owe him? He owes me."

"For what? Getting him in and out of prison?" Paula said.

"I'm not talking to you. I want a lawyer."

John took a plastic bag and collected Wallace's smaller belongings. He sorted them with the end of a pencil; a cell phone, two sets of keys, a watch, and a wallet. John hooked the end of the pencil in one of the rings of keys.

John lifted a set of keys so she could see them—and the *P. N.* monogram on the key fob.

"You son of a bitch. You were the one in my home. You took the hammer and my butcher knife. There's one key missing. You give that to your buddy Sherman?"

Wallace held back his reaction. "I want a lawyer."

"Where's Sherman?" Paula asked.

"Why do you think Sherman cut our good friend Wallace out of his drug business?" John asked Paula.

"He didn't need him anymore. Sherman got what he wanted from him and cut his useless ass loose," Paula said.

A flicker of recognition registered on Wallace's face and dissipated, but he was shaken.

"You heard Sherman: Wallace ran and bailed the first chance he got," John said.

"What do you suppose the deal was that Wallace was crying to Sherman about?" Paula said.

Wallace tried to move, but the splints and neck brace stopped him the second he put pressure against them.

An officer ducked over to the detectives. "Excuse me, Detective Penley, I have some gentlemen here. They say you asked for them to meet you here."

"I'll be right there," John said. Then to Paula, "Can you entertain our guest here for a moment?"

She nodded.

"Why were you trying to kill Sherman?"

"I want a lawyer."

"He made a deal with the AB and left you hanging."

"I want a lawyer."

"How's it feel to be a loose end, worthless and disposable?"

He turned away from her as far as the neck brace allowed.

Two men approached the gurney with John. The first was Bullet, followed by a weakened but stone-faced George Ronland.

"You're a popular man," Paula said.

"So Bullet, what do you say?" John said.

"That's him. That's the guy I saw up on the highway that night."

"You're sure?" John asked. "This guy?" John tapped one of the leg splints.

Wallace grimaced and moaned.

"It's him. Now I remember where I saw him before. He worked at the jail and took my fingerprints the last time I got arrested. I swear, it's him."

"Now, Wallace, you recognize Mr. Ronland here, don't you? You two worked together."

Wallace's glance flicked in Ronland's direction, but he couldn't maintain eye contact.

"Why did you stab Mr. Ronland?" John said.

"Yeah, how come? I tell you I don't want to play in your game to rip off Sherman and you do this?" Ronland gestured to his chest.

"I want a lawyer."

"You always were a weak piece of shit. Scurrying off when things got tough. Like a rat," Ronland said.

"Rat," Paula said the word, and John saw the gears working in her mind. "You were the informant. You're the one who originally tipped off the DA's office about SSPNET," she said.

"The files burned in your house. Those were his informant files. Sherman got ahold of them somehow. He knew what Wallace was up to—Wallace was doing anything he could to avoid being exposed as a rat against his former task force buddies," John said.

"But Sherman planned to expose him the whole time. Sherman wanted us to find those files. That's why he didn't pour gasoline all over the house."

Ronland shuffled forward. "You dropped a dime and ran out? You were as involved as the rest of us, as much as Sherman, Burger, Wing—all of them."

John stepped between Ronland and Wallace's gurney. It didn't take much to hold Ronland back; a palm on the shoulder stopped him short. "George, that's enough. Thanks for your help. Go on back home and finish healing up."

"Come on, man, they got cheap coffee down in the basement," Bullet said to Ronland. "My treat."

Ronland backed away. Bullet nodded to Penley and followed Ronland out of the rotunda.

"I have to ask. Was Junior with you at all the killings, or did he trust you to do it all by yourself like a big boy?" Paula said.

"Screw you, Newberry. The DA isn't about to let me go down like that," Wallace said. "Besides, she knew the task force was skimming the take. She looked the other way as long as she got the convictions."

"You've got nothing left to play. DA Clarke isn't going put her reputation at risk for you. She wanted Sherman, and you can't deliver." Paula let that thought linger for Wallace.

Paula went to his side and ratcheted a pair of handcuffs. She put one on Wallace's wrist and the other on the gurney rail. It wasn't like he could get up and run off, but it felt good.

"An ex-cop in prison is bad enough, but an ex-cop rat in prison? Well, your quality of life is about to take a real nasty turn," she said.

SIXTY-THREE

Paula watched the paramedics wheel Wallace out of the capitol. She met two officers outside and told them to go with the ambulance and not let Wallace out of their sight.

"Until Sherman is off the board, Clarke will keep coming after me for her case falling apart."

"We have Wallace dead to rights on Burger and Ronland and for trying to stab you," John said.

"That's not enough. Sherman put all this together from behind bars and tore my life apart."

"You can't make this personal—"

"The hell I can't. Sherman set me up, burned my home, and tried to have me killed. Of course it's personal."

"We have everyone out looking for him."

Paula pushed past her partner and headed to the exit. "I don't expect you to understand. I have to do this."

He grabbed her by the arm. "I get it. After almost losing Tommy to a killer, there's probably no one who'll understand it more. But we have to be careful about how we go after him. We can't risk screwing up the case against Sherman for revenge. Clarke would love to throw us under the bus."

She tugged her arm back from him, but her resistance weakened.

She pulled her cell phone and stopped short.

"What is it?"

She held the phone and said, "Sherman was texting Simmons, right?"

"Yeah."

"Where's his phone?" she asked.

"Probably still in the capitol rotunda. I think it broke into a million pieces when he tossed it."

"He was making a deal with Simmons for the whole drug stash. If the phone has the information, we might be able to pull the location from it."

"Maybe with some time and a few tubes of super glue. That thing shattered when it hit the marble floor."

The door at the security screening area was locked. They shut the detectives out when they escorted Wallace to the ambulance. A sign notified visitors that the capitol was temporarily closed. Paula noticed a huddle of highway patrol officers inside. She rapped on the glass door, and one of them saw the detectives but returned to the conversation with the others.

Paula banged on the glass with a closed fist. This time, one broke from the group and came to the door. He didn't unlock it; he jabbed at the closed sign with a stiff index finger.

Paula pointed at him, but not with the same finger. In the other hand, she held her badge.

The officer flicked the lock open and parted the door. "You're gonna have to come back some other time."

He started to close the door, and she shoved her foot in the opening.

John cut Paula off before she unleashed an F-bomb on the highway patrolman. "We need to see Sergeant Wilson. It's about the incident in the rotunda."

The patrolman opened the door and told them to wait while he contacted the sergeant. He kept glancing over at them while he was on the phone. He hung up and came back to them.

"The sergeant says you can meet him in the rotunda. You know how to get there?"

"Yeah," Paula said and walked past him.

The sergeant was standing next to the Columbus statue while another patrolman took photos of the floor where Wallace had landed. There was very little blood from the fall against the hard marble surface, but the space was littered with black shards of plastic and gauze wrappers left behind by the paramedics.

"We're all done with the diving competition for today," Brian said.

"Yeah, the degree of difficulty was good, but he lost points for artistic interpretation," John said. "We just left Wallace at the ambulance. He's gonna live to dive another day."

"You able to get a tail on the other guy—Sherman?"

"That's why we're here," Paula said.

"You need to look at more video?"

"Sherman had a phone," she said, pointing to a couple of the larger pieces of the phone spread out on the marble. "Can we take a look?"

Sergeant Wilson looked to the patrolman taking photos, who nodded, meaning he was all done.

"Go ahead. It doesn't look like that phone will be worth much on trade-in."

Paula walked to the first large shard and pulled a glove from her jacket. She pulled it on and picked up the largest piece of phone; the screen and the lip of the bottom case.

She searched for another piece and found the back case. She left it on the ground without bothering to pick it up.

"What are you looking for? You want me to gather up some of these?"

"No. I got it. There. There it is." She bent and picked up a small hunk of phone guts, less than an inch square.

From behind, Brian said, "Smart."

"What am I missing here, guys?" John said.

"If it doesn't have a tin can and a string, he doesn't understand how it works," Paula said.

Paula plucked out the small SIM card and held it between two fingers. "It doesn't look damaged." She looked to John. "Give me your phone."

"Why? Use your own damn phone," he said.

"You have an ancient one that the card will fit. Give it."

John handed his phone to Paula, and he expected her to stomp on it to get what she needed. She pulled the back off and slid an identical card out of his phone. She handed the card back to John, slid the one she recovered in the phone and powered it on.

"You cloned his phone," Brian said.

Paula pulled up the log of recent calls ingoing and outgoing. A few numbers repeated on the list, including one she recognized from the police department. The text messages were saved to the card, and she pulled up the last three messages, all to the same number.

"4587 Seventh Avenue. That's the location he gave Simmons."

SIXTY-FOUR

"You think Simmons will still be there?" John asked.

"Sherman's deal was for a quick score for some traveling money. It will be pretty straight up. How long till SWAT gets there?"

John turned on Franklin heading south. "They're fifteen minutes out. We'll be there in two. We can provide overwatch and direct the tactical team in."

"Sherman will be nearby. He'll want to take out Simmons when he makes the pickup."

"Or, he's halfway to San Francisco and a plane out of the country," John said.

The neighborhood property values diminished with each block. Vacant storefronts gave way to homes in foreclosure and abandoned furniture at the curb. Blocks from their destination, the occupied homes were marked with iron bars over the windows instead of plywood.

"Up on the right. The gray one with the Chevy Nova in the drive," Paula said.

John coasted the sedan to the corner, a few doors down from the address left on Sherman's phone.

"See anything?" John said.

"Nothing. Can you see the plate on that Nova?"

John read it off, and Paula ran the registration on the vehicle.

"The plate comes back to a ninety-nine Toyota truck," she said.

"There's our probable cause."

"Where's Sherman? And what's he up to?" Paula looked over her shoulder and scanned all the homes along the block. The home directly across the street from the address was unoccupied, and its windows were covered with plywood. A gap between the boards on one window was slightly wider than the others. The muddy darkness inside quivered with a flash of gray.

A dark form moved across the opening. "There," Paula said. She darted out to the dark house.

"Dammit, Paula." John leapt from the car and followed his partner.

They crouched below the open window, and Paula pointed up to the torn screen. John nodded. He knew what she intended. As she started to grab the window frame, he grabbed her and pulled her down. He motioned across the street at the dope house. A limping Simmons came out the front of the house carrying a pry bar. He made quick work of the lock on the garage door. The rotten wood splintered away with the first tug.

Simmons shoved the door upward, and his sidekick stood inside, next to the blue van that Paula had lost in the storage yard.

John checked his watch. "Tac is still ten minutes away. We can take one or the other. Your call, partner—Sherman or Simmons."

"Damn, damn, damn. We can't let those drugs get into circulation." Paula paused for a moment, eyeing the open window above them and the blue van across the road. "Something's going on over there."

Simmons had flung open the van's rear doors, and from his angle, John couldn't see what was inside.

Simmons stood at the open van door and pulled at a large bag near the opening. He pulled a second one out to the garage floor, then another with a frantic energy. Whatever he hoped to find in the van wasn't there. He kicked at a bag on the floor, and it split open. It wasn't confiscated drugs that stuck to his boot. It was steer manure. Bags and bags of garden-quality steer manure filled the van.

John and Paula crept up on Simmons while he pawed through a few more bags of manure. The smell was stockyard fresh, made worse by the heat in the enclosed garage.

The skinny biker noticed them first, and his response was hands up, down on his knees with his hands behind his head, without being told. He'd been through the drill before. Simmons saw his sidekick drop and spun around. His hand slipped behind his back.

"Don't do it," John said.

"No use in getting shot over a load of bull shit," Paula said.

Simmons retracted his empty hand from behind his back and faced the detectives. He got down on his knees like his partner.

Paula stepped forward and removed a snub-nosed .38 revolver from the small of Simmons's back. She put him in handcuffs while John provided cover. When she finished with Simmons, John tossed another set of cuffs, and she put them on the skinny biker.

"How much did Sherman take you for?" Paula asked.

"I don't know what you're talking about," Simmons said, but the sharp look in his eye confirmed it was a lot.

Paula dug in the gangster's pockets and pulled out his cell phone. She didn't need to risk opening the text messages without a warrant because a text appeared on the screen: "GOT YA." The message came from an unknown sender, but she had no doubt that Sherman had sent it.

She held it in front of Simmons. "You want me to reply for you?"

"You ain't got nothing on us."

"I'll start with an ex-con in possession of a firearm and go from there," she said.

John stepped into the back of the van and retrieved two large SSPNET evidence bags with pound-sized bindles of meth and heroin. Nowhere near the quantities that Simmons paid for, but enough to ensure he did prison time when he was caught in possession of the contraband.

Support units and the tactical team arrived at the house. The two gang members were stuffed into the back of separate patrol units, and the house was searched.

The tactical team leader reported that there was no sign that the home was occupied, nor was the rest of the cache of stolen drugs in the place.

Simmons was angry but not at being arrested. He rocked back and forth as he sat in the back of the car. He looked worried. His deal with Sherman had gone bad, and he'd obviously been playing with someone else's money—gang money. John picked up on the cues and pressed.

"How much did Sherman take you for?"

Simmons peered up at John and kept a tight jaw.

"You wouldn't be the first, you know."

"I'll damn sure be the last," Simmons growled.

"We haven't turned up anything other than the firearm possession and a midlevel possession beef. Hypothetically, if you did have something going with Sherman, how much was it worth?"

"Hypothetically?"

"Yeah—it means—"

"I know what it means. If—someone had something going on with Sherman, it would have been to take over his inventory."

"He had that much?" John said.

"That's what I hear."

"Where is he now?"

"If I knew, you and I wouldn't be here having this conversation. Sherman screwed some important people."

"How much, hypothetically, did he take from them?"

"Like seven-fifty," Simmons said.

"What happens if you don't make good on the deal?"

The man didn't bother looking up. "Nothing good."

The two prisoners were driven off for booking, and the searches wound down. The house across the street, where Paula saw the shadow, was empty.

Her phone rang. "Newberry."

"You need to come in," Lieutenant Barnes said.

"What's going on, Lieutenant?" she asked, pointing at the phone so John knew whom she was speaking with. She put the call on speaker.

"We've run this as far as it can go, Paula. I'm sorry; it's time to come in."

"Come in? What do you mean—like turn myself in?"

"Where are you?" Barnes asked.

"Detective Penley and I are at the house where Sherman was supposed to have hidden his inventory. Came up dry."

"You're with Penley and not on your way to SFO?"

"What? SFO? Why would I be in San Francisco?"

"The DA's office just got a hit on your credit card for two airline tickets, one in your name and one in Sherman's."

"We're here in Sacramento, Tim," Penley said.

"The DA is hot on this one. It doesn't look good, Paula. You get what I'm saying?"

"Yeah. Sherman did it again, making me look like his accomplice in all this."

"When is the flight he booked?" John asked.

"Ten-oh-five tonight on Singapore Air to Hong Kong."

"We'll get to SFO as fast as we can. Let TSA know—"

"Paula, it's over. You need to come in. It looks bad enough already. Don't go running to the airport. You can see that, right?" Barnes said.

"Where did Sherman make the ticket purchase?" John said.

"Online."

"That means he's probably not at the terminal yet," John said.

"Does the online ticket have an e-mail account or phone number listed? If he wanted to download a boarding pass, or get flight information, he'd need to give a number," Paula said.

"Hold on a sec," Barnes replied. Paper rustled in the background. "Good call, Paula. There's a phone number listed in flight reservation."

"He must have picked up a burner phone," Paula said. "What's the number?"

"Doesn't matter; I'll make a call and the local sheriff's department will pick him up when he hits the security checkpoint. Come in," Barnes said.

"Thank you, Lieutenant." Paula disconnected the call.

John watched Paula shove the phone into her jacket and tuck her head the way she did when she'd made up her mind. He caught up with her halfway up the drive.

"We're not going back to the office, are we?" John said.

Paula's eyes fired. "My whole life, I've had to work twice as hard to get anything, just for someone to come along and destroy it." She tightened her fists until her knuckles paled. "My father left when I was three, and it tore my world apart. Did you know I was engaged once? That asshole drained my checking accounts and took up with some goth chick. In the academy, I worked my ass off, only to have the training sergeant grade me down on a bullshit use-of-force exam—just so I couldn't graduate as number one in my class. Now this." Paula shook with the final words.

"So what are you gonna do about it?" John asked.

It was all the prodding she needed. "I'm sick of letting them win. I'm not gonna go down without a fight this time. Sherman's not getting on a plane tonight."

SIXTY-FIVE

"Hey, you missed the exit," Paula said. The green-and-white Interstate 80 San Francisco sign shot past in a blur.

"Sherman's been all about misdirection and manipulation. He's not going to San Francisco," John said. He stomped on the gas pedal and shot around a lumbering semitruck.

"He bought tickets with my credit card for a flight out of SFO. The lieutenant told us that. We need to get there before Sherman gets on that plane."

"Why would Sherman use your credit card and get tickets in your name and his?"

"Because that ass wipe wants me to take the fall."

"Don't you think he'd know his name would get flagged, along with your credit card? He made certain the DA would be looking for you—at SFO."

"But I'm not there." She tensed in the seat.

"Neither is Sherman. He wants everyone there looking for you I'm betting he's closer to home."

"That's a hell of a long shot," she said.

"It popped into place when you were talking to the lieutenant. He said the DA's office got the hit on your credit card. The DA, not internal affairs. I don't trust Clarke."

"I don't trust her either, but I'm still not following."

"Clarke said she planned a warm vacation next week."

"Yeah, she wants my ass behind bars before she leaves."

"If you were leaving for a flight, where would you leave from?"

"San Francisco wouldn't be my first choice."

"Nope, that's why we're going there." John pointed at the lights in the distance. High-masted poles towered over the parking lots of the Sacramento International Airport.

The airport was international in the sense that it offered three flights a week to Mexican tourist attractions: Guadalajara, Cabo, and Mazatlán. The only "international" carrier, Aeroméxico, had gates located in the newer expansion of Terminal B, a sleek modern structure that featured a fifty-six-foot-tall red rabbit sculpture in the main atrium. Locals never understood the significance of the public art project, and visitors couldn't understand why a city would choose to have the first thing a new arrival saw be a rabbit's butt.

John and Paula cruised the ticket counters in their search for Sherman. The Aeroméxico counter was open, but the line was nothing compared to the other regional, low-budget carriers. As busy as the ticketing and baggage areas were, the late hour hosted fewer outbound flights. Fewer flights meant fewer passengers milling about.

A quick chat and flash of badges with an Aeroméxico ticket agent gave them nothing on Sherman, but the airline had one flight departing for Guadalajara within the hour.

When they cleared the ticketing area, John and Paula rode the long escalator to the upper level, underneath the dusty underbelly of the red rabbit, to the terrace of shops and the tram that connected to the Terminal B gates.

A few of the shops had shuttered their doors for the day, and Sherman wasn't in any of the coffee shops, bars, or waiting areas. The level cleared, the detectives joined a group who looked to be heading for a family reunion somewhere, based on the bright-green "Johnson Family Meetup" T-shirts they all wore.

The tram pulled into the glass enclosure and spit out a few stragglers from arriving flights and TSA workers leaving after their shifts.

"You know, that's pretty smart, when you think about it," Paula said. She tipped her head in the direction of the off-duty TSA screeners. "He'll have our people chasing their tails in the crowds at SFO. Here, it looks like he timed his flight to the shift change, so there are fewer security personnel on duty to deal with. Sherman can slip right through."

The tram ride was two minutes long, hardly worth the effort, but it dropped all the passengers at the entrance to the security checkpoint. When John and Paula rounded the corner, a single conveyor belt for screening was operational. All the foot traffic fed through this single point. A lone TSA screener checked identification and tickets as passengers passed. There were Sacramento sheriff's deputies at the checkpoint—more than usual for this time of day.

Paula pointed at the line of black-and-yellow uniforms behind the metal detectors. "I guess the lieutenant got the message out here too."

John approached the TSA agent at the podium and identified himself and Paula.

"We're looking for Charles Sherman, might be ticketed for an Aeroméxico flight to Guadalajara in less than an hour. Can you tell if he's checked in through here?" John asked.

"Not from here. You'd have to ask the supervisor. She can pull up a passenger manifest for you."

The TSA agent pointed out the supervisor's desk, and John and Paula bypassed the security checkpoint and found her on the phone. From the one side of the conversation they overheard, one of her employees had called in sick, and it wasn't the first time. She hung up the phone and said, "I guess I'm expecting too much asking people to show up." The last two words were said in a loud voice for the benefit of the rest of her staff. "Now, how can I help you?"

Paula pulled up a mugshot photo on her phone. It was older, but it had Sherman dressed in an orange jumpsuit with a California State Prison placard under his face—and that arrangement pleased her.

"We're looking for him—Charles Sherman. He's likely on the next flight to Guadalajara, Mexico," Paula said.

"That narrows it down a bit." The TSA supervisor tapped a keyboard and looked surprised. She tapped a finger on the screen. "He's checked in for his flight—gate twenty—but his traveling companion, Paula Newberry, hasn't checked in yet."

"Yeah, she probably won't," Paula said.

"There's a note here to detain Newberry if she tries to check in."

"What! Why?" John said.

The supervisor shrugged. "You got me. All it says is LEO hold—local law enforcement hold, per the district attorney."

"If she comes in, what happens?" Paula asked.

"We turn her over to the sheriff's department." She pointed at the black-uniformed sheriff's crew. "Kinda explains why there are extra deputies tonight."

"Can you print that manifest for me?" John asked.

"Sure, no problem."

A couple of the deputies stared at John and Paula. They were taking too long, and one of them broke away and came toward the supervisor's desk.

"We're gonna take a walk through and see if we can't put our eyes on this guy," Paula said, putting her phone away.

John took the printed manifest, and Paula grabbed John by the elbow, urging him past the security checkpoint. She whispered, "SO. Coming this way."

"Gate twenty is down that way on the right," the supervisor said.

"Thanks," Paula responded. They'd already started walking.

They passed the sheriff's deputy and heard him ask the supervisor if there was a problem. They couldn't hear her response as they kept moving toward the gate near the end of the concourse.

"Why didn't the DA flag this ticket purchase? They hit on the SFO ticket, but not this one. But she wanted me snatched up, if I showed up. That doesn't make sense," Paula said.

Two gates away, they spotted Sherman. He sat across the aisle watching his gate. He wore a dark-blue hooded sweat shirt, jeans, and a backpack. They ducked into a closed restaurant, and Paula started to make an approach.

John grabbed her shoulder and pulled her back. "You run up on him, and he's gonna bolt."

She shook free and went to the edge of the restaurant, still in the shadows of the closed commercial space, but close enough to see Sherman's leg bounce in a nervous twitch. His eyes darted between loud conversations, to a coffee cup dropped into a trash can, and to the airline gate agent.

"Man, he's wound up," John said.

"Let's see how far we can wind him up before his spring breaks." Paula pulled Simmons's cell phone from her jacket, removed it from an evidence bag, and brought up the message screen. She entered Sherman's new burner cell number from the ticket information the lieutenant had provided and paused while she composed a message. She spoke as she typed. "You have my money."

They watched as Sherman read the new text message. He shoved the phone back in his pocket.

Paula tapped out another message: "You're no better than Simple Simpkins, and you know how that ended."

"Simpkins? The guy the AB had Sherman kill?" John said.

"Yep. Look."

Sherman went for the phone and stiffened in his seat when he saw the message. He shifted, clearly uncomfortable. Sherman paused, then started tapping a response.

The new message came through on Simmons's phone: "Simpkins didn't deserve that."

Paula went into another message. "This one should do it." She typed, "With all my money, why aren't you flying first class?"

Sherman casually looked at the message and shot to his feet. He looked for Simmons or anyone who looked like one of his biker prospects.

"That struck a nerve." John laughed.

A stern voice from behind the detectives sounded. "What's going on here?"

John and Paula turned and faced two sheriff's deputies.

"TSA says you're looking for someone. Anybody we need to be concerned about?"

"Material witness," John said.

"Bail jumper," Paula said, running over John's answer.

The deputy furrowed his brow. "Which is it?"

"A witness who's jumped bail before," Paula responded.

The deputy sidestepped toward the main corridor so he could get a better view of the passenger area. "You see him yet?"

Sherman noticed the cop in a black jumpsuit scanning the waiting area. He stood, slung his backpack, and ambled to the gate counter. When he didn't spot one of Simmons's thugs in the passenger area, Sherman looked back to the deputy. If he kept looking, it wouldn't be long before he spotted John and Paula.

"Could you give us some space here?" Paula said. "We don't want to draw any attention."

"I'm gonna need to see some ID, guys."

"Now?" Paula said.

"Yeah, and why don't you come with me back to security," the deputy said.

John and Paula fished out their badges and showed them.

Sherman seemed to notice the movement in the darkened restaurant. He pulled up the hood on his sweat shirt and turned back toward the seat he'd come from. He made a few steps toward the seat, then bolted to his left to the gate where a plane was preparing to board.

"Shit, there he goes," Paula hissed.

A cry went up from an airline employee who Sherman bowled over in the gateway.

"Down the ramp!" John said.

The deputy tried to grab Paula's arm, but she pulled away, nearly spilling the bigger man to the floor. She ran to the gate, and John was a few steps behind her when a shrill alarm sounded in the jetway.

The ramp's thin metal skin echoed with each pounding footfall. The shrill alarm came from an open door at the base of the corridor. The thick pressure door of the waiting plane was open and ready for boarding.

Paula darted down the metal stairs from the open door to the tarmac. John bounded into the plane.

She caught a glimpse of blue sweat shirt near the landing gear, under the belly of the plane. Blue-and-red lights flared in the distance and headed toward the compromised gate. Sherman ran through a spotlight, across the taxiway in front of a 777 coming into an empty gate. The plane shuddered when the pilot hit the brake to avoid hitting him.

Paula pursued him across the taxiway and took cover behind the 777. The jet exhaust was hot against her skin as she passed under the wing. She had to close her eyes when the dust kicked up behind the plane, and she lost track of Sherman. The roar of the jet engines masked the sound of footfalls on the hard surface.

A light in the distance blacked out, then another. Sherman had run in front of them, headed to the east end of the terminal buildings.

John climbed down the stairs to the tarmac after he cleared the plane. Paula waved at him until she caught his attention, and then she took off in a dead run after Sherman.

Red-and-blue lights came from the east side and forced Sherman to hop a fence into another portion of airport property. Paula arrived at the fence as the airport sheriff's cars skidded to a stop.

She held her badge up so they could see she was one of them.

Spotlights blinded her, and orders were shouted at her from two different officers. "Get down."

"On your knees."

"He's getting away!" she answered.

"Get your ass down, now!"

John ran interference and jogged between Paula and the spotlights. "Sac PD."

Paula hit the fence of an airport fire department training yard and bounded up and over in seconds. She dropped on the other side, and the smell of smoke and burnt plastic hit her senses. The outline of a jet fuselage, ghostly in the dim light, loomed in the center of the enclosure.

Paula ducked behind a storage building, out of the reach of the spotlights, and let her eyes adjust to the shadowed darkness. A few husks of vehicles used in fire simulation training littered the yard with pried-open doors and hoods. More sheriff's units arrived and ringed the fire training area. The red-and-blue lights pulsed through the holes in the broken back of the jet fuselage.

A shadow shifted in one of the windows.

"Gotcha," Paula said under her breath.

She ran to the edge of the plane's airframe, rested her back on the cold metal, and drew her weapon.

"Sherman, it's over," she called.

When he didn't respond, she raised her weapon and peered into the door's oval opening. A cold shock raced up her spine when she saw the huge open gap in the opposite side of the plane.

A rustle in the air behind her. Paula turned as a metal pipe cut through the air and struck her on the right shoulder. Her arm went numb, and her gun toppled from her grip.

Sherman took another step forward and raised the pipe overhead. Paula dropped to the ground, rolling under the plane for cover. The pipe cracked down on the tarmac inches from her head.

She scrambled under the scorched fuselage as far as she could. Trapped under the plane's remains, Paula had no escape. A burning sensation came from her right arm—a jagged piece of steel tubing from the plane's hydraulic lines had jabbed in her arm above her elbow.

Sherman swung the pipe, and the curve of the plane's side kept most of the impact away from Paula's left side, but she got enough of the blow to wince in pain. She caught a glimpse of her weapon on the ground behind Sherman. If he got ahold of it, she was finished.

Paula tugged a section of the steel tube loose and passed it in front of her face to her left hand, the one closest to him.

Another blow from the pipe rained down, and it caught her on the left hip. Sherman got on one knee and grabbed the back of her pants at the waist.

Paula moved and struck like a snake, jabbing the sharp steel pipe into the closest fleshy target—Sherman's upper leg.

The metal pipe cut through the thick muscles on his thigh. He staggered back and stood, looking at the section of pipe that went through his leg.

Paula scrambled out from under the plane and crawled to her weapon.

Sherman staggered to Paula, tried to kick her with his injured leg, and howled in pain.

She inched forward, looking over her shoulder at the movement. Sherman grabbed the pipe he'd dropped and held it overhead with both hands. His eyes glassed over and burned with anger. Paula closed her eyes and grabbed for the gun.

Three quick blasts knocked Sherman backward, legs in the air, dropping him on his back.

Paula held the gun in her hand, but she hadn't pulled the trigger.

John came into view with a 12-gauge shotgun in hand.

"You okay, partner?"

"I will be," she said.

John held the shotgun trained on Sherman while a deputy rolled him over and put handcuffs on the man. Sherman moaned.

"How the hell did he—?" Then Paula saw the blue-colored stock on the shotgun. "Beanbags? You used frickin' beanbags?"

A paramedic came to Paula, and she pushed him away. She got to her feet and wobbled an unsteady step until John held her up.

"Took you long enough," she said to her partner.

"You seemed to have things under control."

Another team of paramedics applied a tourniquet on Sherman's leg and hefted him to a gurney.

"Newberry," Sherman croaked.

"Hold on a sec, guys," she said to the paramedics.

"I've got you now."

"What the hell do you mean?" she snapped.

"I've got you right where I want you. You won't be able to get away with what you've done to me in front of all these witnesses."

"What I've done? We're talking about you here. You tried to kill me."

"I was defending myself."

"Yeah, just like you were defending yourself when you did Simpkins in prison. We have a witness, and you're gonna go down for that too."

Sherman's eyes looked uncertain.

"What did you do with the drug stash?" Paula asked.

Sherman grinned. "You already have it. Unless the DA found it first." He started laughing, more of a mad wail really, and said, "I got you, I got you."

"Get him the hell outta here," John said.

Paula limped to the side, her hip starting to stiffen from the beating.

"That is one crazy asshole," John said.

Paula looked at the side of the burnt-out plane and didn't respond.

"Paula? You okay?"

"I know where the drugs are, and we need to get there fast."

SIXTY-SIX

Lieutenant Barnes arrived at the location Paula gave him over the phone. John's knuckles turned white against the steering wheel when she told the lieutenant the address: her home.

When they pulled up, John couldn't park in the driveway because crime scene tape blocked the entrance and ran to the front of the house. Someone had screwed plywood over the broken front door, but it didn't cover the angry smoke stains that crept out of the threshold.

"I haven't been back here since the fire," Paula said.

John pointed down the driveway to her garage, where the lieutenant and crime scene techs had gathered.

Paula got out of the car and ducked under the tape while John found a spot a few houses down to park. Looking at her own home, soot-stained and violated, she couldn't see a way to rebuild. All the sweat and time she'd poured into the place —and Sherman had taken it away from her.

She took a few steps down the drive, and John trotted to catch up.

"That nosey old busybody next door was watching me like I was going to steal her newspaper," he said.

"Nothing goes on around here without her knowing about it," Paula said.

The lieutenant saw them approach and strode up the drive to meet them.

"You called it, Paula. Sherman's entire stash of stolen drugs is here," Barnes said.

They all walked to the garage door, and the flash from a crime scene tech's camera lit up the dark space. The light reflected off of steel and chrome and plastic reflective surfaces. Karen Baylor moved to take another photo. A blue panel van, identical to the one they found at the bust with Simmons, sat in the center of the garage.

The back doors were thrown open, and SSPNET evidence bags were stacked floor to roof.

"That's what a half million buys on the street these days," John said.

"Probably worth three times that amount," Barnes said.

"That's the other van we saw in Wallace's garage," Paula said.

"Explains why we lost the GPS track. This one never had the tracker, and we got the runaround chasing after a decoy," John said.

"The bullshit van," Paula said.

"Speaking of bullshit," Barnes said. He jutted his jaw up the drive.

The district attorney, Linda Clarke, came down the drive, her heels tapping a self-important cadence. She ignored John and Paula and confronted the lieutenant.

"My informant told me I could find my evidence here. I'm not surprised," Clarke said.

"That's funny. My detectives just arrested your informant trying to leave the country," Barnes said.

"How is it that Sherman got his passport back so fast after getting out of prison?" Paula asked.

"What is she doing here?" Clarke said.

"What are you doing here?" Paula asked.

"Why isn't my prisoner in handcuffs?" DA Clarke turned, hands on hips, and faced Paula. "She is responsible for this." She gestured to the van full of stolen drugs. "Newberry was complicit in the murders of three former law enforcement officials. I have evidence—"

"Newberry was set up by Sherman, your own informant," John said.

"How am I supposed to explain how confiscated drugs ended up on the street?" Clarke stepped within inches of Paula. "You were working with Sherman and the rest of them. You hid their contraband for them."

Lieutenant Barnes looked over his shoulder and gestured. A plain-clothed officer came from behind the van, and when he stepped from the shadows in the garage, Paula stiffened as she recognized Sammy Kamakawa, the IA investigator.

"When my detectives advised me that Wallace was taken into custody, I got a warrant to search his place," Barnes said.

"What warrant? No request for a search warrant came through my office," Clarke said.

"No. It didn't. I got a federal magistrate to issue the warrant to avoid any confusion."

Clarke tensed.

Kamakawa handed Barnes three clear evidence bags. "This explains how detective Newberry's DNA appeared on our murder victims. Wallace had her hair brush." He held up the bag with a woman's brush.

"Is that what I think it is?" asked John, pointing at some red sludge wrapped in a plastic bindle.

"That depends on if you think it's blood. Sherman's blood, to be precise. We think Wallace planted the blood as well, to throw off the investigation. You see, he wasn't looking to frame Newberry. His deal was to keep Sherman from finding out that he was the prime witness against all the SSPNET officers."

"Conjecture," Clarke hissed.

"Here is Burger's written testimony implicating Wallace—and you." Barnes patted the last envelope, which held three hand-scribbled pages from the dead man.

"That's what Wallace took from Burger's locker at the truck stop," Paula said.

"You backed Sherman's play to get out of prison on some bullshit technicality. Did he blackmail you about the missing drugs from the task force prosecutions? Is that why you personally decided not to prosecute Sherman on a frickin' murder?" John said.

"The evidence didn't support—"

"Don't give me that line. Sherman played you. Wallace got rid of potential witnesses who would expose his role and left a trail of breadcrumbs to my doorstep that even you could follow. Sherman set you up because he knew you'd never admit you made a deal with him to not fight his appeal," Paula said.

"How can you explain the check you had cut for Larry Burger's testimony?" Clarke asked. She wasn't nearly as confident as she'd been minutes ago.

"I did some digging into that," Lieutenant Barnes said. "Detective Newberry didn't have anything to do with that. Turns out, Wallace has a girlfriend who worked in the city controller's office. We found the paper trail on that check. She's agreed to cooperate. She's saying the order came from you."

"That's ridiculous. That will never hold up." Clarke's lips thinned, and a lack of conviction appeared in her eyes.

"Try explaining this one." John rustled a copy of the Aeroméxico flight manifest in front of Clarke. "Looks like you missed your flight tonight too." A yellow highlighted name stood out on the page: "Linda Clarke."

Relief set on Paula's face. A few of the creases that had worked their way across her forehead over the past few days started to relax.

"I can travel anywhere I damn well please." The polished veneer wore thin now. "Arrest her. Arrest Newberry for Burger's murder."

No one made a move to cuff Paula. "Remember the spike strip?" Barnes said. "An officer checked it out. He used your name."

"I remember. Who was it?" she asked.

"Bobby Wing. He convinced the desk officer that he was called back in to train staff on spike-strip deployment. He got to chatting up the officer, and she never checked the name he wrote on the log. We found a video that shows him leaving about the time the spike strip was checked out."

Paula's knees buckled slightly.

"Any questions, Ms. Clarke? Or can we get on with our business?" Barnes asked.

A bustle of activity from the front of the house drew attention from the group. A DA's office staffer planted a podium on Paula's front lawn. A news crew van raised a mast satellite antenna for a live broadcast.

"I think your public awaits," John said, waving the flight manifest.

"You planned to perp walk me across my own yard, didn't you?" Paula said.

Clarke bit her lower lip.

Paula stepped away and went to the podium, where the harried DA's staffer was setting up a microphone cable.

"Get your shit off my lawn."

The man looked to his boss, and Clarke nodded. She didn't say anything else to the lieutenant before hurrying back up the drive.

The reporter chased the DA to her car and failed to get so much as a sneeze in response to a barrage of questions. When Clarke's car pulled away, the reporter stood, microphone in hand, with no one to interview for the live broadcast. She walked to the podium and Paula. "What the hell happened? I have a live shot in five."

"Lieutenant?" Paula waved her hand and got his attention.

Five minutes later, a news camera focused on Lieutenant Barnes and the van full of drugs behind him.

"A diligent investigation by Sacramento Police Detectives John Penley and Paula Newberry resulted in the seizure of an estimated one-and-a-half million dollars of illicit drugs tied to the murders of three witnesses and the attempted murder of another witness. Two suspects are in custody. Mark Wallace is being held without bail on three counts of murder, conspiracy, and attempted murder of a peace officer. Charles Sherman is also being held without bail for conspiracy to commit murder and attempted murder of a peace officer. Additionally, Detectives Newberry and Penley have developed sufficient evidence relating to the murder of another individual in prison by Mr. Sherman."

After the broadcast, the news people left, the crime scene techs finished up, and finally, John and Paula were alone in the front yard.

"How did someone like Sherman manage to manipulate the entire system?" Paula said.

"That's what psychopaths do. Sherman was a manipulator when he was a cop. He never stopped being one."

"He almost got away with it. He almost took me down in the process." She looked at her home and all the work that lay ahead if she was going to restore it again. "Maybe he did."

SIXTY-SEVEN

The smell of fresh paint felt like a rebirth of sorts. Paula stood back and surveyed her work, a smudge of color on her cheek. Three months of rehab and the place was almost back to normal. It would take far longer for Paula to recover. In the eyes of some of the cops she worked with, she'd gotten what she deserved when she crossed that line where you didn't rat on others cops, you kept your mouth shut and did your own job.

As much as she told herself that she did her job, and that's all that it was, there was a nagging little itch in the back of her mind that kept trying to convince her that she was responsible for Sherman. She'd created Sherman and his obsession. If she hadn't been assigned to that IA case, would those ex-SSPNET cops still be alive? She stood in the wake of death, destruction, and broken lives—and carried that burden. Another coat of paint may have covered the smoke-stained walls in her home, but the smudge she felt on her soul was darker.

Newsprint taped to the resanded wood floor protected the finish from paint splatter. One headline stood out from the clutter of tape, paint, and rollers: "DA Linda Clarke Withdraws From Reelection Bid: Rumors of Corruption and Pending Grand Jury Indictment." The article featured side-by-side photos of Clarke and Sherman.

A knock sounded on her front door, and she glanced at the brass face of a grandfather clock in the living room. Cleaning the smoke damage from that piece alone had cost a grand. She smiled and laid a paintbrush on the tray and went to the door.

John held a bag of hot bagels, and Melissa balanced a tray of coffee cups.

"God those smell good," Paula said and grabbed the bag from his hands.

"I heard you were cleared by the departmental shrink for return to duty," John said.

"That was a waste of time." Paula's eyes flickered away from his.

"There's no shame in it. Hell, Paula, you were shot, and everything that Sherman put you through—"

"I know what they're saying. I couldn't handle the job. Or I was weak. I'm damaged goods. I don't care. That's the only thing I've taken to heart in the whole mess: people are gonna say what they're gonna say and there's nothing I can do about it. It doesn't matter what they think. Justice matters. Cops like Stark—they're gonna go on being knuckle draggers, no matter what."

John chuckled.

"What?"

"Stark."

"What about him?"

"Stark was the one who found the property logs and video that proved Bobby Wing got that spike strip. Stark cleared your ass."

"Stark did that? Why?"

"Does it matter?"

"Hell yes, it matters."

"Turns out he went through the recordings to prove it was you who took the spike strip from the property room."

"What?"

John nodded. "Anyway, even though he went out looking for you, he saw Bobby Wing get the spike strip. He found the video and turned it over to the lieutenant. If he wanted to screw you, he could have tossed it or just kept his mouth shut."

She stewed on John's last comment for a moment. "Dammit."

"What?"

"I owe Stark. You know how he's gonna ride me—forever?"

"Well, you can start making nice on Monday. Stark's been assigned to IT. Who knew the guy was computer savvy?"

"Lieutenant Barnes told me the chief's office said I could pick my next assignment," Paula said.

"And?"

"I told him I wanted my old job back—with you."

"I'd hoped that's what you'd say. Speaking of which, Ronland is back to work at the car wash. He even got Bullet a job there. Things are finally getting better for them."

"After what those two went through, they deserve more," Paula said.

"The lieutenant is pushing the city to use the settlement money they wanted to give Sherman to work out some kind of housing program for people like Bullet and his friends at the river. They won't have to go back to that old life."

"I just want my old life back—like it was before Sherman turned it inside out."

"Don't we all?"

She glanced at Melissa, who was placing the coffee cups on a table across the room. She noticed a downcast expression on her partner's face. "What's up with you two?"

"Melissa—we've hit a rough patch is all. We're trying—"

"This can't be from the stuff with Kari," Paula said.

"It's that and her guilt over Tommy's health, but mostly she's having trouble forgiving herself."

"She'll get over it."

"We'll see. She's good for a day or two, then the guilt creeps back in. She's talking about needing some space to figure things out."

"I'm sorry, John."

"She'll come around—"

"Paula? Who's that?" a voice echoed from the freshly painted hallway.

Paula's cheeks flushed when Brian Wilson appeared from the hall, his face streaked with paint.

"Well, hello there, Brian," John said.

The CHP sergeant returned a subtle hand wave.

"Old life, huh?" John asked.

"Something like that," she blushed.

"Thing is, after what you went through, life will never be the same. There's no going back. You can only move forward. The direction you take is up to you."

Paula handed John a paintbrush.

"All I know is that I'm not gonna waste any more of my life thinking about the past—or Sherman."

SIXTY-EIGHT

The darkness of a prison cell is where madness is born. Shadows fill corners and inhabit broken minds in these places. Charles Sherman sat on the edge of his bunk in the dark, and his mind cycled fast in spite of the medication prescribed to dull his senses.

He wasn't supposed to have anything in this cell. Suicide watch, they called it. Sherman wore a paper jumpsuit and rubber shower shoes. There were no sheets in the cell that he could shred and try to hang himself with again. A bare, plastic-sheathed mattress, made from materials that prevented burning and were impossible to tear, sat on the concrete bed frame.

His forehead bore a fresh set of sutures from temple to temple, one side to the other, from banging his head on the concrete cell wall. The broken man sat and rocked forward and touched the wall opposite his bed. He traced an outline of a picture that only he could see—the image of the woman who would haunt him for the rest of his life.

ACKNOWLEDGMENTS

I hope you enjoyed *Bury the Past*, the latest Detective Penley novel, one that reminds us of the old premise that you might be through with the past, but the past isn't through with you. In my past, I worked with some of the most dedicated criminal justice professionals who made sure the public remained safe above all else. Most of us got to go home in one piece after our shifts. I'm forever grateful to the hardworking men and women in California's prisons and parole units who go unsung and unnoticed.

I continue to be very fortunate to surround myself with supportive, encouraging people who aren't afraid to tell me the unvarnished truth—even if it hurts.

I remain eternally grateful to my agent, Elizabeth K. Kracht of Kimberley Cameron & Associates Literary Agency, for her unwavering belief in me and our Detective Penley series. Without her, *Bury the Past* would have never seen the light of day. She is every author's dream agent, and I'm so lucky to have her by my side.

Thank you to Karen Crain-Hedger for her reviews and early edits of the book that eventually became *Bury the Past*.

The team at Crooked Lane Books—including Matt Martz, Jenny Chen, and Sarah Poppe—are incredible. Their unwavering support for the book carried me through the process of writing this story, and they pushed me just enough to make sure you read the best book possible. Detectives John Penley and Paula Newberry have found the perfect home at Crooked Lane.

A big thank you to my kids, Jessica Windham and Michael L'Etoile, who continue to tolerate their father's behavior. Keep those "geospastic" forces going. I'm proud of everything you've accomplished, and I love you more than you could ever know.

Thank you to my wife and partner-in-crime, Ann-Marie, for supporting my crazy dreams, for reading endless drafts of the manuscript, and for giving me the freedom to go out and create a fictional series. She keeps me grounded when I need it and kicks me in the ass on a regular basis. Thanks you for being my S.F.F.H. I love you.